"Ryan!"

Heedless of his own injuries, J.B. bolted to his side, firing his Uzi through the veil of smoke. Grabbing Ryan by the legs, he dragged him back to the wall. "How bad is it?"

"Not…good. I know that much," Ryan gritted. He brought his trembling neck muscles under control to look down at his shoulders, seeing a lot of blood and the jagged end of a bone poking up through the skin.

J.B. gingerly explored the wound. "This is going to hurt a lot." The Armorer eased himself under his old friend's right arm, eliciting a groan of pain from him as he gripped his hand tight to keep him in place.

When J.B. stood, Ryan nearly passed out from the agony shooting through his shoulders. The Armorer half dragged the one-eyed man forward, intent on getting clear of the underground pit and getting help for Ryan….

Other titles in the Deathlands saga:

Keepers of the Sun
Circle Thrice
Eclipse at Noon
Stoneface
Bitter Fruit
Skydark
Demons of Eden
The Mars Arena
Watersleep
Nightmare Passage
Freedom Lost
Way of the Wolf
Dark Emblem
Crucible of Time
Starfall
Encounter:
Collector's Edition
Gemini Rising
Gaia's Demise
Dark Reckoning
Shadow World
Pandora's Redoubt
Rat King
Zero City
Savage Armada
Judas Strike
Shadow Fortress
Sunchild
Breakthrough
Salvation Road
Amazon Gate
Destiny's Truth
Skydark Spawn
Damnation Road Show
Devil Riders
Bloodfire
Hellbenders
Separation
Death Hunt
Shaking Earth
Black Harvest
Vengeance Trail
Ritual Chill
Atlantis Reprise
Labyrinth
Strontium Swamp
Shatter Zone
Perdition Valley
Cannibal Moon
Sky Raider
Remember Tomorrow
Sunspot
Desert Kings
Apocalypse Unborn
Thunder Road
Plague Lords
(Empire of Xibalba Book I)
Dark Resurrection
(Empire of Xibalba Book II)
Eden's Twilight
Desolation Crossing
Alpha Wave
Time Castaways
Prophecy
Blood Harvest
Arcadian's Asylum
Baptism of Rage
Doom Helix
Moonfeast
Downrigger Drift
Playfair's Axiom
Tainted Cascade

JAMES AXLER

DEATHLANDS®

Perception Fault

A GOLD EAGLE BOOK FROM
WORLDWIDE®

TORONTO • NEW YORK • LONDON
AMSTERDAM • PARIS • SYDNEY • HAMBURG
STOCKHOLM • ATHENS • TOKYO • MILAN
MADRID • WARSAW • BUDAPEST • AUCKLAND

First edition July 2011

ISBN-13: 978-0-373-62609-0

PERCEPTION FAULT

Printed in U.S.A.

Every new stroke of civilization has cost the lives of countless brave men, who have fallen defeated by the "dragon," in their efforts to win the apples of the Hesperides, or the fleece of gold. Fallen in their efforts to overcome the old, half sordid savagery of the lower stages of creation, and win the next stage.

—D. H. Lawrence
1885–1930

THE DEATHLANDS SAGA

This world is their legacy, a world born in the violent nuclear spasm of 2001 that was the bitter outcome of a struggle for global dominance.

There is no real escape from this shockscape where life always hangs in the balance, vulnerable to newly demonic nature, barbarism, lawlessness.

But they are the warrior survivalists, and they endure—in the way of the lion, the hawk and the tiger, true to nature's heart despite its ruination.

Ryan Cawdor: The privileged son of an East Coast baron. Acquainted with betrayal from a tender age, he is a master of the hard realities.

Krysty Wroth: Harmony ville's own Titian-haired beauty, a woman with the strength of tempered steel. Her premonitions and Gaia powers have been fostered by her Mother Sonja.

J. B. Dix, the Armorer: Weapons master and Ryan's close ally, he, too, honed his skills traversing the Deathlands with the legendary Trader.

Doctor Theophilus Tanner: Torn from his family and a gentler life in 1896, Doc has been thrown into a future he couldn't have imagined.

Dr. Mildred Wyeth: Her father was killed by the Ku Klux Klan, but her fate is not much lighter. Restored from predark cryogenic suspension, she brings twentieth-century healing skills to a nightmare.

Jak Lauren: A true child of the wastelands, reared on adversity, loss and danger, the albino teenager is a fierce fighter and loyal friend.

Dean Cawdor: Ryan's young son by Sharona accepts the only world he knows, and yet he is the seedling bearing the promise of tomorrow.

In a world where all was lost, they are humanity's last hope....

Chapter One

Crouched behind a half-ruined wall, Ryan Cawdor wiped gritty concrete dust from his tanned face, black eye patch and curly black hair. He peeked around the left side of the barrier, searching for the person with the longblaster who'd come within a couple inches of sending him on the last train west.

The day had started well enough. He and his companions had come out of a mat-trans near what they thought were the ruins of what used to be Denver, Colorado. It was an area they were fairly familiar with, since two of their group had grown up around these parts. Traveling north to check out the ville, they had reached the outskirts without incident. The quiet should have been a warning. They had just set up a campsite with an outdoor fire they'd thought was sheltered from passing eyes, and were roasting their freshly killed dinner. But as Krysty Wroth was turning the giant, heronlike bird on their makeshift spit, she had looked up with that shocked expression everyone knew all too well, sending each of the other five diving for weapons, cover or both. The first shot had cracked out a second later, and now the group was pinned down and facing an unknown force.

The ambush had been well planned and executed. But the targets the raiders had chosen weren't farmers or traders traveling the Deathlands hawking their wares.

They weren't even a ragtag band of mercies looking for work, their blasters available for hire to anyone who had the jack.

Ryan and his five companions had spent years roaming the length and breadth of the radiation and chem-ravaged land that had been called America long ago. They had encountered much during their journeys, from mutant animals and humanoids of every shape and size to power-hungry barons carving out their empires from the postholocaust savagery, offering refuge—of a sort—to anyone who could pay or barter for the price of admission.

The companions had met just about every variety of man, mutant or monster inhabiting this world—and had left many of them on their back, staring sightlessly at the sky while their lifeblood leaked into the dirt. Each member of the group was a master of chilling in just about every way, shape and form possible, with Ryan perhaps the best of them all—a fact these coldhearts were about to find out the hard way.

He glanced over at his old friend, J. B. Dix, who held his mini-Uzi tucked into his shoulder. The sallow-faced man was hunched down behind the same wall as Ryan, but his expression was as calm as if he were strolling through a mountain meadow in spring.

Ryan risked another peek out only to draw another bullet for his trouble, the lead slug ricocheting off the side of the wall. "See anything?"

"Not yet. They picked a good time to spring this surprise. Dusk means better cover, and they used the fire as their targeting point, neatly pinning us near it."

"What I really want to know is how we're going to get the drop on them."

The short, bespectacled man adjusted the battered

fedora on his head and half turned to Ryan. "Working on it. You got a line on anyone else?"

"Krysty and Jak took cover to my right, about ten yards out. Don't know where Mildred and Doc."

"Mildred ended up on the other side of the street, in that falling-down house with half a second floor. That could be useful. Probably better that Doc's taken cover. He can man the fort with me."

Ryan wrinkled his nose as he smelled burning meat. Their untended dinner was going up in flames. "Fireblast and fuck! There goes the turkey." Adding insult to injury, another large-caliber round cracked out, and the carcass burst apart in an explosion of half-raw meat, bone fragments and watery liquid. Ryan snarled, his growling stomach adding its own comment on the travesty that had just happened in front of him. "Now they've really pissed me off."

"Sure would help if you could get a bead on where that longblaster is."

"Dammit, I—" Ryan paused, replaying the exploding meal in his mind's eye, particularly where the bullet had come from. The coldheart had gotten cocky—he'd started playing with them and given Ryan valuable information about his position with that last shot. "About twenty-five feet off the ground, probably third-story window or roof, mebbe one hundred yards straight ahead on the other side of this wall."

"All right, then. They'll be running at least two teams of two, mebbe three out to flank us while that longblaster keeps our heads down. Means some of us go hunting."

Ryan's lips peeled back in a wolfish grin. "I'm game. Care to fill me in on your plan?"

J.B. grinned. "We'll outflank the flankers, you go up

the middle and take out the longblaster. Isn't that what we've been discussing?"

Ryan slapped his oldest friend on the shoulder. "Trader always said never to split up your group. Half your force is—"

"Half your firepower, I know, I know. He also said, 'Find yourself ambushed and your best chance of not buying the farm is to go forward like goose shit off a shovel. They won't be expecting that.'"

Ryan nodded. "Just wanna make sure we don't make the wrong choice, that's all."

"Since when have you ever been worried about that? Just make sure you don't get your ticket punched today." J.B. whistled, low yet loud. The couple on Ryan's right, the beautiful, flame-haired Krysty and a skinny, albino teenager, Jak Lauren, glanced over. With a series of hand signals, he instructed them what to do. A pair of nods, and they disappeared around the far corner of the crumbling shop, the glass in its large windows long gone.

J.B. turned to the black woman peeking out from a gaping doorway in a building that still had its walls. He pointed up, held up two fingers, then pantomimed shooting a pistol. With a curt nod, she disappeared into the darkness.

J.B. raised his subgun so the barrel just poked over the top of the wall. "I'll find Doc later. Get ready to move."

Ryan had already done so, securing his Steyr SSG-70 longblaster across his back and checking the broad-bladed eighteen-inch panga sheathed on his left hip and the narrow-bladed flensing knife at his belt before crouch-walking to the far end of the wall, poised for flight. His right hand was filled with his Sig

Sauer P-226 pistol with its integral silencer, the perfect weapon for close-quarter urban hunting—if the sound suppressor worked—which it often didn't. "Ready when you are."

J.B. squeezed his mini-Uzi's trigger three times, sending short bursts in the direction of the sniper. Ryan would have bet that the man known as the Armorer had come close to hitting the building the sniper was holed up in, just by using the brief description of where the last shot had come from.

However, that was of little consequence, since the moment J.B. fired, Ryan had burst from cover to reach the nearest building. Even as he ran, he heard the louder boom of the longblaster in the distance and felt something pluck at his sleeve as he ran to a large pile of debris topped with a still-intact roof.

Taking a moment to get his breath and bearings, the one-eyed man peeked underneath the roof to find a narrow passageway running down its entire length—the perfect hidey-hole for what he needed to do. Dropping to his knees, he peered inside. The tunnel appeared empty in the dim light. Nevertheless, he drew his thin-bladed flensing knife and placed it between his teeth before crawling into the hole, not wanting to be surprised by any occupants that might be resting inside.

AS A CHILD, J.B. HAD ONCE SEEN a working targeting comp that an outlander tinker had managed to get working. Attached to a car battery, it had been able to calculate the trajectory, azimuth and range of something called an M110 self-propelled howitzer to hit targets up to four miles away.

J.B. had been fascinated by the blinking display, ignoring the adults' pointed questions about where the man had gotten the device and how he'd managed to figure out how it worked. He was simply captivated by the complete and utter accuracy of the machine, no emotion, just simple math and logic used in its calculations to place the bomb where it was supposed to go.

Now, some thirty-odd years later, if anyone had said his own mind worked much like that targeting comp, he would have regarded them with a long, flat stare.

The Armorer had already narrowed down what kind of longblaster they were facing—*hunting gun, perhaps* Remington *bolt-action, .308 caliber*—and taken his measure of the person behind the sights. The coldheart was calm, picked his shots well. From Ryan's estimates, he'd triangulated where the coldheart was, and had aimed high to allow the bursts from his mini-Uzi a chance to arc into the building. A long shot, to be sure, but he had faced death so many times he'd lost count of how often he thought he might have glimpsed the shadow of the conductor waiting to take him aboard the last train to the coast. He fully expected this to be one of those times, as well.

A muffled knock on the wall let him know Mildred was in position. Thinking about the stocky, opinionated predark black woman and the relationship they shared caused the corners of his mouth to twitch up in what might have been a smile, flicking across his face before it vanished again as he turned to the task at hand—providing a very noticeable target without actually getting himself shot.

Readying the mini-Uzi again, he fired two single shots, hoping to make the approaching coldhearts think he was running low on ammo. That was only one of the surprises he had in store for any attackers who had the misfortune to stumble across him in the gathering darkness.

He gripped the mini-Uzi tightly and squeezed off two more shots. Knowing exactly how many shots were left in the magazine, J.B. pressed the trigger once, then again, hearing the loud click as the firing pin fell on an empty chamber, and pulled the trigger twice more, wincing at the potential damage the pin might be suffering as he did so. He heard the crackle of the fire and the oily hiss of the shattered bird carcass as it crisped in the flames, but J.B.'s ears were focused on the sounds coming from outside the firelight—the scrape of a boot on concrete, the clink of metal on metal as the leftmost team snuck closer to try to get the drop on their targets. With him on one side and Mildred on the other, it was a perfect situation to take them out in a lethal cross fire.

The soft snick of a full magazine slotting into the mini-Uzi's handle made J.B. look down. Almost of their own accord, his hands had removed the subgun's empty stick mag and replaced it with a full one from the pocket of his jacket while he'd been listening to their enemies approach. Slowly drawing the cocking handle back, he set the weapon beside him and picked up the second surprise he was going to spring on the raiders. They just had to come a few steps closer….

He was just about to roll out and spray lethal lead when a loud stage whisper carried across the campsite to his ears. "John Barrymore, is that you?"

Dark night! he thought as the movement on the other side of the wall stopped. *Doc, you triple-stupe, sometimes you're more trouble than you're worth.*

Before he could alter his plan, J.B. heard running footsteps from behind him, and then a gruff voice calling out, "Move an' yer dead, old man!"

HAIR TIGHTLY COILED AT HER nape, Krysty Wroth moved through the twilight like a panther tracking its prey—swift, intelligent, remorseless. They were out here somewhere, and she was going to find them and put them on the ground before they did the same to her and her friends. The titian-haired beauty's S&W blaster was at her side, held low but ready to fire at a moment's notice. Her hand-tooled blue cowboy boots clicked on debris as she picked her way through what had been an abandoned store, the once spotless and level tile floor now buckled and slanting, covered with dust, dirt and fragments of glass from its shattered windows.

She knew Jak was advancing parallel with her a few paces to her right, his snow-white hair only somewhat muted in the night. She'd suggested that he cover it more than once, but the albino teen had refused, saying he didn't like wearing anything on his head, even though she had seen him wear an old army cap on at least one occasion. She didn't argue, however—if it made him a more likely target to their enemies, so be it. Besides, she knew he could take care of himself, with or without a blaster.

J.B.'s instructions had been clear—*advance under cover and find a place to ambush attackers*—and she intended to follow them to the letter. She knew it was risky, but she trusted the small man almost as much as she trusted Ryan, and knew he wouldn't have placed them here if there was no chance of getting the job done.

A long counter that ran across the room was also warped and collapsing. Behind it was a space where someone had waited on customers long ago, selling whatever goods they had, and another set of counters that lined the back wall. They looked sturdy enough, however, and Krysty would be able to crouch under the window set several feet up on the wall, even using it as a blaster port if necessary.

She hissed at Jak, who had prowled to the gaping back door, making not a whisper of noise as he'd crept through the room. At her signal, he squatted in the shadow next to the opening, his big .357 Magnum Colt Python almost dwarfing his hands. Krysty held up her closed fist, the signal to stay where he was, then pointed to the window. Jak shrugged, watching her lithe form as she climbed up on the shelf, which creaked a bit under her weight, but held. Standing next to the opening, she cautiously leaned out far enough to get a view of the shattered street outside. Nothing seemed to be moving. Where the hell are they? she wondered.

"Bored. Let's go." Jak's whisper made her start, since it came from only a few feet away. She turned just far enough to see his pale face gleam in the rising moon. He was trying very hard not to stare at her ass, currently uncovered by her shaggy bearskin coat, which she had left near the fire.

She shook her head. "We let them come to us, remember?"

The albino teen shook his head. "Too long. Die waitin' fuckers to come."

Krysty took one last look outside—still no one there. She knew they couldn't have passed the pair—there was no way they wouldn't have seen the coldhearts. "All right. Get back to the door, and we'll go to the next building. Wait for me there."

"Sure, sure." He was already at the doorway by the time she got to the floor, and before she could join him, he had peeked out. "Hey, see one!" Without waiting for an answer, he darted outside.

“Jak, get back here!” Krysty stepped forward just as she felt the unmistakable pressure of a blaster barrel pressed to the back of her head.

“Don’t move, girlie, or you won’t have that pretty head no more.”

Chapter Two

"Come on, J.B., what's taking so long down there?" Mildred Wyeth muttered under her breath as she waited in the second story darkness, her ZKR 551 target pistol poised to aim and fire as soon as the Armorer sprung his trap. Except something was delaying the whole plan.

Having been placed into cryogenic suspension after an adverse reaction to anesthetic during what was supposed to have been a routine operation in the year 2000, the last thing Mildred expected to wake to was the devastated remains of America in a blighted world. But when she had opened her eyes in the cryo chamber, the appearance of the motley assortment of men and the woman who surrounded her had immediately let her know that wherever she was, it definitely wasn't Kansas anymore.

Since then, she had undergone a crash course on life in the Deathlands, adapting to survive in this untamed world, with the pockets of civilization they encountered raw and rough around the edges. She had seen and done things that would have made the old Mildred curse or sob or scream, but now they were taken as a matter of survival, if not of everyday life. In addition, she had been a doctor in her old life, working on the very cryogenic machinery that had saved her life, only to deposit her a century in the future into a hellish land. The irony was all too easy to grasp.

In the beginning, there had been times when she had wondered if this was all a long nightmare or some cruel joke that someone was playing on her. She'd never mentioned it to anyone in the rest of the group, not even J.B., but simply soldiered on, hoping the next place they might find would be some kind of refuge against the insanity that had claimed the world she'd known long ago. But as she had become more acclimatized to her surroundings, she'd been able to hone the necessary survival skills. Sometimes, that thought made her proud of how she had adapted.

Sometimes, it scared the hell out of her.

Now, however, wasn't one of those times. From the moment the first bullet had hit the dirt, there was no time for introspection, only the instinct to stay alive. To kill before being killed.

In that, Mildred had been both lucky and unlucky. She'd been foraging for firewood several yards away from the campfire when the shooting had started. The nearest cover had been the half-collapsed building a few steps away—in the opposite direction from the group. J.B., however, had turned that liability into an opportunity, as she was now hidden in an elevated position, ready to drop any enemy who came into her sights.

Normally the target pistol she carried would also have been a detriment in her situation, but Mildred knew it like she knew herself, and what she could do with it. It also helped that she had been an Olympic-medalist target shooter back in the twentieth century. That was how she had gotten through the killing in the early days. She pretended their savage, slavering enemies had big, black targets on them—aim, shoot and knock 'em down.

She hadn't needed to pretend in a long time.

"Come on, come on, J.B." Two shots from his Uzi rang out, then the clack of the pin falling on an empty chamber. Risking exposing her position, Mildred peeked out over the edge in hopes of spotting one of the lurking bastards creeping in. Instead, what she saw made her heart lurch into her throat.

Below her, three men in identical faded olive-drab fatigue shirts with a patch on the right shoulder trained weapons on a scarecrow-limbed figure in an old, stained frock coat, black pants and battered knee boots. The white-haired old man was currently staring at the armed trio with his arms thrust above his head.

Even as she aimed at the nearest man over the sights of her pistol, the words rose unbidden in her throat.

"Goddammit, Doc!"

ALTHOUGH HE KNEW THE REST of the group sometimes differed in their opinion as to whether Dr. Theophilus Algernon Tanner was a help or a hindrance to them, often depending on the day, the old man with the oddly perfect white teeth, known as Doc to his companions, had a surprisingly accurate gauge of his strengths and weaknesses.

When he was lucid, which was more often than not, he was a definite strength, able to recall esoteric bits of arcane lore that could mean the difference between life and death for Ryan and the rest of the group—much like when he had first met them, as the performing prisoner of Baron Jordan Teague in the ville of Mocsin, long, long ago. When they had all ended up trapped in the mountains while searching for the legendary Project

Cerberus, surrounded by a tribe of hostile Indians, who had saved all of them?

Why, Doc Tanner, that's who.

He'd stepped up to that seamless wall of solid steel and punched in the numbers that had allowed access to that very first redoubt. Saved them all, he had. Not that he expected anyone to remember in the incredible onslaught of adventures they had lived through since. But ever since that day, he'd held tight to that memory.

For that had been the day Ryan Cawdor had given him back his life, such as it was.

By far, Doc would have preferred to have his old, original life back. Like Mildred, he was a man from another time. But where she had Rip Van Winkled her way into the future, he had, in the paraphrased words of the great bard himself, from his own existence been untimely ripped.

He'd had a wonderful life as a doctor of science in Vermont, back before skydark, way back in the late nineteenth century. He'd been married, with two beautiful children. The bright smiles of his wife, Emily, and his children, Rachel and Jolyon, still haunted him in his dreams—close enough to touch, to hold, to kiss—then disappearing when he opened his eyes, never to be seen in this world or any other again.

Doc had been trawled—brought forward in time—to around 1998, one of the only successful test subjects of Operation Chronos, a division of the Totality Concept, which had explored every strange way of bending the known laws of science to man's will. The whitecoats had studied him eight ways from Sunday, performed every test known to man on him, trying to find out how he had survived the mind-warping, body-wrenching trip, where others hadn't.

In the beginning, Doc had been patient and cooperative, sure that once they had finished their work, they would send him back. It was the first of several miscalculations on his part. When they kept him there longer than he desired, he tried to send himself back. That was his second mistake. The greedy, black-hearted barons of the Deathlands had much in common with the pitiless, cold-eyed scientists Doc had met in the late twentieth century—in particular, they both knew when a person had outlived his usefulness.

Nowadays, that person would usually meet either a quick or slow death, depending on the perversity of the baron. The scientists of the Totality Concept were infinitely more heartless. Figuring Doc had survived being plucked from his time, they had trawled the now difficult subject again—into the future, and the Deathlands. His mind scrambled from the jumps, Doc had wandered the hell-blasted lands until falling in with Strasser and his ilk, and had been tormented further—he still couldn't hear a pig squeal without his bowels tightening—until being rescued by Ryan and his friends.

Since then he had accompanied his companions around the country and beyond, helping as they moved from place to place, never staying long, but doing what they could to make wherever they visited better however they could. That was one of the things Doc clung to in this sanity-threatening world—that there were still good people in it who could be counted on to do the right thing when it mattered. Ryan Cawdor and his companions were definitely those good people.

To that end, Doc would do whatever he could for them, including risking his life to serve as a distraction for the three ruffians who currently had him in their sights. At the moment, his mind was perfectly sane, and more than aware that he was a finger twitch away from being blasted into oblivion. And yet…they hadn't shot him yet, not even the sniper, to whom he had to have presented a perfect target, outlined in the fire as he was. Why was that?

Doc had no time to ponder that particular mystery. If he didn't keep up his pretense, he'd be lying on the cold ground in an instant, dead as a doornail. His rich baritone voice reverberating in his throat, Doc played the part of a senile old codger as only he could, doffing an imaginary hat and sweeping out his arm in a wide bow.

"I beg your pardon, good sirs, but I seem to have mislaid my companions somewhere around here. If you would kindly assist me in ascertaining their whereabouts, I would be most grateful." His gaze flicked to J.B., who was still lying prone on the ground behind the wall, mostly obscured from the three coldhearts' sight, the long barrel of the autoshotgun he carried clenched in both hands. *Any time now, John Barrymore*, Doc thought.

The three men looked to be just a few more of the ever-present two-legged predators that scourged the Deathlands, looking for anything they could get their hands on—food, weapons, women, wags. Each was unshaved and rank, dressed in a variety of tattered clothes—except for the similar green shirts worn by each one—the man on the far left without boots on his feet, just blackened, tattered rags wrapped halfway up his legs. Their weapons, however, two remade AK-47s and a battered ArmaLite AR-18, appeared to be in fine working order.

"Nuking hell! Gotta be more than just you making

all the racket, white-hair," the furthest one drawled. "Know we saw least three figures here."

Doc spread his arms wide. "As I mentioned, they seem to have up and left me. I would call them back, but the sight of your armament would no doubt cause a veritable state of panic, for they are indeed peace-loving folks." As he spoke, Doc stared daggers at J.B., who had remained motionless during his entire speech. Then, the old man realized exactly why that was.

In his eagerness to serve as the decoy, he had inadvertently advanced too far ahead, and now stood between the weapons master and his targets. Doc was pretty sure that Mildred was in the mostly ruined building on the other side of the ruffians, which meant that he was in her line of sight, as well. To shoot one of them meant risking the bullet passing through her target and perforating him—a fate he wished to avoid at all costs, especially having seen how accurate she was with her target pistol.

No, if anyone was going to get him out of this predicament, it would have to be Doc himself. Ah, well, it wasn't the first time.

The pair serving as the vanguard of the squad cast uneasy looks into the darkness around them, expecting—as was wise—that a bullet might scream out of the night at them at any moment. One of them glanced back at their apparent leader. "What do ya wanna do?"

"Take 'em for interrogation. The boss'll wanna have a chat."

The third man motioned Doc forward with the barrel of his longblaster. "Come on, old man, and keep those arms up."

Hands groping the sky, Doc searched the ground for a suitable depression or obstacle that would lend his second distraction an ounce of credibility. He found it in a large stone right in front of him. Stepping forward, he let his foot land squarely on top of it, and immediately slip off, pitching him heavily to the ground.

As flashes of pain jolted up his knee and elbow, Doc saw all hell erupt around him.

AS HE BURST OUT INTO THE DARK night, Jak shook his head at Krysty's whispered admonishment. Out here, stalking and hunting men, there wasn't no one better, hands down.

For a moment, he was taken back to the steaming, fetid jungles of his birthplace, Louisiana. Trained to chill from the moment he could crawl, he'd grown up fighting Baron Tourment all his life, until Ryan and his companions had appeared and helped him put an end to the man's sick reign of terror. After that, he'd joined Ryan and the others. With the exception of a brief period when he had tried to build a different life, he'd been with them ever since.

When it came to chilling, maybe a fingerwidth separated Jak and Ryan. J.B. and Krysty were both real good in a fight, and Mildred did things with that small pistol that Jak could only dream about, but when it came to straight up, hand-to-hand chilling, Jak and Ryan were tops. Jak sometimes wondered, if it came down to it, whether he could take Ryan in a no weapons fight. He knew he was good, damn good. But Ryan, he was something else. A rough fighter, but with a strength of will that couldn't be believed. He'd seen Ryan survive things that would have reduced a lesser man to shattered pulp. So no, Jak didn't believe he could take the one-eyed man.

But when it came to human vermin like this, there was no contest.

He had taken off after the glimpse of movement before Krysty could stop him, primarily because he didn't want her help. Oh, she could be impressive in a fight as well, but with those damn boots on, she'd signal their approach like a war wag at full throttle. No, this sort of chilling was best done quick and quiet, and no one was better at both than Jak.

The man he was trailing ducked around another shattered building, disappearing from sight for a few moments. Jak trotted to the corner of the wall, every sense alert, his strange, ruby-red eyes seeing his surroundings like it was almost noon. He peeked around the corner, just a fast glance, to make sure the bastard wasn't setting up to coldcock him.

Nothing moved in the gloom. Jak settled himself and listened to the night, his heightened senses straining for the slightest noise.

There. It was the softest of sounds, maybe cloth brushing against cloth, but it was enough. And just in time, too, as the flat cracks of a blaster from behind him shattered the silence. Jak didn't look back, knowing wiry J.B. was doing his part.

And so was he.

Keeping his .357 at his side, the albino teen tiptoed toward his prey as silent as stalking death. The shots died away, and there was only Jak and his soon-to-be victims.

Edging to the next corner of the former building, he listened again and heard more this time—whispers and the soft clicks of blasters being readied. Jak took a deep breath in through his nose, let it pass out through his mouth. He hauled back on the hammer of his blaster with the thumb of his hand, brought the weapon around to grasp it in both his hands and rounded the corner, ready to blast them into hell—

As expected, when they looked up and saw his face, there was a moment of shock at his stark-white hair, pale skin and burning red eyes. He'd surprised a pair of the intruders, both dressed in green, long-sleeved shirts. The one on the left was older, taller, with salt-and-pepper hair and a grizzled look, as if he had seen his share of hard living. A lot of people looked like that in the Deathlands, however. This guy was simply another one who'd chosen the way of the coldheart instead of some other way to live.

His partner was younger, maybe only a few years older than Jak, with a dirty yet unlined face. His movements were unsure as he fumbled with his longblaster, a hunting model with the stock sawed off and black electrical tape wrapped around the foregrip. He looked up at Jak, his mouth hanging open.

The way was as clear as glass—put a bullet into the old man, then follow through on the younger while he was still gaping at the albino apparition that had just appeared. Jak started to squeeze the trigger of his Colt Python when his attention was caught by something else shambling out of the darkness behind the two men.

As soon as he saw it, Jak moved his blaster a fraction to point between the two. Pulling the trigger, he had just enough time to shout, "Stickie!" before the weapon's roar drowned out all other noises. The snap-aimed shot only grazed the mutie's arm as it headed for the taller man.

The two men started at the bullet passing between them, then whirled. Each reacted differently upon seeing the naked, pasty, flabby mutie with its narrow, bulging eyes, vestigial nose, lipless mouth and fleshy hands, each finger tipped with a sucker that could literally tear a man's face off.

The older man pointed his sawed off, double-barreled shotgun at the new threat, following the unwritten law of the land that stickies were to be chilled on sight. The blaster boomed, a cloud of pellets ripping into the mutie's side, but not stopping its advance for an instant.

The second man's reflexes were a bit slower, as he was still bringing his rifle into play, when the stickie barreled into him. One second, the albino teen was staring at his own death, the next the man was on his knees, a guttural scream bursting from his lips as the mutie behind him slapped its hand over his face and brutally yanked his head back, hard enough for the vertebrae in his spine to crack at the impossible angle forced upon them. It was just as well, too, since what happened next would have also put the man on the last train to the coast, just more agonizingly slowly.

The stickie pulled its hand away from the man's face, the skin and flesh on his forehead and cheekbones peeling away from his skull with wet, tearing sounds, as if the creature was removing a mask to see who was underneath. Blood sprayed from his ruined head as the stickie twisted the bloody skull ninety degrees to the left, then let the twitching body drop, raising its head to snarl at the other two men.

But Jak had corrected his aim by then, lining up the Python's sights on that hideous face and squeezing off another round. The slug hit the stickie right in the nose, obliterating it as the hollowpoint round mushroomed inside the skull, plowing through and punching out the back, spraying blood, bone and brains everywhere.

Still, the stickie took a step toward the pair of men, its shattered mouth opening and closing in its ruined face before the grizzled coldheart let fly with his second barrel, pulverizing the rest of the mutie's face and sending it toppling over, dead.

His chest heaving, the older man turned back—to find himself staring down the barrel of Jak's blaster. The empty shotgun less than useless in his hands, the man raised his arms, letting the weapon clatter to the ground at his feet. "C'mon, kid, you can't chill me after we both faced that."

"Shut mouth." Jak had used the distraction of the stickie to move inside the half room, and now had his back against the wall.

"Please, I don't have another blaster—just let me go, and I'll git back where I came from."

"Said shut mouth, fucker." Jak hesitated for a second, considering whether he should take the man prisoner so they could find out what was going on around here. He made up his mind, the muzzle centering on the man's forehead. "Get on knees."

The man collapsed to the ground. "Black dust, no."

"Shut fuck up." Jak stepped out from the wall, then caught a flicker of movement to his left as a shadow dropped over him. Whirling, he was bringing the .357 around when he saw a strange pattern appear in his vision, an oval of fine crosshatching right in front of him.

The rifle butt smacked into his forehead above the right eye, laying the skinny albino out full-length on the ground, the pistol flying from his grasp.

He heard snatches of conversation between the grizzled man and someone else. "Runty little fucker, ain't he?"

"Son of a bitch got the drop on Larssen and me 'fore a stickie jumped us, tore his face off. Larssen told me there's another one thataway, a woman. Let's grab her, too. Now that we got her kin, she'll deal."

The last thing Jak saw was the grizzled man standing over him, holding his Colt Python in his hand, before the world swirled and faded around him.

Chapter Three

Where did he come from? Krysty wondered as she slowly raised her hands, the S&W revolver dangling on her index finger by the trigger guard. Beneath the counter—stupe not to check there first, was her conclusion.

She felt the pressure of the blaster barrel lessen as her captor stepped away. "Set the blaster down, then turn around slowly. Try anythin' dumb, and all you'll get's a third eye in your forehead."

She complied with the orders, turning on her heel, and she heard a small gasp as the man took in her features.

With her long dark crimson hair framing a gorgeous face featuring high cheekbones, a sleek, straight nose, full lips and deep green eyes that glinted in the sunlight like cut emeralds, Krysty had a good idea of what the typical man's thoughts turned to when he first saw her. And that was before they got a look at her body, with its full breasts, narrow waist, long, lithe legs and strong arms. She was any man's wet dream, and she was well aware of it.

While growing up in Harmony, her mother, Sonja, had drilled it into her that her looks would draw attention, most of it unwanted. The elder Wroth had summed it up this way: "Give any man long enough, my child, and he will begin thinking about you with his smaller head rather than his larger one." Mother Sonja had taught her how to read a man's intentions through body language—the majority of them were absurdly easy—and how to turn just about any situation to her advantage. It was the job of her other closest living relative, Uncle Tyas McCann, to teach her how to protect herself from these unwanted advances, and he had taught her very well indeed.

Krysty faced her captor with her head held high and her back straight, which, of course, just happened to show off her high, firm breasts to great effect underneath her dark blue jumpsuit, the zipper lowered down the middle just enough to give a tantalizing glimpse of the creamy-skinned wonders underneath. She watched the expression change on his face, saw his lust war with whatever orders he had been given, and simply bided her time.

"Oh, girlie, the boss will certainly want to see ya, I garan'tee. But first—" his mouth curved open in a knowing leer, revealing several missing teeth, and the remaining ones spotted with yellow and brown "—I best make sure ya ain't hidin' any other weapons. Don't try nothin' stupe, and ya might even enjoy it."

Krysty's face might have been carved from white marble for all the reaction she showed. The man placed his blaster at her stomach, promising a horrible, gut-shot passing if she tried anything. He ran his dirty hands over her lower legs, up her shapely thighs and between the vee of her sex, lingering there much longer than necessary, his callused fingers pinching hard. Krysty's lips tightened, but she made no sound at all.

"Strong, silent type, huh? The boss likes 'em to scream—I'm sure he'll enjoy breakin' you in, bitch."

Krysty didn't deign to make eye contact, but she did speak. "Just get it over with."

"Go fast as I please, girlie. No fire-haired whore tells me what ta do." His hands spidered upward, across her muscular midriff, heading for her breasts. "Almost there, sweetheart."

Krysty's eyes flicked downward just as he grabbed the tab of her jumpsuit zipper and pulled it down, the material parting to reveal more of her breasts, supported by a simple white bra. His eyes were solely on those round globes, and she felt the pressure on her abdomen lessen a bit as he licked his lips, his free hand just inches away. "Course, mebbe you and I could cut a deal right here—"

The moment his hand touched her skin, Krysty moved. Her left hand swept down and across, catching the man's blaster hand and shoving it aside. At the same time, her right leg shot up, the chiseled metal point of silver-toed cowboy boot sinking deep into the man's genitals. The man's grin was replaced by a wide-open O of shock as the brutal assault on his privates short-circuited his brain. His trigger finger spasmed, sending a bullet into the floor as his other hand moved to cup his injured parts. He sank to his knees, retching once, a globule of vomit spraying from his lips to splatter on the floor.

With her right hand, Krysty had snatched her blaster off the counter and brought the butt down on the back of the man's neck, laying him out with one ferocious blow.

Zipping up her jumpsuit, she turned to the doorway just as a shadow fell across it. She saw a flash of white hair and relaxed for a moment, thinking it was just Jak returning, except he was moving oddly, his feet dragging, almost as if—

"Don't move, or he gets a bullet in the head," a voice

said from behind her and to the left. Startled, Krysty half turned, watching both the speaker and the man who had one arm curled around Jak's throat, holding him up, the teen's.357 Magnum blaster pressed to his temple.

Gaia, give me strength, she thought, raising her hands for the second time in as many minutes, just as a profusion of blaster shots erupted in the distance.

DOC HADN'T EVEN FINISHED bouncing in the dirt before J.B. leveled the M-4000 autoshotgun and let loose a hailstorm of death. The razor-sharp steel fléchettes passed over Doc's outstretched body, arrowing through the knees of both coldhearts and sending them crashing to the ground, tormented screams bursting from their throats as they clutched their bloody, crippled legs.

The old man hadn't been idle, either, hauling his massive LeMat single-action blaster out from under his coat and pointing it at the third man, who was standing stock-still on the other side of the wall, staring at the bloody tableau that had unfolded before him. He opened his mouth as if to speak, but all that came out was a huge gout of blood. Eyes rolling back in his head, he collapsed onto the wall, a smaller trickle of blood leaking from the round hole in the top of his skull.

"Upon my word." Doc kept his blaster pointed at the two wounded men as he started to clamber to his feet. In seconds, J.B. was at his side, hauling him back down behind the wall while keeping his M-4000 aimed at the pair, both of whom had stopped rolling on the ground and stared back at the companions with hate-filled eyes.

The Armorer waved at the building across the street

even as he shook his head. "Dark night, Doc, you trying to get yourself killed?"

Doc grinned, showing his peculiarly even, white teeth. "While I will admit that my diversion may not have been well planned, it did do the trick, did it not?"

"These triple-stupe bastards aren't what I'm talking about." J.B. jabbed a thumb at the other side of the wall. "Remember the longblaster out there? Next time, think of something better than playing the hero—sure way to get a bullet through the brainpan."

"Perhaps, but I got the distinct impression that these brigands were not coming to kill us, but to capture as many alive as they could."

"Black dust, Doc, I swear that third guy came within an ass-hair of hitting you with his blaster."

Mildred had come down from the building and run across the street in a crouch to join them, looking at their two prisoners with distaste. "What were you thinking, showing yourself like that?"

Doc shrugged. "I saw a course of action and took it. In hindsight, I concur that may not have been the most prudent avenue to pursue, but it got the job done, so to speak."

The black woman shook her head, her beaded plaits swaying back and forth. "I swear, Doc, you take more words to say 'I fucked up' than anyone I know. What about these two?" She indicated the pair with the barrel of her blaster.

"See if you can patch them up long enough to— Look out!" J.B. shoved Mildred aside and brought up his shotgun even as Doc's LeMat boomed. The slug smashed through the first prisoner's breastbone, sending splinters of bone along with the slug crashing into his heart, stopping it instantly. The crude blaster, tape wrapped around its handle, fell from his hand.

The other coldheart had launched his own diversion by trying to grab Mildred. J.B. didn't waste a shot on him, but instead brought the M-4000's stock around in a short arc, cracking the man in the side of the head. He fell over as if someone had cut his spinal cord, collapsing in a sprawled heap on the ground.

"Damn, J.B." Her blaster out, she checked the man for weapons, then checked his neck for a pulse. "You killed him. Must have crushed his temple with that little love tap of yours."

The Armorer grimaced as he bent over to examine the corpse. "Didn't think I hit him that hard."

"You don't know your own strength, John Barrymore." For some reason Doc found that statement absurdly funny, slapping his knee as he laughed so hard he nearly choked, coughing and spluttering. J.B. glanced at Mildred in puzzlement, but she returned his look with a shrug before craning her neck a bit to peer cautiously over the wall.

"Shouldn't we be finding the others?"

J.B. checked his chron. "Haven't heard any signals—no gunshots or other signal calls yet—but it's only been about three minutes since they left. Let's give them two more, then poke around for them. Ryan's still out there after the sniper. We better leave him a chance to take the coldheart out before we risk our necks going anywhere."

The boom of the sniper rifle echoed all around them, making heads turn toward the no-man's land on the other side of the wall. J.B. frowned. "Or we might have to go a bit sooner than planned."

AS HE RETURNED to consciousness, Jak had the strange sense he was floating over the ground. Then there were the noises—voices nearby—a man, no, two men talking, and a woman whose voice sounded familiar.

The rest of his awareness came back between flashes of pain. First was his swollen head, with a large lump on his forehead that he couldn't touch for some reason. His cheek was wet, too, although he didn't know if that was his blood or someone else's. Also, there was a band of unyielding pressure around his throat, constrictive enough to allow just a bit of air to get through. Lastly, he felt a warm circle of metal pressed against his temple, and the distinct odor of cordite every time he inhaled. His eyes fluttered, but he had the sense to remain as still as possible, trying to pick out what was being said around him.

"Blind norad, we got a live one here!"

"Good-lookin', too. All right, step away from Henney there, and don't do anything stupe, or your kid gets it."

There was a startled cough of surprise, and Jak's mouth twitched as the thought of what the expression on Krysty's face had to look like right now. When she spoke, her voice was lower and rough.

"My kid? You got a funny sense of humor if you think I'd lay claim to that puling whelp. Little bastard's been nothing but trouble since I found him six weeks ago. Now the son of a bitch's got me trapped and cornered, so you can have him for all I care. I just want to get out of this in one piece."

"I think that's something we can talk about later, but just in case, I'll gonna keep your little buddy here. Koons, get in here and see if you can rouse Johnny."

Jak heard footsteps approaching from outside, and

another person entered the room, crossing in front of him to behind the counter.

"Ah-ah—don't even twitch toward that blaster. See where this is pointed?" Jak felt his head being wrenched back and quickly closed his eyes in case the other man was looking at him. The circle of metal pressed hard into the skin over his temple, but Jak hadn't heard the hammer being cocked—yet. "I'll vent his head if you move the wrong way. Come out from over there and stand right here. Dammit, Koons, you almost let her get the drop on us."

"Thought you had her under control, ya stupe. I got my own problems right now. Johnny ain't looking too good—breathin' shallow and fast. Got a lump on his head the size of my fist, seems like."

"Shit." The man hawked up a wad of phlegm and spit. "You lay Johnny out, bitch?"

"He didn't know how to keep his hands to himself."

Jak felt the man behind him shift his weight. "Nukeshit, I knew this was gonna be more trouble than it was worth." Cracking open one eye, he peeked out through his lashes to see Krysty with her hands up, standing in the middle of the room. Sounds of movement came from behind the counter as the second man tended to the third one.

"If we don't get him back pronto, he's gonna die. Might not make it anyway."

Jak opened his eye farther, willing Krysty to look at his face, to know he was conscious. At last she did, but betrayed no reaction upon seeing his intense stare.

"All right, let's bind these two and take them both back. If there's more, the other team should take care of them. We got enough."

"Look, can't you just let me go?" Krysty stepped forward, her hands held out beseechingly.

"Nukin' hell, bitch, stay right where you are, or I'll pull this trigger and spray his brains all over the room!"

While she moved closer, Krysty arched one eyebrow at Jak in an unspoken question. Jak rolled his eyes, indicating what he thought of her query.

Krysty shrugged at the threat. "All right. It's your funeral."

"What—" was all the coldheart got out before Jak's right hand shot up and grabbed his captor's hand, levering the large blaster away from his temple before he could shoot. At the same time, the albino lowered his head against the man's forearm, gagging for a moment as his air was cut off, then powered it backward with all his strength, slamming the back of his skull into the man's nose. His right leg shot straight out ahead of him, then snapped backward, smashing his heel into the man's knee. Lastly, a twitch of his left wrist had dropped a narrow, leaf-bladed throwing blade into his hand, the tip of which adroitly found its way into the man's abdomen, under his rib cage, penetrating deep into his stomach.

Separately, any of the attacks would have been disorienting or crippling at the least. Together, they were an onslaught that spelled the man's doom. Too stunned from his crushed nose to squeeze the Python's trigger, he let his hostage go as he found himself falling to the right, his crippled knee unable to support his weight. The heavy blaster was plucked from his hand as he toppled over, suddenly aware of the sharp flash of pain blooming in his side, draining all his strength away as if it was leaking out along with his blood. The last thing he saw was the weird albino kid leaning over him, a thin, dripping blade in his pale hand, and those eyes, those slitted, red eyes, underneath that shock of white hair gleaming like some kind of demon….

Jak opened his throat with a slash, and the man's eyes dulled, glazing into the sightlessness of death. Blaster in hand, he turned to see that Krysty hadn't been idle while he was freeing himself. In one graceful bound, she had leaped on top of the crooked counter just as the third man's head had popped back up at the commotion.

"Trey—" he began before Krysty's muscled leg lashed out in a devastating front kick, the silver point of her boot catching him right in the lower jaw. The crack was loud in the silence as the bone shattered under the impact. The man spun and fell to the ground, clasping his hands to his ruined face as he rolled around, grunting and whuffling in pain. Without pausing, Krysty jumped down behind the counter, there was another crack, and then silence. She came out from behind it with her blaster in hand.

"Let's go."

"Works for me." His voice was hoarse, and Jak stepped carefully as a brief wave of nausea hit him, making him see stars and blackness for a moment.

"You all right?"

"Yeah, let's get back camp. Seen men and stickies. Warn others."

"Stickies? Where?"

"Pulled guy's face off next building. Blew its head off 'fore his buddies got drop on me and brought here."

"Shit, we better get back double-quick. Come on."

The tall redhead and the lean, white-haired teen slipped out of the room and back toward the campsite, leaving only the dead and dying behind.

Chapter Four

Knife gripped between his teeth, Ryan squirmed into the small tunnel, which seemed solid, if tight enough that his shoulders brushed the walls on both sides. He wouldn't shoot from here—the position was too confining—but it would give him enough cover to scan the area ahead and try to spot the sniper.

Levering himself forward on his elbows, he powered up the slight slope, staying low to the ground so the Steyr longblaster wouldn't get caught on the makeshift roof above his head. When he reached the top, the one-eyed man made sure he wasn't visible by anyone outside, sheathed his knife again and took out his new toy, which he'd found in the redoubt. He carefully unwrapped the bundle to reveal a black plastic and metal tube a bit over a foot long and four inches in diameter. Ryan took off the soft rubber cap at one end and hit a small button covered by a protective rubber cap. He heard the high-pitched whine of the rechargeable battery coming to life, then placed the device to his eye and gazed out on a transformed world.

The moonless night had been replaced by an eerie, lambent green as the night-vision scope amplified the invisible infrared light it was projecting more than twenty thousand times, turning the darkness into neon-green day. Ryan scanned the high points first, adjusting the 4x zoom to try to pick out any sign of movement.

At first, he didn't see anything. The guy might have left when night fell, he thought, but kept looking anyway, staring at the ruined hulks of buildings as if he could bring out anyone inside by sheer force of will. Long minutes passed without any sign of life. About to give up, Ryan decided to give it thirty more seconds before turning off the device to preserve the battery. He kept as still as possible, examining every aspect of the building he had chosen, from its empty windows, which looked like gaping, glowing eyesockets in the night-vision scope's lens, to the pole sticking off the roof, attached to the side of the building by a length of wood.

Ryan blinked and refocused on the "pole," pushing the magnifier to its maximum limit. He took one last long look. The man with the longblaster had camouflaged his position to look like part of the building, indistinguishable from the rest of the crumbling rubble. Ryan frowned. Whoever these guys were, they were well-trained, much better than the everyday, ragged bands of coldhearts.

He was still peering at the sniper's position when a dark shadow obscured the scope's vision. Thinking the unit had malfunctioned, he started to remove it from his eye, only to have it torn out of his hand to crash into the floor beneath him, the tinkle of broken glass telling him it was now just another piece of junk like everything else around him.

Instinctively, Ryan scooted down, hunching back into the tunnel. The action saved his life. A dirty, greasy hand slapped down on the tunnel floor right in front of him. The fingers wriggled on the dusty surface, then pulled free with a wet, sucking sound.

Stickie! Ryan looked up in time to see a hulking form block out the dim starlight. Hoarse breathing echoed in the small corridor, and Ryan caught the fetid scent of rotting meat wafting from the mutie's gaping maw. With a bestial grunt, the mutie grabbed both sides of the tunnel and began crawling inside, intent on destroying its prey.

Ryan was about to shove himself down to the other end when the entire tunnel rocked at the bottom. With a sinking feeling, the one-eyed man knew what was at the other end.

Forcing his right hand down to his hip, Ryan drew the P-226 Sig Sauer and aimed between his spread legs, all too aware of the slavering death only a yard or two away from his head. He fired blindly five times, the muzzle-flash illuminating the face of the stickie at the bottom of the tunnel, each burst of light revealing the destruction wrought upon its face as the 9 mm hollowpoint bullets slammed into it. Only when the last one punched through its eye did it whine shrilly and, expelling a fist-size wad of blood and phlegm, crumple to the floor, effectively blocking his retreat.

Ryan tried to bring the blaster back up, but found himself wedged in the tunnel, and couldn't straighten before the top stickie was almost upon him, its gluey hand slapping at his shirt and starting to pull him toward it. Above the pressure of being dragged to his death, the Deathlands warrior felt the sheath of the thin-bladed knife pressing against his neck.

He pushed at the stickie's rubbery arm with his left arm as hard as he could, trying to pin it against the tunnel wall, while he dropped his blaster and went for the blade at his neck with his right. As he brought his free hand around, the one-eyed smacked into something wet and slobbering, and he didn't hesitate. He curled his fingers into a fist and smashed them three times into what could only be the mutie's face, causing a howl of pain to reverberate through the passageway.

The mutie pulled back enough for Ryan to free his blade from its sheath and slash up with it. He met resistance and struck again and again, not giving the stickie a chance to recover or launch its own offensive. At one point, he felt the tip of the blade scrape bone, and felt warm, thin fluid run down his hand. The stickie screamed in pain and thrashed around in the passageway, bucking back and forth against the walls. Squealing in pain and surprise, the mutie retreated back up the tunnel.

When it was halfway out, it jerked in surprise, then slumped limply in the opening as the boom of the sniper's longblaster echoed off the walls. The stickie flailed feebly, then stiffened as its head seemed to explode, showering Ryan with gore from its shattered skull. The mutie's corpse sagged toward the floor of the tunnel, held up by the sucker pads of one of its fingers, still adhered to the wall.

Ryan wiped foul-smelling gore from his face and eyes and considered his current predicament. The big question now was, why didn't the sniper shoot the stickie when it was trying to climb in and tear Ryan's face off? But there was no time to ponder an answer. The stench of dead mutie, combined with burned cordite, was overpowering, and Ryan began to cough and choke as he slid to the bottom of the tunnel to retrieve his blaster—after first making sure the bottom stickie was dead by kicking it in the head several times. Only when he was sure did he crouch to feel for his Sig Sauer, finally retrieving it from the mush that had been the mutie's head and wiping off the gunk as best as he could. Then he tried shifting the body out of the tunnel, but even heaving at it with all his strength didn't budge it—the corpse was wedged fast.

Breathing through his mouth, Ryan knew there was only one way out. Panting with each movement, he began the laborious climb back up, the tunnel floor now slick with the stinking liquid dripping on him from the corpse above. At last he reached the sodden form and wedged his legs up into the tunnel to give himself a bit of a rest while he figured out the best way to escape the trap he found himself in.

Over, under, around or through, he thought, remembering one of the Trader's favorite axioms. With the other three options unavailable to him, there was only straight through, up and out, hoping the distraction of the stickie's suddenly animated body would be enough to cover his scramble to shelter.

The preparation for his escape attempt was almost overwhelming by itself. Ryan forced himself to get as close to the dead body as he could stand, after first confirming its deceased state by the simple expedient of putting a bullet in its brain. While there, he noticed something that made him pause. Stickies usually didn't wear much clothing, maybe a tattered pair of pants, if anything, but this one had a black nylon collar with a small box around its neck. He reminded himself to check it out if possible once he was out of this stifling, would-be tomb.

When he was wedged uncomfortably close, he heaved at the sticky, flabby body with all his strength, shoving it up and back until gravity took over, and the dead stickie slithered out of the opening to the ground below. Gagging on the stink, Ryan scrambled out as quickly as he could, diving to the ground and landing on the corpse, which expelled a loud, rank blast of stale air. He heard a crack over his head, followed immediately by the sting of concrete chips flying at his head, then the boom of the longblaster's report all around him.

Ryan was already moving, crawling over the debris to the nearest cover, a pile of concrete pieces that might have been a sidewalk a century ago. He'd just reached cover when the ground near his left arm puffed up dust, and the crack of the large-bore rifle exploded in the distance again.

"This is gettin' bastard old," Ryan muttered. Going back wasn't an option. As long that that keen-eyed coldheart held the high ground, they couldn't leave the area without someone taking a bullet or two.

The nearest cover was a copse of stunted trees, their thin trunks intertwined into a gnarled knot of wood that sprouted sickly branches reaching up to the sky. It was only a couple of feet wide, but it had to serve as shelter until Ryan could get to the half-standing house on the other side of it. Selecting a suitably large chunk of concrete, he tossed it to the left, then rolled right as fast as he could.

The shooter was no slouch. Ryan had just stopped behind the tree when he felt something tug at his boot, and heard the thunder of the longblaster's report again. Unslinging his own weapon, he felt the bottom of his combat boot and discovered the heel had been shot away.

"Bastard." Ryan slowly rose to a crouch, about to experiment with pushing the barrel through the tangled tree to see if he could draw a bead on his opponent, but a sudden explosion of wood above his head made him hit the dirt again. Looking up, he saw a fist-size hole in the profusion of tree trunks and immediately took off again, crawling like a snake through the rough terrain to the wall of the house.

Steyr clutched to his chest, Ryan circled around the house's right side, senses alert for signs of men, stickies or anything else that might try to kill him. The decaying landscape around him was eerily silent, considering all the recent activity, and the one-eyed man's shoulder blades itched, as if in anticipation of a bullet drilling between them. Shaking off the ominous feeling, he kept moving, drawing closer to the building where the sniper was holed up.

Stalking closer, he rounded a corner and ran smack into a pair of men coming the other way. The surprise was equal on both sides, but Ryan reacted faster, swinging his SSG's stock into the first man's jaw, slamming him into the wall and then to the ground, out cold. The second man was just bringing his rusty revolver up when Ryan jabbed the butt of the longblaster into the man's forehead, breaking the skin and sending him staggering backward, the blaster flying from his hand. Ryan followed right after him, but he didn't need to hit him again. When the man landed on the rocky ground, the snap of his broken neck was plainly audible to the one-eyed man. Nudging the now-limp body aside with his boot, he saw the sharp edge of the rock the guy had landed on.

Straightening, he scanned the shadows, looking for a scout or flanking team creeping up on him. A quick peek around the corner revealed the three-story building about twenty yards away. The long way to it meant going twice that distance, but it also kept him under cover almost the entire way. Slinging his Steyr, Ryan drew his Sig Sauer and replaced the half-full magazine with a full one from his pocket. Checking his back one last time, he scanned the windows of the building for movement, then hunched over and ran the last few yards to the wall, putting his back to it and hiding in the shadows as he listened for any kind of alarm. After several quiet seconds, he worked his way to the entrance, where a battered metal door hung on one hinge. Ryan listened to the pitch-blackness inside and, hearing nothing, edged into the room, leading with his blaster, careful not to touch or move the door.

He waited just inside until his eye adjusted to the gloom. When he could discern the walls instead of simply blank blackness, he began to advance cautiously, heading for the staircase he spotted on the back wall. The ground floor was completely bare of any furnishings or debris, just empty floor and support pillars throughout. He stepped quietly and listened for anyone coming after him, but heard nothing.

Reaching the stairs, Ryan began to climb, staying near the wall so the steps wouldn't give his position away with a telltale creak. Once he reached the top, Ryan was pleased to see the starlight streaming weakly in through the glassless windows. The next staircase was right above him, its entrance at the far end of the room. He had just taken his second step when a section of the floor gave way under his foot with a snap, the weak boards crashing to the ground. Cat-quick, he wrenched himself back before his leg fell through.

Ryan froze, hearing the rapid clomp of quick footfalls. This floor was empty, as well, with nowhere and nothing to hide him. The steps grew louder, and Ryan knew the coldhearts were seconds away from flushing him. A glance at the ceiling revealed a latticework of metal bars under tangles of metal pipes and ducts. He had no idea if it was strong enough to hold his weight, but it was the only option available. Shoving his blaster into his belt, he sprang up with all his strength, grabbing the thin metal and hoisting himself up as quickly as he dared. He had managed to pull his chin up when he heard the sound of boots on the stairs. The bar settled for a moment, and he feared it would pull loose, but it held, and he kept climbing, swinging his leg up and over and pulling himself onto the bar, balancing there just as the advance team hit the floor.

Like the others, they were swift and silent, quartering the room and sweeping and clearing each section with rapid movements. The pair moved well, always covering one another's back, and each man never out of sight of the other. They were completely covered from head to toe, one with a scarf wrapped around his head, and the other wearing what looked like an old gas mask, which gave Ryan an uncomfortable feeling. If they had gas weapons, he could be in for a world of hurt. Then he noticed there was no filtering canister on the end, and realized the hunter was wearing it as some kind of decoration or trophy.

So far, Ryan had been lucky. From what he could see, they hadn't looked up once. Of course, that didn't mean they wouldn't at any moment, but he couldn't move. If he tried for his blaster, he'd probably make enough noise to alert them, and that'd be all she wrote. So he waited and watched them come closer, trying to figure out some kind of plan.

At the far end, one of the coldhearts looked out the window and drew back in alarm, signaling to his partner about the lack of guards, apparently. There was a brief, signaled argument, then they headed back toward the stairway leading to the first floor, their weapons—two well-maintained short-barreled machine guns—held at their waist, muzzles pointing in front of them.

They were a few steps away when the glimmerings of a plan formed in Ryan's mind. It would require split-second timing, but if he could pull it off… He watched as they came closer…three steps…two steps…one step away…

When the coldhearts were right below him, about to take their first step onto the staircase, he let his feet swing free and dropped to the floor, barely making a sound as he landed right behind them, drawing his Sig Sauer as he landed.

There was a moment's surprise as both whirled to see their deaths in the single, icy-cold blue eye of the tall, black-haired man less than an arm's length away. Still, they tried to bring their blasters to bear on him before he put a bullet into their heads, knowing it was hopeless, but trying anyway.

And it was. Even before the man on the right could finish turning, a 9 mm slug had entered his eye socket, drilling straight back into his brain and out the back of his skull, splattering the wall with red-gray gore as he slumped against the wall, his feet trembling and kicking as his limbs slowly registered his death.

Ryan switched his aim to Gas Mask and triggered two shots, knowing that the plastic lens of its eyepieces could sometimes deflect a bullet enough to prevent a kill shot. One or the other had to have done the job, since his attacker froze, standing stock-still at the top of the stairs, blaster clenched in his hands. Ryan kept his weapon aimed at the bandit, just in case he was faking, but it seemed the coldheart was on the last train west, even if his body hadn't quite registered the fact yet.

From inside the gas mask came a small sigh, as if

the coldheart had exhaled his last breath, and he started to fall backward, down the stairs. Ryan was aware that something was wrong; then he noticed it, and threw himself to the side, just as the corpse's finger spasmed on the trigger of his blaster, emptying the entire magazine into the back of the staircase. The body disappeared, thumping its way down the stairs to land with a crash at the bottom as the roar from the blaster died away.

Sig Sauer covering the staircase, Ryan opened his eye to see the slumped body of the first raider, and dust and plaster trickling down from the blaster. The scarf, now askew over the head of the corpse, gave him another idea, and he got up and went over to the body, unwrapping the sodden garment and wrapping it around his head so that the gore-soaked section was over his face. He stripped the corpse of its drab-green shirt and slipped it on, finding the sleeves a couple inches too short, but figuring no one would notice. The smell of the scarf was overpowering, but he breathed through his mouth and walked to the stairs leading to the third floor, listening for anyone coming to investigate.

Only silence greeted him. Steeling himself, Ryan bent over and staggered up the stairs, breathing loudly with each step. At the top, he crawled out onto the landing, wheezing as if severely injured while looking around at the room.

The sniper's position was ahead and to the right, a form still bent over the longblaster, scanning outside. Another figure was in the window next to him, next to a small scope mounted on a tripod, but looking back at the staircase, a weapon pointed at the crawling form that had just appeared.

"Hey, stop right— Jeez, Carly, is that you? What

happened?" The voice turned from commanding to concerned, and Ryan felt a small hand on his arm, trying to help him up. "Come on. Let's get you over—Hey, you're not—"

The mistake was realized too late, as Ryan had already grabbed the spotter's arm in a steely grip while he shoved his Sig Sauer into the man's chest and pulled the trigger twice, shattering ribs and holing vital organs. The coldheart let out a startled grunt and collapsed to the floor. Ryan kicked the blaster out of his hand and aimed at the sniper, who had heard the commotion and was drawing a small blaster of his own. Their weapons went off almost simultaneously, and Ryan felt a small puff of air against the side of his head from the bullet's passage as his own shot hit his target in the upper chest. The shooter fell back against his blind and tried to lift his blaster again, but his second shot went wild into the darkness. Panting with the effort, he stared at the weapon in his hand as if it weighed a thousand pounds, then lifted his gaze back to Ryan.

"Bastard…." was his last, high-pitched word, then his head lolled, and the blaster slipped from his lifeless fingers. Ryan had been covering him while scanning the rest of the room, but finding no one else here, went over to the sniper's body. Something about him had caught his attention, and Ryan removed the drab-green cap from the body's head to find a surprise underneath.

A woman. Not even a woman, a girl, maybe in her late teens at most. Ryan didn't feel that much of a twang of conscience. Women were just as lethal in the Deathlands as men, more so a lot of times. And there was the fact that she had been trying to kill him just a few minutes ago. No, what he was more concerned about was who was training what should have been a ragtag group of bandits to have this much skill and precision.

Something had definitely changed in Denver, and Ryan was suddenly very curious to find out what.

Chapter Five

J.B. poked at the charred remains of what had been their dinner with the blade of his knife, shaking his head. "Damn shame."

"Got that right." Ryan had made his way back to the rest of the group to find them all puzzling over the unusual fight.

Mildred arched an eyebrow at both of them. "You talking about the turkey or that paramilitary force we just encountered?"

"Bit of both." Ryan exchanged a glance with J.B., who nodded. "Someone's got a base of operations here, and is supplying people with quality weapons—" he indicated the pile of blasters and magazines he'd taken from the bodies on his way out of the sniper's building "—and the training to use them well."

"Too well." J.B. was methodically sorting the pile of weapons into types, then calibers. "Wide range, from an AK-47 to a Webley revolver—wonder where that came from?—but all are well-tended, oiled and everything." He hefted the longblaster Ryan had brought back. "Remington 700, composite stock, 10x sight, very clean. Good trading value."

Mildred grimaced. "Whoever sent those people out here probably has a difference of opinion on that."

"Mebbe, but we're holding them now. Possession's a hundred percent of the law out here, you know that."

"Speaking of, what about the coldhearts themselves?" Krysty waved at the three corpses that had died trying to capture J.B., Mildred and Doc. "Some are in ragged uniforms, and others—like the ones you ran into—well dressed, and all with matching shirts. What about that?"

Ryan took off the shirt he'd worn back to his friends and examined the embroidered insignia on the right sleeve. Not a patch, the symbol—a lightning bolt diagonally bisecting a field that was red, with a small sword on the upper left, and blue with what looked like an unrolled scroll of paper on the lower right—was stitched directly into the cloth. He had no idea what it meant. Wealthy barons with delusions of grandeur often outfitted their sec men in matching uniforms, thinking it gave their ville an appearance of respectability and power. Ryan often thought it simply made the hired thugs easier to identify and kill.

Doc rubbed his temples with his long fingers. "And, except for the ones that our good man Ryan took out, they did not seem all that interested in chilling us, but rather were looking for captives. Standard operating procedure, if they were out to collect slaves, but that was not the impression I got. It is all most peculiar."

"Don't forget stickies," Jak piped up from the other side of the fire as he cast long looks into the darkness.

"And those collars they were wearing. What's that about? Is someone controlling them? We have a whole lot of questions, and no answers." Ryan shoved the weapons into a large backpack he had liberated from the sniper's building. "We'll move to the high building and hole up there for the night. Between the bastard stickies and what looks like the vanguard of an army, there's too much trouble around to be staying out in the open. Let's strip the rest of the bodies along the way. No sense letting anyone else find these blasters. Once we're secure, we'll rig a few alarms, and take turns watching throughout the night. In the morning, we'll head farther into the city—carefully—and see if we can get some idea of what's going on here."

"What we eat?" Jak asked.

Ryan jerked his thumb behind him. "Rations back at the sniper position."

"Great."

There were no further objections, and they all packed up, doused the fire and headed for cover.

GUNFIRE AWOKE RYAN the next morning, jolting him out of bed with his Sig Sauer in his hand before he realized it was off in the distance. Looking around, he saw most of the others were also awake, from a sleepy-eyed Mildred to a yawning Jak, who had taken the most recent watch. Only Doc's stentorian snoring continued unabated.

After a quick sweep of the building to ensure no one had entered during the night, the other five broke their fast over a small fire built in a section of aluminum vent that Ryan and J.B. had taken apart and reshaped to form a rough chimney. After choking down the vacuum-packed, nearly indestructible rations that tasted bland whether they were hot or cold, spiced or plain, the five ascended to the roof to see if they could spot where the shots were coming from.

The remains of the former neighborhood around them were flanked by hills to the north and west. Now that day had broken, columns of smoke to the north were easily visible as black plumes dotting the horizon. The blasterfire continued, single shots echoing over the foothills of the Rockies, interspersed with bursts of automatic weapons fire here and there, interspersed with the sustained roar of a light machine gun, followed by the heavier boom of another automatic weapon.

J.B. identified the various sounds as if he was listening to bird calls. "M-60 belt-fed dueling with a .50-caliber heavy. Someone's got a bit of firepower on their side. The pops we're hearing are AK-47s, and I also caught a few M-16s and some lighter caliber weapons, .38s, .45s."

Krysty stood at the edge of the rooftop, the cool morning breeze blowing her hair away from her face. "Doesn't sound like anything we want to get mixed up in, lover."

"Mebbe, mebbe not. Been thinking about it since last night. It looks like someone's raising an army, or trying to, and every time that happens, it leads to all kinds of trouble."

"Trouble to whom?" Mildred asked, shading her eyes with her hand as she gazed north. "We slip out now, head back to the redoubt, jump somewhere else, and leave whoever's out there to kill each other however they want. So far I'm siding with Krysty on this one, boys. I'm all for fighting the good fight, doing what we can when we can, but that doesn't involve marching into what sounds like a war zone up there."

Ryan eyed the black woman for a moment. "You're right, it may not be our kind of trouble, but there's plenty of places around here where it could be their kind—and Krysty and J.B. know of two of them."

"Not fair, Ryan." Krysty hadn't taken her eyes from the horizon, but her tone carried unmistakable reproach.

"Neither is the world." Ryan didn't have to look at

J.B. to know he'd already come to a similar conclusion. He didn't know how the Armorer felt about Cripple Creek, the town he grew up in, but he doubted the man would simply walk away from a potential threat to it. And he was sure that Krysty wouldn't put up with invaders swooping down on the ville of Harmony, where she grew up, to steal conscripts and turn them into trained killers, if there was anything she could do to stop it.

"I'm about as keen as you all are to go walking into what might be our deaths, but I think we need to check out what's going on up there. Besides, someone came after us last night, and I want to find out who's holding the other end of that leash."

"And take them out?" J.B. stared at him speculatively. "If we head up there, it won't be a pleasure trip. Don't want to get caught between two barons feuding. We'd be like a bug between two rocks—squashed."

Ryan digested his friend's take on the situation and nodded. "If we didn't like what we saw once there, we either head out or do what we can. Lots of times we don't really have a choice, but here we do. What about you, Jak? You been quiet ever since we came up here."

The albino youth was also shading his eyes against the morning light, the rising wind from the mountains to the west ruffling his white hair. "My people not been free if you not come stop Baron Tourment and men. We fight, we move, we survive all time. Not think much 'bout tomorrow. Comes if when comes. Got chance help people, mebbe we should. But only if good fight. One we got chance winnin'."

"Amen to that, my snowy-haired young friend." Everyone turned to see Doc, dressed for travel, ascend the last of the stairs to the roof. "My apologies for tarrying in bed so long. Methinks the porter had not received my wake-up call last night. But it is a glorious morning, and after we enjoy a fine repast, I, for one, am looking forward to seeing more of this 'Wild West' as they refer to it in the newspapers back east."

"Doc?" Krysty approached him warily, aware of how fragile he could be when he regressed to this past state. "You're not back in the nineteenth century anymore, you're here, with us, remember?"

For a moment, the old man stared at Krysty as if she was the one who had lost all reason, not him. Then his mouth split into a wide grin, revealing his peculiar set of teeth, and he laughed, long and loud, the joyous sound echoing off the deserted ruins of the buildings around them.

Along with everyone else, Ryan was surprised by Doc's reaction. Normally he responded to being wrenched back into the present with depression, and usually denial, rambling and tears. This sort of reaction made him fear the white-haired old man had finally slipped over the edge of sanity once and for all. He caught J.B.'s eye, who nodded and casually took three steps to the left to stand on Doc's flank, ready to tackle him if needed.

And indeed, Doc was trying to speak, but wheezing and gasping as he was, he couldn't get any words out. He held up one hand while resting the other on his knee as he whooped and coughed. "Just a…just a minute… dear friends…oh, the looks on your faces…" At that he broke into a fresh gale of hilarity, nearly falling over in his mirth.

Ryan gave J.B. a hand signal to stand down. Crossing his arms over his chest, he waited for the latest jocularity to subside.

"Upon my soul…that is as good a jape as I have had in many a long year…"

Mildred caught it first. "Jape? That was a joke, old man?"

"Indeed it was, my ebony-skinned companion. I am aware that I trip the time fantastic now and again, and I thought it might be good for a chuckle if I only pretended to have gamboled down memory lane once more." The stony looks on the faces of his companions made him sober up quickly. "Er, perhaps it was not quite as amusing to you all as it was to me."

"Oh, yeah, it was amusing all right—about as funny as a dead baby on a pitchfork." Brushing roughly by the old man, Mildred stomped down the stairs to the floor of their camp.

Krysty simply sighed and followed the other woman down, while Jak muttered something about, "fuckin' senile white-haired bastards," and followed. J.B., phlegmatic as usual, patted the scholar on the shoulder. "Good one, Doc."

That left him and Ryan alone on the rooftop. Ryan stared at Doc, nonplussed. He thought he'd seen every kind of quirk from the old man in their travels together, but once again, Doc had pulled the rug out from under him. He didn't know whether to be angry, disappointed, stoic or what, so he settled for asking the obvious question. "What the fuck was that all about, Doc?"

And the old man's lined countenance, which had maintained its composure in the face of the mixed emotions of the other group, finally broke, collapsing into an expression of profound sadness. He walked over to Ryan, his hand reaching out to the other man's shoulder, his fingers curved to grip his flesh like the talons of a hawk. But when his rheumy-eyed gaze bored into

Ryan's lone good eye, it had the unsettling clarity of a man who knew exactly what he was doing.

"Don't you see, my dear Ryan? Do you truly not see the irony of it all? It is either make jokes when I can, even when the subjects are my trusted friends, or one day I shall truly go insane in this place."

He relaxed his hand and headed to the stairs, singing some sort of ballad under his breath in a language Ryan didn't understand, and leaving the even more confused man alone on the rooftop. With a shrug, he took one last look at the pillars of smoke to the north before heading down to help pack up.

Chapter Six

Between the various weapons they'd found, everyone had gotten the chance to top off their ammo. They decided to cache the weapons in the ductwork of the building, figuring they'd come back for them later.

Ryan also suggested they each take one of the shirts—not to wear right away, but to use as camouflage in case they ran into more of the green militia first. Everyone had one hidden on their person, ready to pull on if necessary.

The one-eyed man took the lead as they headed out, holding J.B.'s M-4000, the Steyr slung. If he surprised anyone, he wanted the shotgun's overwhelming firepower to be available at a moment's notice. Krysty followed, her crimson hair tucked away, then Doc, then Mildred, with J.B. and Jak bringing up the rear.

His plan was simple—head north until they reached the top of the hills, which should give them a better view of what was going on below. Once they had accomplished that, then what came next all depended on who was doing what to whom.

Ryan took a moment to lay down the ground rules. "Everyone keep your eyes wide-open, and remember, it's not just coldhearts we're watching out for. Those stickies may be running around, too, so anyone sees anything out of the ordinary, pass the word triple-quick. If we encounter overwhelming force or get split up, circle around to the cache building to regroup. Give any stragglers twelve hours, then head for the redoubt."

He saw the dark looks that came his way upon hearing the last words, but pretended not to. What they were heading into was too dangerous for a divided group to try to take on. It was better to run away and live to fight another day. Besides, even as he gave the orders, he was pretty sure none of the others would follow them if anyone did get caught.

The first hour was slow going. Ryan had removed the scope from the Remington and used it to scout the terrain ahead—block after block of dilapidated suburbs consisting of crumbling, falling-down houses that could hide a veritable army of coldhearts. He made sure to scan each building along the path they took, watching for any sign of movement. Only when he was sure it was safe did he give the signal to move out, and even then they took it one house at a time, leapfrogging in rotation and covering one another.

The sounds of fighting grew louder as the morning sun ascended into the light purple sky. By the time it was overhead, they'd left the housing neighborhood behind and were climbing up their target hill, which was larger than it had first looked, when they heard the rough roar of ill-maintained engines coming their way. Ryan gave the signal to seek cover wherever they could, but the group was caught in the worst position possible, on an upslope, with the nearest cover at least one hundred yards away. Everyone scattered, hitting the ground and trying to camouflage themselves as best as they could in the knee-high grass covering the hill. Ryan dived to the dirt and rolled left, shotgun out and aimed at where he thought the wag might come over the hill.

But instead of a wag cresting the top, the first thing

they saw was a running human, sobbing with fear and exhaustion as he fairly flew over the top and began leaping down the other side of the hill—right toward Ryan. The approaching person wasn't wearing the green shirt of the force that had ambushed them the previous night, which meant they were probably part of the opposing side.

Only one way to find out, Ryan thought. The runner was now only a few steps away and moving so fast he was one misstep from tripping and falling the rest of the way down the hill. Ryan let him take two more huge leaps, then rose and put out his arm to clothesline the fleeing man, careful to catch him across the chest instead of the neck.

Although he was at least six inches taller and probably fifty pounds heavier, the runner hit Ryan with enough force to nearly bowl him over. They collapsed in a pile, with the one-eyed man scrambling on top of his captive and clamping a hand over his mouth to keep him quiet.

"Stop fighting! We're not your enemy!" He grunted as the person writhed and bucked underneath him. Sky-blue eyes glared at him from under a mottled green-and-brown cap that fell off as they struggled, revealing long blond hair framing what was undeniably a woman's face.

"Wait—" was all Ryan got out before feeling her leg tense, and turned his thigh just in time to block a shot to his groin from her knee. "Stop it. We're not with the green shirts!"

"Then who the fuck are you?"

Ryan didn't have time to answer, as the racket from the pursuing wag was now ear-shattering as the first of them roared over the hill, sailing through the air to land with a crash on the downslope. The battered Hummer's paint was faded to a light tan, but what caught Ryan's eye was the open weapon mount on top, which contained a .50-caliber heavy machine gun, and even worse, a man behind it.

"Fireblast! Get down!" Ryan crushed the woman to the ground as he brought up the M-4000, aiming at the windshield and letting the weapon's recoil ride the barrel up over the roof to the gunner's position. The weapon turret began swiveling toward him, but Ryan also heard the stutter of J.B.'s mini-Uzi on his left, and the man behind the big Fifty suddenly slumped over his weapon.

Unfortunately, Ryan's bold attack had attracted the driver's attention. He swung the wheel of the armored wag over, sending the heavy vehicle barreling at him and the woman.

"Run!" Ryan rose and triggered the M-4000 again, trying to draw the driver off and give the woman a chance to get away. The fléchettes ricocheted off the windshield as Ryan ran the magazine dry, but as the woman got up and scrambled away across the hill, the mil wag altered course to pursue her instead.

"Fire blast!" Ryan turned to pursue both of them, but saw Jak standing on the hill about twenty yards away, his legs apart, his left hand bracing his right, which held the .357 Colt Python at arm's length. The wag raced toward the woman, the driver seemingly oblivious to the albino teen with the blaster. The passenger, however, leaned out and aimed an automatic rifle at him just in time to take the first shot from Jak's blaster in the face, making him drop his weapon and slump over, dangling out the passenger door. The albino youth kept firing, the heavy slugs fragmenting the windshield, then punching through.

The Hummer suddenly slowed and turned down the hill. "Shit! Get it, get it!" Jak shouted as he ran toward the driverless wag. Ryan slung the shotgun and followed, drawing his Sig Sauer on the move. Krysty and Mildred were also pursuing, but Ryan and Jak were the closest.

The mil wag gathered speed as it rolled toward the bottom of the hill, then hit the flat plain and tried to climb up a small hillock, the engine spluttering in protest at not having enough power to finish the job. Jak reached the stopped wag a few steps ahead of Ryan, and paused at the back of the off-roader, waiting for the older man to catch up. The moment Ryan got there, Jak bent over and crept to the driver's door, slipping around to the other side and grabbing the handle. At Ryan's nod, he popped the door open, allowing the one-eyed man to cover the driver with his blaster.

Ryan saw a flash of black metal and fired three times, the trio of bullets slamming into the wounded driver's bloody side, breaking his arm and burrowing into his chest, one lodging in his heart. The black Beretta blaster fell from his grasp into the dust as Ryan grabbed the body and threw it out, then unslung the Steyr and set it behind the driver's seat.

"Come on!" Ryan jumped into the front seat while Jak clambered onto the hood and headed for the turret, only to be met by J.B., who had climbed up the back and was already hauling the dead man out.

"Not today, Jak. Take the passenger seat."

"Hey, was—"

"Jak, sit your ass down *now!*" Ryan's tone brooked no argument, and the albino teen ripped the dead body out of the passenger window and slid in, fuming silently. Ryan shoved the M-4000 shotgun and a full mag at him. “Reload, and keep your eyes peeled.”

Jak’s red eyes widened at receiving the weapon, then he yanked out the magazine, inserted another one and pulled back the cocking lever. “What waiting for?”

Shaking his head, Ryan was about to head out when J.B. slapped the roof. “Hold on, the others are coming!” His words were immediately followed by the deafening roar of the .50-caliber machine gun, its recoil shaking the wag’s entire cab, and Jak, who’d been watching out the passenger window, whooped in glee.

“Got him!”

“Course.”

Ryan stole a look out the passenger side to see another mil wag on the ridge, stopped and aflame. The rear passenger door opened, and a figure wreathed in orange flame fell out, rolling on the ground to try to extinguish the fire crisping his body. Bullets started cooking off in the heat with dull pops, and one of them had to have struck the flamer, as he suddenly jerked and lay still on the ground.

The back doors of Ryan’s transport popped open, and Krysty, Mildred and Doc squeezed into the cramped compartment. The women went in back, leaving Doc to try to crowd into the front. “Nukeshit, Doc, put stork legs somewhere not crotch!” Jak shouted as the lanky-legged timer traveler tried to arrange himself in the passenger seat. Ryan didn’t wait, but had popped the clutch and was moving the wag forward, his eyes on the fleeing figure pulling away from them with every step.

“I say, Jak, if you would just place that shotgun elsewhere—”

“Not happen—hold still!” Jak had squirmed out

from under Doc, and was now sitting on his lap, a position neither one was enjoying. He stuck the barrel out the passenger window as the wag began to accelerate and fired five quick blasts into a group of running men, downing two and making the rest scatter for cover. J.B.'s fifty had also joined the fray, the weapon's deeper roar overwhelming the S&W's reports.

"Come on! Could get out run faster!" Jak egged Ryan on as he scanned for another target.

Ryan gritted his teeth as he forced the gearshift into Second. "Overloaded as we are, I might just take you up on that." The Hummer was finally starting to catch up with their target when J.B. called out from the turret. "Wags at three o'clock!"

The one-eyed man glanced right to see two more mil wags crest the hill and speed toward them, one peeling off to chase the running woman, the other on a course to intercept Ryan's hijacked wag. "Get them off us, J.B.!"

"No prob—" The Armorer depressed the trigger of the Fifty, which spit a short burst before going silent. He cleared the action and tried again, with similar results. "Black dust! Blaster's jammed!"

"Marvelous." Doc was pressed back into the passenger seat, fending off Jak's elbow in his face as the teenager tried to get a better angle on the approaching wag. "Nothing like riding in style."

"Better than hoofing it like she is, Doc." Ryan struggled to shift into third, the engine whining with the effort. Krysty was already shooting at the enemy wag, but a burst from their turret, manned with a green shirt toting an automatic rifle, quickly made her duck back inside.

"If you're going to fire that thing, Jak, any time now would be great!"

"Yeah, yeah." He stuck the shotgun out again and let fly, the fléchettes sparking off the hood and roof of the other mil wag. Just as quickly, Jak jerked the blaster back inside as bullets hit all around the window, one even penetrating to lodge in the dashboard next to him.

"How close, J.B.?" Ryan shouted.

"Ten yards and coming up fast—they're gonna ram us!"

"Not if I can help it." Ryan waited one more moment, then jammed on the brakes with both feet as he downshifted, decelerating so fast Jak and Doc were thrown against the windshield. Caught by surprise, the other driver tried to compensate, but couldn't slow down in time. The rear quarter panel of the other mil wag smacked against the right front fender of Ryan's, but didn't do any serious damage. "Chill that bastard!" Ryan snapped as he wrestled the obstinate vehicle back into motion.

Jak recovered faster than the turret gunner, poking his head out with the M-4000 tucked into his shoulder. The man's eyes widened when he saw the shotgun's maw pointed at him, but he still tried to bring the AK-47 to bear on his opponent.

He failed.

The albino teen squeezed the trigger, sending dozens of razor-sharp steel darts flying into the man's chest, piercing his lungs and slicing between his ribs, shredding his stomach, liver and kidneys into pulp. The man fell forward, and was immediately pushed out of the turret by someone else inside, the body rolling off the sloped back to land in front of Ryan's wag. Bracing himself, the one-eyed man didn't stop, feeling the heavy thump as the wheels rolled over the body, finishing him off if he hadn't been dead already.

"Where's that big blaster, J.B.?" Ryan shouted, seeing the other mil wag begin to pull away from them. His question was answered a moment later by a long burst of bullets from up top that chewed into the back of the Hummer in front of them, blowing off the spare tire and punching large holes into the armored top. The squat wag slewed from side-to-side, but kept going, so J.B. aimed another two-second burst at the left rear corner. The cluster of shells disintegrated the armored fender and continued into the tire, blowing it apart in a cloud of flying rubber. The driver lost control of his vehicle, which swerved around in a 180-degree turn and stalled.

Suddenly face-to-face with the coldheart through his side door window, Ryan scrambled to draw his Sig Sauer and aim it at the wheelman, who was just as frantically lining up his own blaster. A single shot cracked out, and the enemy driver's head snapped back, a small hole appearing in his forehead. If anyone else was inside the wag, they were staying put behind the armored doors.

Ryan reholstered his blaster and hit the gas. "Thanks, Mildred."

"No problem. Now let's get that woman."

Squinting through the dust-covered windshield, Ryan spotted the second mil wag pulling alongside the woman, who tried to dodge away, but was grabbed by a man in the rear passenger seat who drew the kicking, screaming woman into the back. "Nuking hell, they got her!"

"Well, then, my dear Ryan, I suggest that we get

her back." With a feral grin, Doc had his LeMat drawn and ready, and seemed to be fully in the moment. "Tallyho!"

"Tallyho indeed, whatever the fuck that means." Ryan goosed the accelerator, and the ancient mil wag, as if sensing his urgency, now leaped forward, straining to catch up to the vehicle ahead of them.

"J.B., can you take them out without hitting anyone in the rear?" Ryan shouted.

"Ask me to shoot off their hats without mussin' their hair, why don't ya!" J.B. yelled back. "This is a machine gun, not a bastard scalpel!"

"All right, all right, we'll do it the hard way." Ryan heard sniggering from the passenger seat and glanced over to find both Jak and Doc apparently sharing a private joke. "Want to tell me what's so bastard funny?"

"You said…hit anyone…in rear," Jak got out between chortles. Doc's laugh grated on Ryan's nerves, as well, but he ignored it and concentrated on getting closer to the wag ahead of them.

"Shut your mouths and look sharp—mebbe snipers above."

His words sobered the two up, and they returned to watching the surrounding countryside as it blurred past. They'd left the long hillside behind now, and were jouncing through a series of smaller foothills, the wag's engine growling as it powered up one side and down another. Ryan followed them into a narrow valley, where there was barely enough room for both vehicles to drive side-by-side.

"Watch it, Ryan, could be a trap," J.B. called down from the top.

"Better keep that longblaster ready then, shouldn't you?" he yelled back.

"Hope your plan to get her out of there is better than the one that got us into this," the Armorer shouted, holding on to his beloved fedora with one hand.

"Better, no, crazy, yeah!"

A few hundred yards ahead, Ryan spotted what he was looking for. "J.B., keep a lookout behind us! Jak, give Doc the shotgun!"

The albino teen frowned at the order. "What, why?"

"'Cause you're going to take the wheel in a few seconds. Now hand it over!"

Dumping the blaster into Doc's lap, Jak prepared to move over and take command.

"Doc, just point and shoot to keep that turret gunner's head down. And for fuck's sake, don't drop it!" For once Ryan was pleased that fléchette rounds were in the shotgun, as they wouldn't penetrate the armor. "Now!"

The old man stuck his face and upper body out of the window, his long hair swirling around his face like a demented, blaster-toting prophet. He unloaded on the back of the mil wag as Ryan mashed the pedal to the floor, drawing a burst of speed from the ancient machine he would have thought impossible a few moments ago.

The two mil wags hit the widened plain at the same time, Ryan having pulled them abreast of the other Hummer. "Take it, Jak!" Ryan said, waiting until he felt the teen's foot stomp down on the gas pedal before releasing it and handing over the wheel, as well. There was a slight sway as Jak maneuvered himself into the driver's seat, but the 4x4 steadied soon enough, and Ryan pushed the driver's door open, pulling himself up and out using the hinges of the door as steps.

Krysty leaned forward. "Lover, what the hell are you doing?"

Ryan glanced back at her, but didn't stop. "Back in a sec."

Before she could protest further, he stepped out onto the roof and let the door slam shut under him. J.B. had his back turned, sniping with the .50-caliber blaster as best he could at the far-off mob of green shirts streaming down the hill like rows of ants. Ryan didn't spare him a second glance, as his attention was focused on the dull brown mil wag slowly pulling away from his own vehicle. The hot, dry wind whipped at his face, making him squint as he watched the other wag come closer.

Only a couple yards separated them, and as Ryan gauged his timing, Jak drifted slowly right, bringing the back of the mil wag to within a yard of their front bumper. Doc let loose one more blast from the autoshotgun at the turret, ruffling the hair of the man inside, who had just started to poke his head back up.

It was now or never.

Ryan took two large steps across the hood of the Hummer and leaped into space.

Chapter Seven

The trip across seemed to be over in a second and stretch on forever at the same time. Ryan felt the brief, strange sensation of weightlessness for a moment, and didn't dare look down at the ground blurring underneath him, but kept his eye on the prize—the rim of the turret atop the mil wag he was sailing toward.

He hit the slanted back of the Hummer feet-first and threw himself forward, straining to reach the metal lip before he slid off. His fingers locked onto the raised edge just as the gunner inside poked his head up to see what had landed on the back of his ride. Eyes widening in surprise, he yanked a knife from an upside-down sheath on his web gear and thrust it at Ryan's face.

Jerking his head aside, Ryan grabbed the man's wrist and pulled it toward him, twisting at the same time until the man's fingers popped open, and the blade clattered free, skittering away to fall to the ground. He turned back to the coldheart in time to take a blow to the side of his head from the man's wild swing. The green shirt cocked his free hand back for another punch, but as he brought his fist forward, Ryan blocked it with his left hand, then pulled the guy forward, head-butting him in the face. Drawing back his head, Ryan drove it forward again, cracking his adversary in the mouth this time, and drawing blood from his mashed lips.

His lower face crushed into a red smear, the man

sagged from the blows, giving Ryan time to pull his own blade and drive it into the man's heart, stilling him for good. Removing the blade and pulling his feet up under him, Ryan dragged the body from the turret and tossed him over the side, then drew his Sig Sauer and paused for a moment. As he expected, a shadow appeared in the turret as another man poked his head up, blaster in hand, to see what was going on. The moment Ryan saw him, he jumped feet-first into the open space.

Seeing the combat boots aimed straight at his face, the coldheart tried to pull back into the recesses of the passenger compartment while aiming his blaster at the intruder. He accomplished neither, and his gun hand was caught underneath the heavy rubber soles, which crushed it to the deck with the snap of several broken wrist bones. The man howled in pain, giving Ryan a perfect target—his wide-open mouth. One bullet later, brains splashed against the rear door, and the coldheart stopped screaming permanently.

Ryan was trusting that the blonde woman was behind him—and that she wouldn't try to backstab him as he whirled to take on the front seat pair. The passenger seat was empty, but the driver was half turned in his seat, the revolver in his hand swinging toward Ryan's head. Close enough to touch, he grabbed the blaster's cylinder, preventing it from firing, and aimed the muzzle of his own weapon between the wheelman's eyes before pulling the trigger.

"Are you crazy!" He heard before the mil wag surged ahead as the spasming driver's foot floored the gas pedal while the steering wheel turned hard left—aiming the vehicle straight toward the steep hillside. Ryan shoved the driver's body down as he lunged over the seat for the wheel, but he was too late. With a roar, the off-roader tried to drive up the slope, making it a few yards before gravity took over and brought it tipping over on its side. The wag hung there for a moment before slowly falling over on its roof, the engine stalling as it crashed to a stop.

Ryan ended up on the ceiling with the driver's leaking body on top of him. Hearing scrabbling sounds nearby, he shoved off the corpse and rose to find the woman pushing at the passenger door, which wasn't budging, with all her strength.

"Come on!" she panted in the heat. Glancing back at Ryan, she whirled to face him while putting her back against the door and shoving. "Come any closer and you'll regret it!"

Ryan sat back on his haunches and showed his blaster, careful not to point it directly at her. "Strange way to thank the man who just saved your life."

"Are you shittin' me? Have you seen the army running around these fuckin' hills? You haven't saved me at all, stupe! By getting' in the way, you're just in for a world of trouble." She didn't let up on the door at all, but kept straining at it, jerking at the handle. "Why won't this fuckin' thing move?"

"If you give my friends a minute, they'll get us both out."

"Sure, and you'll end up ransoming me to my father instead of them—don't think I don't know what you're up to."

Ryan frowned. "Girl, I don't even know who you are."

That stopped her, just in time for Ryan to hear J.B.'s voice outside. "Ryan, you alive in there?"

"Yeah, but the doors are jammed. Can you bust them?"

"Sure thing."

Ryan heard fading footsteps, then a strange whine, like metal rasping on metal, then a clink on the other side of the door. "So, who are you?"

Puzzlement clouded her features. "You really don't know?"

Ryan poked the body of the driver next to him. "I know you're important to these green shirts, since they went to a lot of trouble to capture you alive, but other than that, you're just another outland woman to me."

"Just another— I'm Rachel Carrington, the daughter of Josiah Carrington, the leader of Free Denver."

Ryan nodded. "And the green shirts are fighting against your father, right?"

"Yeah, lousy traitors. They want what my father's spent his whole life building. They just think they can come in and take over. Not if I can help it."

J.B.'s voice sounded from outside. "Keep away from the door." The engine of the other mil wag revved outside, followed by a sudden jerk on the frame of the upside-down 4x4. The engine revved again, and with another lurch, the door tore away from its hinges, letting in bright sunlight.

Ryan motioned toward the door. "There you go."

"You're letting me go?"

"I don't kidnap people for ransom. It looked like you were in trouble back there, and I thought you could use some help."

She stared at him for long seconds. "Who are you?"

Ryan grinned. "No one of consequence."

Her expression changed from exasperated to puzzled. "I very much doubt that."

J.B.'s voice sounded from outside. "Company's

almost here, Ryan. You coming out, or fixing to stay in there for the rest of your bastard short life?"

"You can go with us, or take your chances with the green shirts outside. It's up to you."

"Choice like that isn't any choice at all." She scooted to the opening, scooping up the dead gunner's blaster as she did so. But instead of pointing it at him, she extended a tanned hand, still oozing blood from a scraped knuckle. "Let's go."

Taking it, Ryan was surprised by the strength in her wiry form. "Thanks." He got up and glanced at J.B., who was regarding the woman with his habitual expressionless face. "J. B. Dix, Rachel Carrington, Rachel, J.B."

Dropping the metal cable and hook, which began retracting into the winch at the front of the mil wag, the Armorer nodded, receiving a curt one in return. "Rest of the group's about two minutes behind us. This gully'll be swarming with them soon, and I'd rather not be here when they arrive."

Ryan eyed Rachel. "Let me guess. If they were taking you that way—" he pointed in the direction the Hummer had been driving "—I'd guess your ville is back that way, right?" He jerked his thumb back the way they had come.

"Yeah." She saw J.B. about to ask the obvious question, and spoke first. "I got cut off from my unit, and it was either light out this way or try to break back through the enemy line. I thought I'd like to live another day, rather than kill myself trying to get back."

"But if we reach the ville, you can get us inside, right?"

"Yeah, *if* we can reach it. There must be a hundred of those bastards between us and them."

"Then you might not like the idea I got in mind. Come on." Ryan ran back to the wag. "Move over, Jak. Rachel, find a hole in the back. And everyone put on your green shirts right now!"

Jak grimaced as he climbed over the gearshift. "Where? More here, be assholes and elbows ever'where."

"Just move. Get in the turret with J.B. if you have to. Take the shotgun if you head topside."

Both men spoke at the same time. "How am I supposed to shoot with him—"

"Too crowded aim anythin'—"

"I don't care if you have to reach under each other's legs to pull the trigger, just figure it out!" Ryan slammed the driver's door shut and spun the wheel. Already sluggish with six aboard, the off-roader moved even more slowly with another person, the engine developing a nasty rattle as he maneuvered the way around and started heading back the way they had come. "J.B., how much ammo left in the Fifty?"

"About a hundred rounds, which I'm going to need if you're doing what I think you're doing."

"You got it." Ryan raised his voice to be heard over the growling engine. "Everyone get out your blasters and be ready to lay down a curtain of lead when we see the coldhearts. Should blow right through them before they can get their acts together, make a run for the main gate or entryway or wherever Rachel's going to tell me to go."

In the back, he heard Rachel ask Krysty, "Is he always this nuts?"

Krysty cocked the hammer on her revolver, her expression calmly grim. "I have a hard time deciding between just nuts and plain bat-shit crazy sometimes."

Ryan just grinned as he pressed the gas pedal to the floor. In all respects, she was probably right—it was a crazy idea, but he also knew the almost incalculable value of surprise, and that was his ace in the hole. All they needed to do was punch a hole in the line and squirt through, and they'd be inside the ville in no time. Assuming the people they faced didn't have RPGs or mortars or any of a dozen other things that would end his little surprise run before it began.

The mil wag slowly but steadily picked up speed, until the speedometer needle had crept up to a shaky fifty miles per hour. The rattle from the engine had grown louder, and Ryan prayed to the invisible gods of machinery that it would last a few minutes longer. It wouldn't do to have them coast to a stop right in front of the approaching enemy force.

"Ryan, I do hope you know what you're doing," Doc said as he readied his ponderous LeMat to shoot out of the passenger window.

"Trust me. I'll be the last thing they expect. Besides, how many wags can they have left?"

He thought he heard Rachel mutter something in the back, but couldn't make it out over the wind and the engine noise. Glancing down, he noticed a red warning light flickering on the instrument panel, and gripped the steering wheel tighter.

"All right, we're coming up on the last turn! J.B., aim for any wags that look like they could come after us! The rest of you just keep shooting to keep their heads down. If you chill one, great, but we're really just looking for a distraction. Here we go!"

Chapter Eight

The opening to the canyon was covered in shadow, and Ryan felt a brief chill wash over him as they shot through it and into the hot, bright sunlight beyond. When he did, however, his jaw dropped, and the thought that his plan might not have been the smartest crossed his mind.

The entire hillside was covered with green shirts—more than a hundred, coming down the hill in loose units. Scattered among them were several mil wags, apparently serving as rally points, since each one had a large group clustered around it.

Ryan's packed Hummer burst out of the rocky valley like a rabid wolf among sheep, sowing panic and confusion from the moment it appeared.

J.B. started the carnage with a touch on the trigger of the .50-caliber blaster that sent a short burst into the nearest vehicle, the bullets carving through the warm bodies of the sec men and into the armor-plated hood and windshield, reducing the driver and passengers to blood-soaked meat. One of the bullets had to have hit something incendiary or explosive, because there was a dull *whump* and the wag suddenly erupted in a large fireball, tossing the rest of the nearby green shirts through the air, many of them also on fire.

The explosion made every head on the hill look their way. Cranking the wheel hard left, Ryan gunned the engine, trying to reach the top of the hill as fast as possible. The crack of multiple small-arms fire roared in his ears as Krysty, Mildred, Jak, Doc and Rachel unloaded on the nearby soldiers, caught flat-footed with no cover except the featureless, unforgiving ground.

The roaring mil wag, bristling with weapons, rampaged through the herd—a herd armed with blasters, but a herd nonetheless. Although a few managed to draw or aim their weapons, they were either cut down by bullets or mowed down by the vehicle itself, Ryan plowing through them in his relentless quest to reach the top.

J.B.'s machine gun stuttered out its relentless death song, hammering another mil wag trying to make a run at them, this one unfortunately topless, especially for the men inside. They didn't make it within fifty yards before the heavy slugs turned the driver and passengers inside to bloody corpses. The Armorer put another short burst into the front grille, the burst of steam jetting from under the hood confirming another one down.

By now other vehicle-mounted blasters were coming into play, with streams of bullets kicking up dirt and grass near the fleeing wag. Ryan jogged the wheel left, trying to zigzag up the slope, but almost put them into the side of the rocky escarpment for his trouble.

"Almost out. Mebbe fifty shells left!" J.B. shouted from above.

"Keep hitting them—we're almost there!" Ryan was hunched over the wheel, trying to will the shrilling engine to carry the wag the last dozen or so yards to the top. Bullets spanged off the armor, small pings of blasterfire interspersed with heavier *ponks* of automatic rifle round ricocheting off the armor plate.

"Shit!" Jak pulled himself back inside from the turret, clutching his bleeding arm. "Bouncer got me!"

"Doc, cover fire!" Ryan could see the top of the hill now, but the engine was making unhealthy grinding noises. Doc's LeMat boomed, and he heard screams from outside, followed by a more ominous lack of noise—the .50-caliber blaster on top wasn't firing anymore.

"I'm out!" J.B. shouted.

"We're over!" Ryan exclaimed.

Unfortunately, although they had crested the hill, they were far from being out of danger. The other side leading down to a refinery was not choked quite as much with fighters or wags, but there was enough to make them pause, all of them charging up the hillside. In the distance, on the other side of the mob, was a ville wreathed in smoke and fire, behind what looked like a long wall made of some kind of crushed ruins of cars blocking the streets, forming a ten-foot-high barrier. How his group could reach it alive, Ryan barely had an idea.

"Hold your fire!" he hissed at his group just as the nearest green shirt reached the window.

"What the hell's going on over there?"

"Ambush by people from the hills. We got wounded we're bringing back." Ryan nodded at Jak, who picked up on the cue, and moaned loudly, clutching his arm.

The soldier drew back at Jak's appearance. "Never seen him before."

"New conscript—just got him in our unit last week. Look, they need reinforcements quick. Get over there and help them. We gotta fly!" Ryan released the brake and stepped on the gas, letting gravity help get the overloaded wag moving.

"Make a hole! Wounded coming through!" the green shirt shouted after them. Men and wags moved out of the way as the vehicle began to descend the hill.

"Pretty clever, Ryan," Mildred acknowledged while reloading her Czech target pistol and snapping the cylinder shut.

"Yeah, well, we aren't even close to out of the woods yet." Ryan heard shouts and shots from the top of the hill and grimaced. "There goes our cover. Hang on!"

He tromped on the gas, and the 4x4 leaped forward, sending slower green shirts tumbling in his wake as the steel fenders clipped their legs and waists. The confusion worked in their favor again as the men either froze, wondering why one of their own seemed to be attacking them, or looking to their commanding officer as to what to do about the marauding vehicle.

Ryan and his crew were able to make it halfway down the hill before any kind of organized action occurred around them. But when it came, it was heavy. Everyone was forced to duck for cover as it seemed every blaster on the hill opened up on them. Ryan felt the jolt as both tires on the right side were flattened, but he kept going, knowing the standard wheels on a mil wag could travel up to thirty miles, even when punctured. The vehicle listed to the right for a few seconds, then the tires on the left side were shot out, as well, and it leveled off.

They roared down to the bottom of the hill, and Ryan hung a hard right, aiming for the barricade.

Rachel leaned forward, so close Ryan felt her breath on his neck. "Hey, Ryan, how you gonna get inside? You're driving an enemy wag and dressed in enemy clothes."

"That's where you come in. Since you're the baron's

daughter, I figure once they get a look at your pretty head, they'll welcome us with open arms."

"If they don't blow you to pieces before you get within a hundred yards of that wall."

Right then the engine hitched, knocked loudly and stopped working with a jerk that made the whole wag shake as it coasted to a stop—still at least a hundred yards from the wall.

"Fireblast! Everyone out. Head to the abandoned buildings over there."

Rachel grabbed his arm. "No, we run for the wall, full-out. With me in the lead, they'll give covering fire. We go into the old refinery, we're all dead!" When he turned to ask her why, she said, "Stickies live there. When you get to the wall, look for the pink metal. That's the ground entrance."

"Okay, everyone out, move, move, move!" Ryan spilled out of the driver's seat, grabbing his Steyr. He hurried to the wag's back fender, tearing off the green shirt and throwing it away, his Sig Sauer a reassuring weight in his hand. "Krysty, Mildred, Rachel, get out and head for the wall. J.B., you all right up there?"

"Don't freak." When Ryan spared a glance at his old friend, he nearly sat down in surprise. The left side of the Armorer's face was a mask of blood, covering his forehead, eye, cheek, nose and jaw. J.B. jumped from the turret just as a burst from the nearest green shirts thunked into the back of the Hummer. "Shrapnel sliced my forehead. Looks worse than it is. Here." He thrust the M-4000 into Ryan's free hand. "Can't see shit." He took his precious glasses off and cleaned them on his shirt. Better. "Okay, what's the plan?"

Ryan shoved his blaster into his belt and checked the load on the shotgun. "You and everyone else haul ass to that wall. I'll hold them off for a minute, then be right behind you."

"See you there." J.B. readied his mini-Uzi and moved toward the front of the wag. Ryan holstered his Sig Sauer and snugged the butt of the shotgun into his armpit. An enemy wag roared up and skidded to a stop in a cloud of dust, inadvertently providing cover for Ryan and his people from the other green shirts. The turret swung over, with what looked like an M-60 light machine gun on top, the gunner about to lay into the companions' wag. It hadn't quite gotten aligned when Ryan poked the M-4000's muzzle out and unleashed a firestorm of hell.

The blaster bucked hard in his grasp, and Ryan realized when half the magazine was gone that this one was loaded with double-00 buckshot. The scything cloud of pellets enveloped the wag, taking out the gunner in the turret, shredding both tires and starring the thick windshield. After the bellow of the M-4000 had died away, he still heard loud booms coming from the other side of his wag, and saw large stars appear in the already-shattered windshield. Ryan ducked his head under the vehicle to see a familiar set of combat boots near the front wheel.

"Jak!" Ryan retreated back to the hood to find the albino youth aiming his .357 through the window of the open passenger door, squeezing off shots with one hand, despite the recoil jacking his hand back every time. "What part of 'haul ass to that wall' didn't you fucking understand?"

The albino teen fired one last shot and ducked down to reload. "Bullets left. 'Sides, run faster than you."

"Well, I hope you run really bastard fast this time, 'cause I think we got everyone who's left out there on our tail now." Ryan peeked up above the top edge of the door, and immediately ducked as a hail of gunfire nearly clipped his hair.

Jak smirked. "Bet you not do that again."

Ryan raised his Sig Sauer and fired several shots in the direction of their enemy, and was rewarded with what sounded like a shout of pain. "Why don't you make yourself useful and put a hole in the gas tank so we can make a distraction to get the hell out of here? Leave that hand blaster with me. It'll give them something to think about, at least."

Jak flipped the large weapon around and offered it to Ryan butt-first. "Five left. Don't scratch the finish."

"Only if I lay the barrel alongside your triple-stupe head. Get down there." A blaster in each hand, Ryan kept watch as Jak hit the ground and slithered under the wag. Sounds of metal on metal could be heard, followed by the youth swearing loudly. Ryan snapped off the occasional shot, wondering where the nuking hell the backup fire was from that stupe wall. Finally, Jak's feet appeared from under the front of the wag, but he didn't come out yet. After a few more seconds, and with a strangled curse, Jak rolled out from under the vehicle, spluttering and wiping gas from his face.

"'Kay, leaking now. Bastard tank, can't get through first."

The roar of a light machine gun almost drowned out Jak's last words, but Ryan smiled with relief. The stream of bullets was coming from behind them, not in front. "Cavalry's arrived. Okay, I light this, and after you take off that green shirt so you don't get shot, we scoot. When you get there, look for a pink car or piece of metal. The door's supposed to be there."

"Be inside wall 'fore you reach, old man."

Ryan gave Jak's blaster back to him. "That's a bet. Ready…set…" Ryan leaned down and triggered his Sig, the flash from the muzzle igniting the pool of gas under the wag. "Go!"

The two broke from cover as the pool of fuel went up with a whoosh, licking at the underside of the armored mil wag. The lone blaster on the wall was joined by others, but Ryan didn't spare a second to look up, as he was too busy making sure he didn't twist an ankle on the rough ground leading to the wall.

The fighting here had been intense, with green-clad bodies lying everywhere, many with blasters near their hands. The wall itself was on fire in several places, with the attacking force using some kind of jellied gas that stuck to the metal barricade. Ryan juked and ducked in a zigzag pattern. Although the closer soldiers might be keeping their heads down, there was no reason someone higher on the hill wouldn't hesitate to take him out if they could get a shot.

It was the longest run he could remember, expecting with every step to feel the punch of a bullet explode his heart and rib cage, but Ryan made it to the wall in one piece. Jak was already hunting around for the key piece that would get them inside. "Here it is!" Slapping his hand on a bright pink piece of metal about three feet by three feet square. He pushed, then pulled on it with all his strength. "Fucker's stuck!"

Ryan lent his muscles to the attempt, but didn't have any more success than Jak. He looked at the forbidding wall looming above them, studded with razor-sharp shafts of metal and jagged pieces of old cars that has been turned into spikes, many stained a dark red. "Looks like we'll have to climb."

The firing from above had died down, and Ryan

heard voices off in the smoky distance. "They're going to make a run at us. Persistent bastards." He raised his blaster, ready to shoot the first one that came out of the smoke and dust.

Something landed on his right shoulder, making Ryan twist away in surprise. He glanced back to see a rope hanging down from the wall. Jak looked back at him. "Go up, now!" he whispered urgently. The teen needed no encouragement, but when he tried to climb, his wounded arm buckled, and he fell back.

"Sorry, Ryan. Can't hold weight."

"Shit, Jak, get me killed out here and I'm coming back after you. That's a promise." Ryan quickly fashioned a rope sling and looped it under Jak's shoulders, then yanked on the rope twice. "Watch yourself on that metal."

Jak was lifted into the air, heading toward the top of the wall and disappearing over it. Ryan kept his back to the towering barrier, ears straining to hear where the rush would come from.

With a dull *whump,* the wag exploded, showering the area around with glass and metal fragments. The green shirts chose that exact moment to attack, charging Ryan with their longblasters at the ready, but not firing as they came at him.

The one-eyed man waited until he got a clear sight of them bursting out of the smoke, then he went to work, sighting on each man and squeezing off a shot. They went down with each bullet fired, skidding into ungainly heaps or spinning and crumpling where they dropped. Only two remained, but they still kept coming when the rope again dropped on Ryan. Wrapping it securely around his free arm, he yanked twice and was hoisted into the air, his blaster out and aimed at the remaining green shirts, who didn't even try to shoot him, but retreated back into the swirling smoke left over from the fight.

Once sure he was clear, Ryan managed to turn himself so he didn't get torn to shreds on the spikes in the wall. At the top, he was grabbed by several obliging hands—and slammed facedown onto an iron-grated section of parapet, his blaster torn from his grasp.

Flipped over before he could say anything, Ryan froze as he stared up into the muzzles of a half dozen smoking longblasters.

Chapter Nine

"Move and you're dead, prisoner!" a man snapped as he regarded Ryan down the sights of his M-16 rifle.

A form appeared out of the smoke, a large man, dressed in a mix of camouflage; desert tans and browns on his legs, a patterned green, black and brown jacket covering his upper body. He moved with easy command, the various men holding Ryan at bay stiffening slightly at his approach. Under a flattop haircut was a face like a brick; square, broad and hard. Cold brown eyes stared at him from above a flattened nose, and a hand-rolled cheroot dangled from one corner of his mouth.

"Identify yourself."

Ryan stared up at him, lifting a hand to slap the nearest blaster barrel out of his face—since the overeager man holding it seemed to be trying to pick his prisoner's nose—and pushed himself up on his elbows. The ring of men around him all tensed, their weapons not budging an inch, but, as Ryan had guessed, not moving a muscle until their leader gave the order.

He glared at the camo-clad sec man and jerked a thumb back over the wall. "I'm the man who just saved the baron's daughter from that mob out there."

"Ryan! Ryan!" He heard Krysty's voice as the tall redhead stormed up onto the parapet, her green eyes flashing. "That's Ryan! He's with us, you asses!"

Rachel followed suit, nodding at the tall man. "At ease, Major. This is the man who rescued me from Tellen's forces."

"Yeah, and almost got chilled by them myself for the trouble. What happened with that special panel you mentioned?"

Rachel flushed. "The wall shifted and jammed it closed. I'm sorry you were caught out there like that. We tried to get you to safety as fast as possible."

Ryan waved off her apology. "Better the door's stuck closed than open, I suppose."

For a moment, everyone stared at him. Then Rachel chuckled, getting the joke. Her laughter was infectious, with many of the men nodding in agreement, and a few even chuckling.

The brick-faced man didn't even change expression. "Second squad, stand down. Squads one and three, return to overwatch." The squad of riflemen pulled back, letting their leader lean over and extend a callused, nail-bitten hand. "My apologies for the rough entry. It wouldn't have been the first time they'd tried to infiltrate using outlanders."

Ryan looked at the hand for a moment, then accepted it, planting his feet as the major pulled him up. The man was as solid as he looked—not an ounce of fat on him—and his hand felt like bands of steel with skin and a bit of flesh stretched over them. "Forget it. Not as bad as some places I've seen."

"That's the spirit. The name's Major Quind Kelor."

"Ryan Cawdor." He pumped the major's hand once, giving as good as he got, and nodding when the major didn't try to turn the handshake into a pissing contest. "That's Krysty Wroth, and the others—" He glanced around, suddenly aware that J.B., Jak and the others were missing.

Rachel stepped forward. "Your friends are safe, Ryan. After what you did out there, you and the rest of your group are our honored guests."

"Do they know that?"

"I told the men with them that they were under my own personal protection—" Rachel's words were cut off as a commotion at the end of the walkway caught everyone's attention.

"Where is Rachel?" The man striding toward them—flanked by two lean, wary men who were obviously bodyguards—was also tall and thin almost to the point of gauntness. He was clad in combat boots, gray-and-black camouflage, a bulletproof vest bulking his chest and a blaster holstered at his left side. His hair was short and iron-gray, and his expression would have been stern if not for the left side of his face. The muscles there hung slack on his skull, even his downturned mouth and drooping eyelid, lending that half of his expression a sleepy look, which was completely belied both by the strong gaze of his deep blue eyes and the tone of his voice—hard steel underlaid with a tremor of true concern.

"Father." Rachel turned to face him, her back straightening and her boots coming together, almost standing at attention as he approached.

He crossed to her and clasped his arms around her shoulders. "Damn it, child, I've told you that you are not to go out into the field like that..." He stopped before his voice broke and crushed her to him in a bear hug. "I'm very glad you've come back to us safely."

"Thanks to these people, Father," Rachel replied once he had released her and she'd regained her breath.

"This is Ryan Cawdor, the man who helped me get back. Ryan, this is my father, Josiah Carrington, the leader of the Free City of Denver."

Josiah regarded Ryan, his gaze calm and intent. "So you're the one I have to thank for returning my daughter safe and sound."

Ryan nodded. "Seemed like the right thing to do."

The baron rubbed his chin as he considered Ryan's words. "Far too little of that sentiment to be found today. Come, you and your group must be hungry. You'll dine at my table this evening, after you've had a chance to wash up. If there's anything you need—weapons, ammunition, supplies, a wag—just let me know, and it will be yours."

"Very kind of you, Baron."

Josiah had turned to head back down, but stopped when he heard Ryan's words. "I'm sorry, what did you say?"

"Sir, we should get you down, there are still snipers—" The major began, but was stopped by Josiah's upraised hand as he whirled.

"I'll ask you once more, Ryan Cawdor—what did you say?"

Outwardly Ryan remained calm, but his mind raced, already planning tactics and escape routes should this meeting head any further south. Carrington was close enough to reach out and grab, and that would be the only way out—eliminate the bodyguard on the left and take the leader hostage before the other one could react. Krysty could probably get Rachel in the same instant, and then they could negotiate for the others, but that would be fraught with complications. But before he knew whether to strike or split, there was the matter of answering the man who seemed poised to throw down on him.

Squaring his shoulders, Ryan answered, "I said 'very kind of you, Baron.'"

Josiah walked up to Ryan, staring him straight in the eye. The black-haired man was aware of the men around him holding their weapons ready enough to cover him again in a moment's notice if necessary, and despite the potential danger, he had to admire their training. He didn't even have to look at the bodyguards to know they would try to chill him if he even made the slightest move toward their baron.

"As my daughter mentioned, you are fortunate enough to find yourself in the Free City of Denver. We have a few simple rules here—respect your fellow men and women as you respect yourself, and do not take that which doesn't belong to you. The other rule we have, my own personal edict, if you will—" Josiah's previously calm air vanished, replaced by an expression of pure, unadulterated fury that was astonishing in its savagery "—is *never* compare me to those power-hungry, bloodthirsty, psychopathic, inbred whoresons out there who claw their way to dominance on the backs of innocent men and women, breaking them for their own amusement and throwing them away to die in squalor and misery. Do you understand?"

Have to respect his convictions, if they're real, Ryan thought. He nodded again. "Perfectly, Josiah. I apologize for any insult. It wasn't intentional."

The other man held his gaze for a long moment, then drew back and clapped Ryan's shoulder. "Excellent! Major, escort Ryan and his companions to the Magnolia, and make sure their every need is seen to. Shall we say dinner at 0600 hours?"

"We look forward to it," Ryan said, walking over to Krysty and slipping an arm around her waist. "Until then."

"Indeed. Rachel?" Josiah took his daughter firmly by the arm and brought her with him, the pair of bodyguards falling in behind them.

"As you were, men." The major surveyed his troops one last time before turning back to Ryan and Krysty. "Well, let's get you back to the rest of your group, and then we'll take you into the city proper."

He motioned for them to walk ahead of him toward the end of the steel-framed parapet, where a walkway going the opposite way sloped down the wall. Ryan and Krysty descended casually, keeping their eyes and ears open and their mouths shut for the time being.

The wall was a beehive of activity around them. Men and women were everywhere. Some attended to the wounded, treating them where they lay or helping move them away from the fortifications. Others were busy fighting the stubborn fire on the exterior, flooding sections with water or beating at the flames that were coming through with blankets. Everywhere Ryan looked, people were working together, all joined in a common cause—the defense of their city. Although there were plenty of sec men around, the majority of them atop the wall, no one had to be forced to do their job. Indeed, everyone was executing their duties with swift efficiency, a far cry from what he'd seen in most dirty, squalid villes.

And that was another thing: the Free City of Denver was clean. It had taken him a few seconds to put that together as they had come off the last ramp onto the ground. From the people, all dressed in a variety of utilitarian clothes—tough coveralls and handmade jumpsuits, work shirts, heavy boots in decent condition and even helmets on several men busy with more dangerous work—to the streets, which, apart from bloodstains from the dead and wounded and the occasional piece of shrapnel or twisted piece of metal that was obviously from the wall, the entire place was otherwise neat and orderly.

J.B., Mildred and Doc were all waiting off to one side, with Jak nowhere to be found. Ryan made a casual inquiring signal to J.B. about how everyone was, and received the answering all-clear sign. For once, the Armorer wasn't yawning, a good sign that he felt they weren't in any immediate danger.

Major Kelor noticed Ryan's raised eyebrow. "Your other associate—the snow-haired one—is being treated by our healer. I'll be sure to leave word to have him transported to the Magnolia once he's ready to go." He flagged down a young man and instructed him to bring around a wag for transporting their guests, and also to find Jak at the hospital and make sure he was escorted to the Magnolia. "Do you want to send your man any sort of message?"

Ryan thought for a moment. "Just tell him to behave himself."

The major nodded, and the sec man ran off with a quizzical frown on his face.

"Right kind of you, Major," Ryan said before introducing the rest of his party. When he was done, he asked the sec man, "Expecting any more trouble from those green shirts?"

Kelor turned and looked at Ryan in surprise, then chuckled. "That's as good a name as any for Tellen's bastards. That was the largest offensive we've seen from them in a long while. They must've been planning it for quite some time."

"True enough. We ran into some of them south of here, on the very outskirts of the city. They seemed to be clearing the area, looking for prisoners."

Turning his head, Kelor spit into the dust. "Yeah, that sounds like Tellen all right. He sweeps the surrounding area with patrols, looking for anyone he can capture and conscript into his little army. 'Course, if they don't know about us, most go willingly, if only for the food and protection."

"Do you know where he gets his wags from? Or his fuel?"

"Don't know for sure. It's rumored he's running out of Boulder. It's close enough for him to keep an eye on us, and we him, but far enough away that we can't risk sending a large enough force to eradicate him without— Ah, here's the wag."

One of the open-topped trucks came to a halt in front of them, and the major opened the rear door. "After you."

Chapter Ten

The companions climbed in, and the major got in afterward, muttered a few words to the driver, then sat down on the bench nearest to the driver's seat.

"There's no need to stick with us the whole way, Major. I'm sure you have plenty to do elsewhere," Ryan said.

Kelor smiled, but his expression didn't soothe Ryan. It seemed real, but thin, as if it had been pasted on his face. "Orders of the commander say I'm to escort you personally to the Magnolia, and that is exactly what I intend to do."

"Fair enough." Ryan leaned back against the slats of wood and caught J.B.'s eye. The Armorer, his face clean now and a neat bandage covering his head wound, regarded him from across the flatbed. Ryan nodded slightly toward the major, his question clear: What do you think?

J.B. rubbed his right jacket sleeve with his index finger, where a patch would be sewn on a uniform: Sec man, what do you expect?

Ryan touched the corner of his right eye: Stay alert.

J.B.'s brows narrowed, and he gave a brief A-OK sign as he passed his hand across his chest.

With that, Ryan watched the blocks pass by. Everyone was looking outside the truck now, staring in wonder at the relatively untouched buildings around them.

"Hey, look at that!" Krysty pointed, but there was really no need to, as the thing she was indicating was clearly visible to the rest.

They were passing a large, glass-walled building that stretched for several blocks. It had suffered some damage over the decades, with sheets of plywood filling large, empty holes on the lower levels. But that wasn't the strange part.

A huge blue bear, at least forty feet tall, stood in front of the building, its paws raised as if it was shielding its eyes to peer into the windows of the building. Ryan simply stared at the fanciful creation, wondering if his eyes were deceiving him. As they passed, he saw that the right paw had been broken off, and what had looked to be flawless blue paint was actually chipped and scarred, with bits of incomprehensible graffiti covering the huge animal's legs.

"What the nuking hell is that? You guys have a bit of free time on your hands?"

The major barely glanced at the large statue. "Nope, it was here when we arrived. The citizens claim it's the city's mascot. They call it the Free City's Blue Bear."

Doc coughed, his head swiveling on his scrawny neck as he tried to look everywhere at once. "I must say, for your city's location, I am surprised at the small amount of collateral damage. What with NORAD and Cheyenne Mountain so close by, surely Denver would have been targeted as a primary eradication site, and yet— Ow!"

Seeing the major lean forward to better hear Doc's rambling, Ryan shifted his position, as well, using the movement to jab a swift kick at Doc's shin. "Watch it, Doc. Don't be talking the major's ear off with your boring bullshit."

Kelor's muddy-brown eyes flicked from Doc's seamed, lined face to Ryan's impassive one, but he didn't say anything. The old man rubbed his injured leg and remained silent for the rest of the ride. When he turned to watch the street passing, Ryan caught the major's gaze and tapped his temple, then shook his head in the traditional "not all there" gesture. The major nodded slowly, but Ryan was pretty sure he hadn't fooled the canny sec man.

"You said you came from the south of here. Whereabouts, exactly?"

"We were trading down near the border, but pickings were slim, so we thought we'd try our luck north. Our steam wag gave up the ghost about fifty miles south of here, and we been walking ever since. It was a good thing we came on Denver when we did. We were about to roast under that sun."

"Traders, huh? What you dealing in?"

Too late, Ryan realized the subtle trap the major had laid. The sec man was far smarter than Ryan had given him credit for. Like recognized like, and he knew Ryan was anything but a trader. Any sort of regular trade goods would be a clear lie, given their appearance, and anything exotic like weapons or explosives would mark them as a threat.

"As I'd said, pickings were slim. We barely made it out of the last ville we entered with our lives, and had to leave a lot of stuff behind. Since then, we were more in the line of doing odd jobs. My friend there—" he pointed at J.B. "—is an excellent weaponsmith, able to fix just about anything. We're all decent shots—" that was no lie, whenever possible, everyone who could get their hands on a weapon learned shooting early in the Deathlands "—so we were hiring on as sec for small villes, ranches, anyone who needed a few extra sec men."

"But you ended up here instead."

"Yeah. Not much to the south, either. Place called Colorado Springs is pretty much empty."

"Hmm." The major leaned back, leaving Ryan to wonder if his concocted story would hold up. He reminded himself to go over it with everyone else once they were alone.

They rumbled up to a multistory building that also had people bustling in and out of it through the revolving door and side doors, both civilians and those dressed in military fatigues. Major Kelor hopped out and held the door for the others. Once they had all exited, the major had another brief conference with the driver, then the wag took off down the street.

"You're now in the heart of the Free City. Relax and enjoy yourselves. You couldn't be any safer."

"Thank you, Major, and please thank Mr. Carrington for us, as well. We look forward to dining with him this evening," Krysty replied.

"Yes, a wag will be here for you at a quarter to the hour. For now, relax and enjoy yourselves. I'm sure you'll find the Magnolia has plenty to keep you entertained." The major smiled again, this one knowing. Raising two fingers to his brow, he gave them all a sly salute, turned and walked down the street.

"Cheeky one, isn't he?" J.B. muttered out of the side of his mouth.

"Too clever by half. I don't know how much he heard of Doc's rambling, but I think it was more than enough."

"Trouble?"

"Won't know just yet. Might be at dinner tonight."

Krysty watched the retreating figure as he rounded a corner and disappeared. "I wonder what the good major would do if we didn't go inside."

Mildred snorted. "Oh, I imagine we're being watched this very minute, and if we were to go anywhere else, a mil wag and a very polite sec man or two would 'escort' us back right where we belonged."

Another wag came to a stop in front of the hotel, and the passenger door opened to disgorge Jak. The albino teen's face looked clean, and his left arm was in a sling, which he immediately removed and tossed back into the wag before walking over, his thin-lipped mouth set against the pain his arm was causing him.

"Sure hope he didn't chill the healer," J.B. observed as they all watched the skinny, ghost-faced youth approach.

"What waitin' for? Let's go." Jak shouldered his way through and headed toward the doors.

Shrugging, Ryan followed. "Might as well."

The interior of the place was smaller than he'd expected, with a lobby opening up to a bank of elevators ahead and to the right. Directly to their left was a long desk with three people behind it, and to the right was what appeared to be a curving staircase that led to the floor below. Like everything else in the city, the room was spotless.

Jak stood in the middle, his mouth slightly agape, staring at the shining yellow lights in the chandelier. "Got 'lectric here."

Mildred frowned. "Yeah, so? It isn't anything you haven't seen before."

"Mebbe so, but—" Jak looked around to make sure

no one overheard him, "Usually only redoubts, ya know?"

Ryan stopped as the implication struck him. Jak was right. Only the strongest and wealthiest barons had access to generators, but even then they usually only lit their own houses, letting the rest of the populace make do with smoky fireplaces, crude tallow candles or, if they were lucky, kerosene lamps. To have access to enough power to light a building like this meant they didn't just have a generator, but some kind of power plant.

"Power indeed," Ryan breathed. "Boy, we are all kinds of triple-stupe. That's why Tellen's so all-fired hot to move in here. With a plant like that under his thumb, he could dictate terms to anyone he wanted."

"Can I help you folks?" one of the desk men, dressed in a white-collared shirt and threadbare but well-maintained vest, asked.

"We'll talk about this later." Ryan strode over to the desk. "Major Kelor said we're expected. Name's Ryan Cawdor." He gave the names of the others, as well.

"Yes, Mr. Cawdor, you and your friends are expected. My name's Carter, and it's my pleasure to welcome all of you to the Magnolia. Three suites have been prepared for your group. Will that be acceptable?"

"Sure." Ryan shrugged, since he and the rest of the group could sleep anywhere from a pest-hole bed to a hole in the ground and anyplace in between.

Carter was inserting three small cards into a machine on the desk that buzzed as it accepted each one, then he came around the desk. "I'll be happy to take you up and show you around."

Ryan placed his hand on the man's shoulder. "We've seen bedrooms before, friend."

The young man didn't take offense, but simply smiled. "Not like these you haven't."

His matter-of-fact tone made Ryan frown slightly, but he removed his hand. "Okay, let's go."

Carter walked to the elevators and pressed the button. The light above one, in the shape of an upward-pointing arrow, lit up. Ryan and the others moved over and waited for the car to arrive.

Doc reached out hesitantly and tapped on the door with the ferrule of his swordstick. "Pardon my lack of delicacy, my good man, but there, ah, has there been any failures of yon conveyance recently?"

The clerk's confident mask slipped a bit at Doc's odd phrasing of the question, but his intended meaning was clear enough. "We get that question a lot, and the answer is no, the elevator's never failed. It has three separate stopping mechanisms in case anything goes wrong with the machinery."

"Most reassuring." With an electronic ding, the doors opened as the elevator arrived. Ryan swallowed hard as he entered the small room. He wasn't claustrophobic, but Jak's words in the lobby had been right on target—electricity and elevators were the province of the mysterious redoubts that housed the mat-trans units that they used to travel around the Deathlands. Elevators sometimes meant trouble.

Mebbe this time it'll be different, he thought, but his hand still sought out the holstered Sig Sauer at his hip, reassuring himself that it was still there.

The elevator traveled smoothly upward until it stopped with another ding, opening into a small hallway lined with a half dozen heavy wooden doors, with another at the far end. Carter led the way along a worn carpet, talking as soon as he stepped out into the corridor. "This is a treat. Mr. Carrington has these held only for very special guests of our Free City." He showed everyone how to open the doors by inserting the key card into the slot above the door handle, watching as the light changed from red to green, then opening the door.

The interior of the rooms, however, were absolutely magnificent. Ryan doubted he had ever seen anything finer outside a baron's bedroom, which was usually overdecorated with the gaudiest crap they could find, piled up everywhere until it overwhelmed the place. But this place—from the plush, clean carpet covering the floor to the huge bed against the center of the main wall, featuring a feather comforter and real sheets, to the marble-inlaid bathroom with what looked like a whirlpool bath large enough for two, if they were willing to get very cozy—was exactly like the clerk had said. It was truly like nothing any of them had ever seen.

Carter had more surprises in store, walking to the large floor-to-ceiling curtains and pulling them apart to let in the afternoon light. "You have an incredible view of the city from here, including the outskirts. It's advisable to keep them closed at night, however. Some folks have been picked off by Tellen's snipers, I'm afraid."

"Can we see the power plant from here?" J.B. asked, his tone completely expressionless.

The clerk hesitated for the barest second before replying. "That isn't visible at this location, but one of the best things it powers is." He walked to a large cabinet that stood against the wall opposite of the bed and opened the double doors, revealing a large monitor. Pressing a button on a small machine underneath it, he waited for the red light to turn green, opened a small tray and placed a small golden disk in it, closed the tray and waited for a few seconds again until the screen lit up with pictures and sounds.

"We have a large selection of videos dating from the twentieth century for your viewing pleasure." Carter turned to face them, his expression growing serious. "We do keep track of them whenever guests reside in these suites, however."

"Like we can play 'em anywhere else," Jak muttered.

"Of course," Krysty said. "Everything will be left just as we found it."

"Naturally. Are there any questions, or is there anything we can do for you? Clothes cleaning or mending, perhaps a new outfit altogether?"

Ryan and the rest of his group exchanged glance before Doc spoke up. "Now that would be heavenly. What is the procedure?"

"Once you've selected a room, simply use the phone besides the bed—" Carter demonstrated with the unit in the room "—and press the front desk button. Let us know you're ready for laundry service, and we'll take care of the rest."

"You'll have them ready for this evening?" Ryan asked.

"Yes, otherwise we would be happy to outfit you in alternate attire, if you so desire."

"Jeez, talk like Doc now." Jak had torn his attention away from the wondrous video player to whisper to J.B.

Ryan spoke over the albino teen's words. "Might take you up on that offer, thanks. For now I think we'll just relax a bit until dinner."

"Very well then. If you should require anything, the

front desk button again will connect you. I hope your stay at the Magnolia is a pleasant one."

Me, too, Ryan thought, watching the clerk walk to the door and leave, closing it behind him.

Chapter Eleven

As soon as the major rounded the corner of the Magnolia, his pace quickened until he was almost trotting down the street, nodding to civilians as he passed, tossing off quick answering salutes to fellow sec men.

"Bastard rank-and-file," he muttered. Times like this—when he'd actually prefer to be inconspicuous—the uniform impeded him to no end. But going in civilian clothes would take too much time now. If he wanted to make his rendezvous, he'd have to hurry.

Stepping quickly to the back of the building, he saw the squat, hulking shape of the mil wag and driver he'd told to meet him here. "Where to, sir?" the sec man asked, about to turn the key.

"That's a negative. I'm commandeering this vehicle myself. You're to report back to your quarters, and tell no one about this. I'll return this vehicle to the motor pool after I'm finished."

The man's salute was firm at first, but wavered as he heard his instructions. "Yes, sir. Um, sir, permission to speak freely?"

Kelor stifled a sigh and nodded. "Yes?"

"Given the recent attack, the regs say that no one should be out by themselves. Requesting permission to accompany you on your mission."

Kelor smiled. It was all too easy. Just give the average man something to believe in, something larger than himself, and he'd gladly risk his own life to save another. "I appreciate your devotion to duty, Private Hanstead. Tell you what. I've got a turn in the Magnolia coming up, but as a reward for your adherence to the regulations, I'd like you to go in my place."

The young man's eyes goggled. "Sir, do you really mean that?"

Kelor smiled again, this one easy and real. "I wouldn't have said it if I didn't, Hanstead. Why don't you head back to barracks and get cleaned up. Once I've finished my business, I'll head back here and arrange for that pass to be waiting."

"Sir, yes, sir!" Hanstead scampered off, and Kelor swung into the driver's seat, hitting the ignition and easing the wag into gear. The vehicle balked a bit before accelerating, and Kelor frowned as he listened to the rough engine. Stores of gas are getting worse and worse every day, he thought. Got to see about tracking down more from somewhere. Need to get updated numbers on the summer crops and cattle, too. If that bastard Tellen keeps rustling heads, it's gonna be a long, meatless winter.

His thoughts turned from logistics and supply problems to the new arrivals in town. They were stone-cold chillers, every one of them, even the old man. And that redhead was damn fine. But he'd bet she'd feed any man's nuts to him if she didn't want to play.

He'd been paralleling the main wall a few blocks to the west, but as he left he angled deeper into the city, away from the main fortifications and into the ring of houses still protected by the metal wall. He scanned the deserted streets, an ancient, creased map on his knee, looking for a tumbledown house at a particular intersection.

The wag sputtered as he rounded a corner, and Kelor fed it more gas to keep the vehicle going. The last thing he wanted to be was on foot this far out from the main cordon. Just because they were behind the wall didn't mean there weren't predators that found their way inside.

"Bastard place's gotta be around here somewhere—Ah, there it is."

The houses here were little more than crumbling ruins, ravaged by a century of harsh Rocky Mountain weather. One in particular, a weathered, pale gray ranch listing to one side, caught his attention, primarily due to the large, white X that had been painted on the door, looking fresh and clean as if it had been done the day before, which probably wasn't too far from the truth.

Kelor grimaced as he pulled up to the worn curb in front of the house, checking that his Beretta PX4 .40-caliber blaster was secure in its hip holster before moving in. It was unnerving how they got inside the perimeter so easily, even with the random patrols through certain neighborhoods. After all, if one or two could get in here, what's to stop ten, or twenty, or fifty? But he was in too deep now to stop—too much was riding on his ability to produce what was needed.

Halfway up the cracked sidewalk, he thought he heard a skittering noise around the left side of the house. Easing his blaster out of the holster, he pulled back the slide to chamber a round and crept to the corner of the house, raising his blaster before lunging around the corner of the building, pistol extended to aim at…

Nothing. Dried brown grass crunched under his feet, and a few yards away a weathered wooden fence stood, gaps in the barrier providing a glimpse into the next yard, but no signs of life. Kelor exhaled and raised his blaster, shaking his head. All that skulking around was making him paranoid.

Glancing around warily nonetheless, he walked back to the front door and listened at it before trying the knob. As soon as he touched it, the slab of wood fell into the room with a crash, sending a cloud of dust into the air.

As soon as the door hit, Kelor stepped inside and swept the room with the laser sight on his Beretta, looking for the slightest movement. Every time he went out for one of these meetings, he expected a double-cross to be pulled, with him chilled on the floor. So far the information he had provided had been invaluable, but Kelor wasn't stupe enough to think his usefulness would last forever, especially given what his contact had in mind.

The living room was desert-dry, with a thick layer of dust on the carpeted floor, revealing two sets of footprints heading toward the entryway to the room beyond. Kelor approached the entryway on the right-hand side, skirting the perimeter of the room until he was next to the opening, close enough to see the faded white counters of a kitchen inside. Peeking his head in for a moment, the major established that no one was waiting in the room for him, then ducked through the doorway, checking each corner, just to make sure.

When Kelor was certain the room was empty and secure, he looked at the aluminum-legged table in the middle of the kitchen. Unlike everything else, the tabletop was free of dust and debris. On it rested a rectangular, dark green box with a keypad and illuminated screen on the front, right next to a handset. Approaching it warily, Kelor picked up the handset and put it to his ear. "Hello?"

"You're late." The voice was cool and controlled, causing a shiver to run down Kelor's spine every time he heard it.

"Yeah, I had to oversee cleaning up the mess your people created when they attacked early. I warned you the shift change was at 1:00 p.m., and going any earlier would jeopardize the entire timeline, but they just couldn't wait, could they?"

"That's inconsequential in the face of the results. The Carrington girl was supposed to be lured out and cut off so she could be captured. Instead, I lose even more men while providing the diversion so she can be taken, only to have her snatched out from under my nose by some ragtag group of outlanders?"

"Hey, I gave you everything you needed. How in the nuking hell was I supposed to account for a group wandering in to upset your plan? Besides, as I saw it, they carved through your men like a knife through butter, not to mention going through your entire force to get to the wall, so if anything, that says more about your men than my intel."

There was silence from the other end of the radio, and Kelor forced himself to keep breathing, aware he'd scored a minor victory. The voice on the other end changed tack. "What have you found out about them?"

"Group of six, two women, four men, all more than able. Led by a black-haired, rangy son of a bitch named Ryan Cawdor—"

"Ryan Cawdor! Are you sure?"

"Sure as I shook his hand while he introduced himself. Why, do you know him?"

"Only by reputation. He used to travel with the Trader years back, till he struck out on his own. Thought he was dead, but every so often his name seems to pop up here or there. He's a dangerous man."

"They're all having dinner with Carrington tonight. Perhaps I should be there."

"No, if the old man didn't invite you, don't insert yourself. You may have other things to attend to. Anything else of interest?"

"Yeah, they got an old man with them. Didn't catch his name, Doc something or other. White hair, maybe in his late fifties, early sixties, hard to tell. Anyway, he seemed to know more about this area than he should have, particularly given that they hadn't been here before."

"That you know of," the voice interjected.

"Regardless, Cawdor mentioned Colorado Springs as being abandoned. Nothing about stickies in the area, which your men encountered last month. Anyway, the old man mentioned some sites that he *definitely* shouldn't have known about—like Cheyenne Mountain and NORAD."

"Hmm, now that *is* interesting. That settles it—I want to meet Cawdor. Tonight."

It was a good thing Kelor's throat was already dry, because he didn't choke when he heard the request, but only coughed instead. Although it was stifling inside the small room, the chill he'd felt earlier reappeared, dancing along his spine up to the nape and back down again. "Are you out of your mind? Slipping out to these little meetings is one thing, but trying to get you in the city would get me killed if we get caught."

"Well, then, you'd simply better make sure you *don't* get caught, Major. Set it up, and let me know how and when you're ready to bring us in. And don't even think about trying to hand me over, or the first bullet out of my blaster'll go right between your eyes."

"Don't be stupe, who's going to believe I happened to capture you while driving around the city? I've got as much to lose here as you do, you know."

"Yes, and as much to gain by staying the course, as well."

"Only if you can pull off taking the city."

"That's why I have you on the inside, Major. However, the lack of progress made so far has been a bit—disturbing. Perhaps these new arrivals will be exactly what I need. Set up the meeting, but don't tell Cawdor. It's always better to have the element of surprise on one's side."

Kelor couldn't help himself. "Yeah, like when he surprised your men on the hillside."

Instead of anger, the tone turned thoughtful. "Hmm, no doubt. A man like that could prove useful if he can be persuaded to join the right side. Get it done, and take the radio with you so you can report directly to me once it's done."

Kelor was about to twist the power knob off when the voice spoke once more. "Oh, and Major, my men reported signs of stickies near the house, so I'd be careful out there if I were you. I look forward to hearing from you shortly."

There was a click as the voice on the other end switched off. Kelor did the same, then reached over to pick up the radio. As he did, he heard the scrape of something crossing the threshold of the front door.

Already pissed off by what he was being forced to do, Kelor raised his blaster as he whirled to see a naked female stickie shambling toward him, suckered hands outstretched to tear the skin from his body. Instinct took over, and the major put three rounds into the mutie when it was just a few feet away, the .40-caliber rounds smashing through its forehead and exploding out the back of the creature's skull. The corpse swayed on its feet for a moment, then crashed into dust, ichor leaking out of its shattered head, dripping over the black collar around its neck and onto the floor.

"Nuking hell, where do these fuckers keep coming from?" Kelor wondered as he replaced his low magazine with a fresh one. Keeping his blaster at the ready, he left the house, radio tucked under his arm, his mind whirling at the task he'd been assigned. His senses sharp for any more muties, he trotted to the wag, got in and drove back toward the center of the city.

Chapter Twelve

"Well, no reason for everyone to hang out here," Ryan said, catching Mildred and J.B. edging toward the door out of the corner of his eye. "Why don't we all take it easy, but not too easy, until, say—" he looked at the marvel that was a working digital clock near the bedside, which read 2:03 p.m. "—five-thirty, when we all regroup here, okay?"

J.B. had kept his eyes on the television screen when he paused at the door. "You aren't worried about being watched here? These guys got tech we haven't seen in years, 'cept like Jak said before. Strange we haven't heard about them elsewhere. With riches like this, you'd think traders would carry the word far and wide."

Ryan motioned everyone close. "Mebbe, mebbe not. After all, it's not like a lot of folks are humping up to or over the Rockies anymore. There's just not that much left on the Cific worth anyone's time. Might be another question for Mr. Carrington tonight. But before anyone goes strolling around, here's our cover story." He related the improvised tale he'd spun for Major Kelor earlier, making sure everyone got what little of it there was down pat. "Obviously, no talk of redoubts or any of that stuff. Our meal tonight will be interesting enough without us pouring fuel on the fire." He distributed the various key cards to the rest of the group, then took Krysty's hand. "Now all of you can scram."

The others filed out, leaving Krysty and Ryan alone. "Subtle, lover, real subtle."

"What do you mean? I don't know about you, but I'm planning on taking a nap till dinner."

"Oh, no, you're not. I refuse to let that filthy body of yours ruin these clean sheets just yet." Krysty spread the comforter back and bent to smell the clean cotton beneath. "Gaia, smells just like lemons and springtime. How do they do all this?"

"I don't know yet, but it'll make for some interesting dinner conversation." Ryan looked down at the front of his dust and sweat-stained shirt and caught a whiff of himself. "Phew. Okay, you just might have something there. Tell you what—why don't we take them up on that offer to wash our clothes while we clean up here ourselves." Picking up the phone receiver, he pressed the button for the front desk and was immediately rewarded by a familiar voice on the other end. "Front desk, this is Carter, how may I help you, Mr. Cawdor?"

Ryan stared at the piece of plastic in his hand, wondering how the clerk had known who was calling. "Uh, yeah, we'd like to get our clothes cleaned."

"Excellent, we'd be happy to take care of that for you. If you'd like, you may leave them in the main room, and someone will be along shortly to collect them."

"Tell you what, we'll leave them outside the door. We're likely to be occupied."

"Very well, Mr. Cawdor."

Ryan replaced the phone and turned to Krysty, a satisfied smile on his face. "That takes care of that."

Kicking off her boots, Krysty unzipped the front of her jumpsuit, revealing her full breasts contained by her simple cotton bra. "Best idea you've had all day, lover."

Having slipped off his longcoat, Ryan was doing the same with his combat boots, feeling secure enough to actually let his feet breathe for once. He shucked his drab-green fatigue pants and pulled off the black T-shirt. Scooping up both his and Krysty's clothes, he headed to the door and cracked it open. Peeking outside to see the hallway deserted, he placed the clothes next to the door, then closed it again. "Better than the one that got us in here?"

Krysty had been heading to the bathroom, but turned at the door to regard him with her penetrating, emerald-eyed gaze. "Yeah, loads better. That one took Gaia's own grace to get us through without one of us getting chilled. I'll follow you to the gates of hell, lover, you know that, but sometimes I do wonder what goes on in that head of yours, to think charging into an army is a good idea."

Ryan walked to the bathroom, pausing in the doorway to admire Krysty's voluptuousness as she fiddled with the tub controls. "Simple enough. If we kept going west, we'd be stuck with what was left of Tellen's army between us and the city. When an army's been repelled from their target, they're already beaten and demoralized. They're not paying attention to their surroundings anymore, they just want to go home. Done fast and hard, a single unit—like ours—can break through the line before they can regroup and reach our objective. Just like we did back there."

Krysty was running the bath water, smiling in delight when the water came out clear and clean. "All right, all right, enough with the tactics lesson. Just get your lanky ass in here." She examined small bottles near the side of the bathtub, selected one and dumped its entire contents into the swirling water.

"Lanky? Lanky? Doc is lanky. Jak is—well, skinny as a two-sided rail, I guess." Ryan padded barefoot up behind Krysty and scooped her up in his arms, relishing the feel of her skin against his, even as sweaty and dirty as they both were. But that would just make getting clean that much more fun. "I am anything but lanky."

"No, I suppose you're not." Snaking an arm around his neck, Krysty turned her face to his, her mouth seeking his in a firm kiss that, as usual, almost made his toes curl. He gently let her down, enjoying the lip-to-lip contact as their bodies pressed together, her breasts brushing against his chest while her other hand snaked lower, seeking another part of his anatomy. "And there's some parts of you that are definitely anything *but* lanky."

"Glad you approve. What do you say we get into that big tub and soap each other all over before heading to that even bigger bed for an hour or two?"

"I'd like nothing better, lover."

"WHAT'S THE RUSH, Mildred?" J.B. asked with a small smile as she tugged him by the hand toward the room at the far end of the hall.

"John, John, John. If you have to ask, it's obvious we haven't had enough privacy in the past few weeks." Snatching the key card from his hand, she inserted it into the slot and pushed the door open. "Showers in military bases or baths in freezing mountain streams at sunrise are one thing, but a working bathroom in a five-star luxury hotel in this day and age is better than winning the lottery, and I intend to take full advantage of it."

"I'm all for that." J.B. shook his head at her strange terminology. Even after all this time, Mildred's speech could sometimes be as confusing as Doc's. Shrugging off his battered leather jacket, he located the closet—behind a six-foot-high, intact, mirrored door—and hung it on a hanger, sliding the door closed.

"Also, I want my clothes cleaned—hell, I think I might just have them burned and get all new ones…." Mildred's patter trailed off, and he turned to see her with her hands clapped to her mouth, staring at the phone.

Immediately his hands went to his mini-Uzi, and he trotted to her side. "Hey, what's the matter?"

She took her hands away, and he was startled to see she was smiling, even as tears were welling up in the corners of her eyes. "Nothing, nothing at all. Everything is just fine." She gently removed the submachine gun from his hands and walked over to the desk next to the closet, setting it down on top before coming back to him and taking both of his hands in hers. "For the next two hours, I do not want to hear a single word about power plants, enemy armies, this Carrington dude, his daughter, that creepy major what's-his-name, chilling, stickies, blasters, or anything else we have to endure in this godforsaken world every single day. You understand me?"

Taking off his fedora, J.B. sent it across the room with a flick of his wrist, landing it on the wingback armchair in the corner. Leaning over, he kissed her on the mouth, quick and light at first, then deeper and with more urgency as her hands snuck around his waist to hold him tight and her mouth opened to his. Moving her to the bed, he peeled her shirt off, revealing a body that had once been a bit soft and fleshy when they had first found her in that cryo-chamber in the jungles of Minnesota all those months ago, but which had been honed to hard planes of muscle by life in the Deathlands since. J.B. ran his hands, implements that knew dozens of ways of taking life, over her breasts, smiling as she moaned in response to his gentle ministrations. Bending lower, he took the enlarged nipple of her left one in his mouth, teasing it with deft flicks of his tongue.

"Ryan always said you were a man of few words, and I certainly know why—your actions speak a thousand times louder than any words ever could." Her hands were busy at his belt, unbuckling the metal clasp and sliding his pants down his pale legs, where they met his boots. "Damn it. Just a sec." She reached down to unlace his boots and wrench them off his feet, letting them thump to the floor.

J.B. supported her with his right arm as he laid her down on the bed. Straightening, he pulled off his own shirt and tossed it aside as he gazed down on her. "Sure you don't want a bath first?"

"Hell, no, right now all I want is you. We'll have plenty of time to get cleaned up later. Besides, I like the way you smell."

J.B. took an experimental whiff of his pit and wrinkled his nose. "Cordite, sweat, dust and blood. If my stink is turning you on, you've got to get that nose checked out."

"There's nothing wrong with my nose, John. Now come here." Reaching for him, Mildred pulled J.B. down onto the very soft, very comfortable bed.

AS THE SINGLES, Jak and Doc got the middle room by default. Jak cast an envious look at Ryan's door as they headed into their room. "Wonder if got gaudies here?"

Doc clucked his tongue. "If they are anything like the rest of this gilded city, they will probably cost more than a bereft lad such as yourself could afford. And then there is the potential problem of the major's men keeping an eye on us, as I figure they will be doing anyway."

Jak ran into the room and flopped on the bed. "Not scared him. Gets in way, chill him."

"Which also would not endear us to the citizens of this remarkable ville." Doc had picked up a small pamphlet on the nightstand near the side of the bed and was flipping through it. "If you are not going to get cleaned up, perhaps there is something on that devil's box that can keep you entertained until dinner."

His eyes widening, Doc picked up the phone and hit a button. "Yes, Carter, this is Dr. Tanner. Did my eyes deceive me, or do you actually have a working barbershop in this establishment? Halleujah! Yes, I will be right down, thank you. Please notify them to have a chair waiting upon my arrival."

He hung up the phone and turned to Jak, who was already engrossed in the television and its remote control. "I take it you will be fine by yourself for a couple hours?"

With a grunt, Jak dismissed him with the wave of a hand, lost in the strange kaleidoscoping colors on the screen. Doc shrugged out of his frock coat, revealing a stained, torn, ivory-colored shirt that looked almost as old as he was, and trousers that had been washed and worn so many times they had faded from whatever their original color has been to a uniform dull gray. "I myself am about to sample the pleasures of this fine establishment."

With that, he took up his frock coat and left the room and strolled to the elevator, his lion's-head cane thudding softly on the floor with each step. At the polished steel doors, he hit the button with the end of his cane, whistling softly as he waited. When the doors opened, he strolled in and pushed the button for the basement, still whistling his nameless tune as he descended.

When the doors opened, he strolled out into a large room with several columns spaced throughout the area. A bar stretched across the wall to his left, and several reclining barber chairs were arrayed around the space, a few occupied, and several others that were empty. The scent of soap, leather and aftershave hung in the air. A tear came to Doc's eye along with unbidden memories of a time long, long ago, and he blinked it away with an effort.

A short Hispanic man with close-cropped hair and a white towel over his shoulder walked over. "Welcome to the barbershop, Mr. Tanner. Mr. Carter said to expect you. My name is Jésus, and I'll be your barber. Anything special you would like?"

Doc puffed out his skinny chest and eyed the young man with an air of grandeur. "Sir, I want the whole shebang."

Jésus didn't bat an eye. "Very well. I suggest a quick steam while we clean those clothes."

"Actually, you may toss this shirt and the trousers on the nearest dung pile, if you have one. I will be requiring a new white shirt, and trousers from your finest broadcloth."

Jésus turned and picked up a thick, white, terrycloth bathrobe from a nearby chair. "In the meantime, perhaps this will be comfortable."

Doc was one step ahead of him, pulling off the soiled shirt and handing it to him, then kicking off his boots and sending them skittering across the floor next to an empty chair. His pants were next, which were so dirty they could have stood up by themselves. "Perhaps you could provide new drawers, sir."

"Indeed. And I'll arrange to have your coat cleaned."

"Excellent."

The next ninety minutes passed for Doc in a haze of relaxation like he hadn't known since the nineteenth century. After his long steam, which relaxed every tight muscle in his body, he took a bracingly cold shower, then toweled off and slipped into the thick, soft, warm white robe. Jésus led him over to the chair and had him sit down. He wrapped a moist, hot towel around Doc's face, arranging it to leave a small air hole near his nose, and let him sit for a few minutes, until Doc almost fell asleep. Then he whisked the towel away and stropped his old-fashioned razor until the edge gleamed in the light. Lathering up soap in a small container, he brushed it onto Doc's chin and cheeks, then shaved him with sure, steady strokes, cleaning the blade on his towel after each stroke and going back until the old man's face was as smooth as a newborn's. He splashed on just a touch of aftershave, enough to cool Doc's skin and wake him up, then sat him up and cut his hair. Finally, Jésus turned his chair around so Doc could get a glimpse of the new man he had become.

"Dear God..." Doc stared at himself, rubbing his weathered chin and forehead, examining the hollows of his cheeks, the jutting planes of his cheekbones and slightly sunken eyes under his neatly trimmed white hair. "I look...so old..."

Jésus quickly whirled the chair back around. "Not at all, sir, you simply look distinguished. How about we take a look at clothes to fit the rest of you, as well?"

Doc shook his head and looked up at him. "Yes, yes, let's do that, shall we?"

"If you'll follow me, sir."

Squaring his shoulders, Doc rose from the chair and trailed the short man into the next room, leaving the mirror and its haunting image behind.

Thirty minutes later, dressed in clean underwear, a crisp white shirt and black pants cut to fit his cracked knee boots, which had also been cleaned and polished, Doc walked back along the corridor to his suite. A large plastic bag containing his clean frock suit, among other things, was slung over his shoulder. Fumbling for his key card, Doc inserted it into the slot, frowning when the light failed to change, then turned the card around and tried it again. This time the light turned green, and he pushed the door open.

The moment he slipped inside, he was assaulted by a blast of noise unlike anything he'd ever heard before, a strange combination of whine and howl that made the hairs on the back of his neck stand on end. Strange voices could also be heard over the din, men snapping out commands to one another, punctuated by more strange sounds that resembled some of the odder weapons he had seen during his travels throughout the Deathlands. The main room of the suite was dark except for waves of flickering light and noise emanating from the television.

Doc stopped, grabbing for his LeMat, which he had left behind in the room, and stood transfixed as he watched the incredible action unfold on the screen—strange vessels soaring against the backdrop of space as they whirled and dived above a gigantic planet that seemed to be a massive artificial space station.

"Have you been here the entire time?"

"Shh! Good part's comin'."

"That's quite impossible. Any ships in space couldn't move that quickly, not without an opposing force to push against. Newton's laws would still be in effect, even in a vacuum."

Jak turned his cold ruby eyes on Doc. "Said shut mouth." With that he turned back to the television.

Absorbed in spite of himself, Doc watched as a young man with a dome-headed, silver-and-white robot as his copilot flew a harrowing course down a large trench while being menaced by a sinister man clad in black armor wearing a vicious-looking helmet and face mask that made him sound like he was speaking through a box or screen of some kind. The masked enemy was driven off by another ship that swooped in at the last minute to save the day, making Doc roll his eyes in disbelief.

At the climax, the pilot aimed his "photon torpedoes" at a small opening that apparently destroyed the entire structure when it was hit. While his scientific mind tallied up the many impossibilities of what he'd just seen, Doc's romantic mind soared with the young man as he came back to his friends' hidden base and received a reward from a pretty, brown-haired woman, along with his friend, a dark-haired hired blaster and his partner, a tall, hirsute mutant who resembled a shaggy, walking carpet.

When the triumphant swell of trumpets sounded over the credits of the movie, Doc shook himself out of his reverie and turned on the lights. "It's almost time to head down to dinner, and you haven't even washed up yet."

Jak shook his head in denial. "Yeah, did. Stuck

head under faucet. 'Sides, healer cleaned me. Better 'n you—stink like gaudy house slut."

"Yes, but you could at least have gotten your clothes— Ah, why do I even bother? All right, if that is how you want to go, who am I to stop you?"

"Yeah, who?" Jak was already ejecting the golden disk and putting it back in the folder, and choosing another one. "Not want go. Two more vids after this one. You not see the—what'd they call it?—'lightsaber' scenes. Awesome!"

"Now, Jak, I am sure there will be plenty of time to watch the rest of those, but we should really pay our respects to the leader of this ville tonight. Besides, are you not hungry?"

With a long sigh, Jak turned off the television and plodded over. "Rather eat here. Not want sit at table and listen people jaw heads off."

Doc sat on the soft bed and regarded his roommate with sad eyes. "Sometimes, my young friend, I could not agree with you more."

Chapter Thirteen

The group met at Ryan's room around five-thirty as agreed. J.B. and Mildred were first, their intertwined hands and relaxed smiles leaving no doubt as to how they had passed the time.

"Come on in." Ryan answered the door, still admiring the neat sewing job the hotel's tailors had done on his pants and shirt. "Where's Jak and Doc?"

"I imagine they'll be along soon enough. Quite the arrangements, huh?"

"A far cry from where we slept last night, that's for damn sure. I didn't think places like this still existed."

"Haven't seen buildings in this good shape since we were down south in Cajun country—the very first time, not recently," Krysty amended with a grimace, not wanting to think about the time they'd almost lost Mildred to the oozie plague. "You both look…well-rested."

"Was about to say the same thing about you two," Mildred said with a crooked smile. Krysty grinned back, while the men cast about for anything to change the subject.

"How do you figure Carrington keeps this place and the people in line?" J.B. asked.

"The lure of a power plant might be enough to get people to fall in line, or it brings raiders like this guy Tellen they're fighting, looking to take over. If they're raising cattle or buffalo out here, there's enough grass to feed them, so there's your food. Vegetables still grow everywhere, and if Doc's right, and the city didn't get tagged by the nukes during skydark, and the people either fled or figured out how to get along, no reason others couldn't come along and make a go of it, I suppose."

"What you think we should carry to dinner?" Mildred asked.

"Figured we'd stick to handblasters only, and let them go if necessary. Don't make sense for us to tote heavy firepower to the meal, and since we brought the baron's little girl back safe and sound, I figure they shouldn't be too wary of us."

"Yeah, shouldn't be," J.B. repeated. "I don't know. Carrington seemed wound pretty tight to me."

Mildred shook her head. "You would be, too, if your people had just pushed back a major assault on your city. It's the natural lull after an adrenaline high. I wouldn't be surprised if we find him falling asleep in the soup tonight."

Ryan's eye widened as he saw past Mildred to their other companions coming down the hall. "Speaking of surprises, would you get a look at this."

Jak and Doc approached. Jak was dressed in his usual clothes, including the jacket with its bits of metal sewn into it to provide a nasty surprise to anyone who tried to grab him. His hair was sleeked back, making him look like an unusually alert, albino, humanoid cat.

Beside him, Doc had been transformed from the scruffy Deathlands denizen he'd been when they had first arrived to a character out of a twentieth century movie. Besides his haircut and shave, he was also decked out in a sky-blue suit with wide lapels over a white, ruffled shirt, a sky-blue bow tie at his throat and a broad blue band around his waist. Matching pants and even light blue shoes completed the ensemble, which actually went pretty well with his white hair and tanned skin, Ryan had to admit. Even so…

"I hope you're not planning on wearing that anywhere else besides dinner tonight, Doc."

His malacca cane tucked under his arm, the old man sketched a formal bow to the rest of the group. "Of course not, my dear Ryan. Such a tuxedo would be most unsuitable for any sort of activity other than the one upon we are about to embark."

Jak jerked a thumb at the eye-catching costume. "That's why took long."

Mildred had hidden a smile behind her hand, but now she lowered it and stared at him, shaking her head in either amusement or admiration, Ryan couldn't tell which. "It suits you, Doc. It definitely suits you."

"If the rest of you have time, I strongly suggest that you all see what they have. It's truly quite amazing," Doc said. "I had hoped we would all be dressed more suitably for the occasion—"

"Thought clean clothes were suitable," J.B. muttered.

"However, you could not possibly have known, and no doubt our hosts will take that into consideration. Shall we?"

With Doc leading the way, the companions walked to the elevators and made their way down to the lobby. Carter was still on duty, and came around the desk to see them.

"Good evening, ladies and gentlemen. I trust all of you have found the Magnolia's facilities acceptable?"

Ryan nodded. "Just fine, thanks. The major said

there'd be someone here who would be driving us to dinner."

"Yes, I received word that they'll be here in approximately ten minutes. In the meantime, perhaps you'd care for a drink at the bar?" He indicated a small room on the other side of the lobby, almost hidden by the traffic coming in and out of the busy hotel. "Feel free to sample one of our local beers."

Ryan hid his grimace, knowing from experience what local brewing usually turned out to be in the Deathlands—flat, tasteless and warm. Still, when the host insisted… The group walked over to the small room, which was tended by a lone man dressed in a white collared shirt and black bow tie who was polishing the bar with a clean white rag. Behind him was a tall rack, filled with several dozen bottles containing various liquids from clear to dark amber and everything in between, including one blue one and one colored bright green. Other than him and the group, the bar was empty.

"Evening, folks, have a seat." Carter caught the bartender's attention after his greeting, whispering a few words in his ear and slipping a small stack of what looked like bronze coins into his hand. The man nodded before he turned back to Ryan's group while the clerk walked out of the room. "My name is Trace, and I'll be serving you this evening. What would you like?"

Ryan jerked his thumb at the still-swinging doors. "What was that about?"

The bartender's amiable smile faltered just a bit before he spoke. "Carter was just telling me that your drinks are on the house this evening."

"Pricey, are they? That would explain why it's so quiet in here."

"You are correct, sir. The Magnolia prides itself on its collection of aged liquors—that is, liquors bottled predark."

Doc's face lit up. "You do not say? However did that happen?"

"Mr. Carrington will be happy to answer any questions you may have about the town's history. I just pour the drinks." He presented a neat, handwritten list of the available liquors. "As I said, on the house, ladies and gentlemen."

"Do you do mixed drinks?" Mildred asked, leaning forward on her stool.

"It would depend on the ingredients, but I'll try to create whatever you ask for."

"I would love what to have a White Russian. My father let me try a version of it when I was a teenager, and I never forgot the taste." Her face fell. "But I supposed you'd need cream for that."

Trace's smile never left his face. "That one I can do. As long as you don't mind buffalo cream."

"That isn't some kind of joke, is it?" the black woman asked, her face darkening.

Trace held up his hand to head her off. "Not at all. Buffalo do better on the plains out here, so we've been tending them as best we can, including raising females and calves for meat and milk. So…" He busied himself with a glass and three bottles, including one of thick, white cream, taken from a small refrigerator under the bar. Layering the vodka, coffee liqueur and cream over ice, he set the finished drink down in front of her. "Enjoy."

Mildred took the glass and sipped, her eyes closing in pleasure. "My God, it's like I'm back home again. It's very good, thank you. You guys have to try this.

It's unbelievable." She passed the glass down, and they all took a small sip. Ryan found it incredibly sweet, but said nothing. Of them all, Krysty seemed to enjoy it the most after Mildred, with Doc abstaining and Jak making a face and pronouncing it "sweet-bitter."

"And for you, miss?" Trace asked Krysty.

"Carter recommended your beer."

"Rightly so. I'm afraid that we're limited to only a few selections at the moment, notably our golden pilsner, along with a refreshing wheat beer you might like. Take your pick."

"The pilsner sounds good."

"Make that two," Ryan said.

Trace produced two chilled glass mugs and filled them from the tap, letting the head settle before sliding them across the bar. "There you are."

Ryan eyed his glass, finding the liquid inside a far cry from most of the crudely distilled alcohols he'd sampled during his travels. It was much clearer and a uniform light gold color. Bringing it to his lips, he sniffed lightly, surprised to enjoy the clear, tangy aroma. Sipping, he was rewarded with a light, crisp taste with a bit of unidentifiable fruit notes in the back. Swallowing, he took another drink before setting the glass down on the bar. "Damn good."

"None better in this area, that's for sure. To your liking, miss?"

Krysty had been as cautious as Ryan, but was also enjoying her glass. "You can call me Krysty, and yes, this is incredible. You folks brew it here?"

"Only way to do it. There were lots of small breweries in the area, and between all of them we were able to cobble together a place to make our own. With the fields around, we can grow plenty of wheat and barley. The only problem is the hops, which we have to get from out west when we can, and they cost a pretty penny, but as I'm sure you agree, are more than worth it."

Trace turned to J.B., Doc and Jak. "And for you gentlemen?"

"Anything you have from the Emerald Isle would be just fine, thank you," Doc said. At the bartender's puzzled look, he shook his head. "Sorry. What do you have for whiskey?"

"I think I have a bit of Bushmills lurking about. Let me check." Trace turned to the back wall and scanned it, then brought down a bottle with a black-and-white label. "Ah, here it is. Neat, or on the rocks?"

"You have ice?" Doc shook his head, apparently not remembering that Mildred's drink had contained cubes, as well. "On the rocks, please."

Trace prepared the drink, which was much simpler than Mildred's—simply pouring the dark amber liquid over a short, heavy-bottomed glass filled with clear ice. He pushed the glass forward, and Doc accepted it with a hand that only trembled once as he raised it.

"I never thought I would see the likes of this again in all my days." He sipped, almost delicately, and held the liquid in his mouth for a few seconds before swallowing. "That's a good burn, that is." He moved off to one side and sat on a stool away from the others, staring into his drink.

"He all right?" Trace asked, watching the old man with not quite a frown on his face.

Ryan was quick to get the bartender's attention. "He'll be just fine. He has, spells of a sort every so often. Never know what'll set him off."

Trace nodded. "My wife's sister used to be the same

way. Well, two left who haven't chosen. The bar is still open, sirs."

Jak alternated between looking at the man behind the bar and the bottles themselves. "What blue stuff?"

"That, young sir, is what's known as curaçao, orange liqueur with a hint of bitterness. People used to use it in mixed drinks, although you can take it on its own, I suppose."

"Never had blue liquor before. Try it."

The bartender poured him a shot over ice. Jak picked up the glass and mimicked the others' behavior, sipping instead of pounding the entire drink down in a single gulp. His face wrinkled, then returned to its normal suspicious expression. "Orange, and bitter like said." He sipped again. "Not bad."

"And for the last gentleman?"

J.B. adjusted his glasses as he regarded the man in front of him. "I don't suppose you have a brand called Grey Goose, do you?"

"Grey Goose?" Trace turned again to look at the shelves. "Nothing up here, but wait a moment..." He knelt and rummaged in a cabinet behind the bar, coming up with a tiny bottle featuring a small goose on the label above three tiny squares of red, white and blue. "I believe this is what you're looking for."

J.B. leaned forward and nodded. "That's the one."

"Most vodkas are best served ice-cold, so if you'll allow me." Trace filled another glass with ice, then twisted off the cap and emptied the tiny bottle into it, the liquid barely rising a third of the way up. "Let that sit for a minute or two to chill to the proper temperature, and enjoy."

Ryan drained his glass, finding the last swallow of beer as pleasurable as the first. "Fireblast, that was probably the best beer I've ever had. You folks really have something here."

"Thank you, sir, we certainly like to think so."

"So what was with those coins Carter passed to you when we came in?" Mildred asked, having finished her drink and sucking on a piece of liquor-coated ice.

Trace grinned again. "You mean Carrington's Coins?" He took one of the smooth-edged circles of metal out from under the counter and set it spinning on the surface with a flick of his finger. "Mr. Carrington came up with these a couple years ago, as an incentive program for excellent work or service to the community. He doles them out as he sees fit, and the recipient can exchange them for certain goods or services. They are difficult to obtain, but not impossible. One will get you an entire day off from work or duty—or one drink at this very bar. Speaking of drinks, yours should be just about ready now, sir."

J.B. sipped the colorless liquid in his glass and smiled. "Almost like I remember it."

"Vodka doesn't taste like anything, as I recall," Mildred said.

"It's not the taste, but what it's associated with." J.B.'s gaze grew distant as he stared into his glass.

"Want to share a memory, J.B.?"

"Nope, Millie. Just want to savor the drink and think back to when I was fifteen."

No one pressed the Armorer for details. He had never spoken about his youth, not even to Mildred.

J.B. remained silent for a few minutes.

"So, how does the vodka taste?" Ryan asked.

"About the same as it did then—something, yet nothing. If I had to describe it, I'd say it's like drinking pure, liquid coldness." He sipped again.

Everyone was quiet after that, those who had them sipping their drinks until their glasses were empty. Trace caught the vibe the group was giving off, and was content to give them their space and silence, cleaning up the bar and polishing glasses until the door swung open to reveal Carter standing in the entryway.

"Your escort has arrived, Mr. Cawdor."

Chapter Fourteen

Ryan led his group through the lobby and out the hotel's main doors, where a mil wag with its top removed, much like the one that had brought them here, idled outside. An older black man with a lined, careworn face and sergeant's chevrons on his shoulder waited by the passenger door, hands clasped behind his back. "Ryan Cawdor?"

"That's me."

"My name is Sergeant Pard Caddeus. I'm here to escort you and your group to dinner with Mr. Carrington. If you will all please step up into the vehicle, we can be on our way."

Ryan helped Krysty board, then climbed in himself, receiving a small smile at his gallant gesture. J.B. did the same for Mildred, leaving Jak and Doc to scramble up as best as they could. Once everyone was situated, Caddeus closed the door, walked around to the driver's side, got in and they headed out.

The heat of the day had dissipated somewhat. While it was no longer as blazingly hot as the afternoon had been, the early evening hadn't shed all of the day's warmth yet. Combined with the light breeze, the open-air trip was refreshing after the closeness of the well-preserved hotel. The six members looked around again at the streets they passed through, lit by electric lights instead of smoking torches or fuel-burning lanterns, and watched various people going about their business. There was a noticeable absence of unruly behavior—no public drunkenness, gaudy houses or violence in the street, either by citizens, sec men or both.

As he looked around, Ryan realized another difference between other villes and this one—there weren't any sec men patrolling what would be considered the downtown area. The fatigue-clad men and women were certainly around, but they were often performing other duties. Here it seemed like everyone followed an unspoken but understood rule not to get in each other's business. It was strange, but comfortable in a way, knowing that they didn't have to constantly be on the lookout for the eyes of the law watching them.

Of course, Ryan thought, remembering his conversation with J.B. back at their rooms, that doesn't mean they aren't watching us by other means. As the vehicle wound its way through the city streets, he kept an eye out for cameras or other surveillance gear, but didn't see any, which didn't mean anything, either. The powers that be had come up with plenty of ways to hide the spy cams and other equipment back in the day, and smart, enterprising people all over the Deathlands had come up with ways to modify the old tech to new uses.

The wag pulled up to a small, old, two-story building that looked as if it had been standing on the same spot forever, from predark and even before that. The thick, weather-beaten brick walls and small windows made it look like a building that had been wrenched out of time and deposited here in the twenty-second century. A large green canvas awning stretched from one side of the first floor to the other, and on it was written Buckhorn Exchange in neat, white letters.

Turning off the wag, Caddeus turned to the group.

"We're here. I'll be around for the evening, as well as other members of my squad posted around the building. So if you see one of them near a door or window, don't be alarmed. Mr. Carrington is waiting for you inside."

He got out and opened the passenger door again, letting everyone file out before closing the door. Leading them to the front of the building, the sergeant returned the salute of an armed private in front of the entrance, then pulled the thick wood and glass door open and held it as the group walked into the building.

The place-out-of-time motif continued in here, as well, with the interior covered in rich, real wood that had been lovingly maintained, creating a look straight out of history. The floor, walls and furniture were made out of the same heavy, dark walnut, lending a sense of eternity to the entire place, while the upper half of the main room was covered in red velvet and adorned with dozens of mounted heads of various animals, including buffalo, pronghorn antelope, deer, elk and other game animals. More animals were mounted on stands around the room, including a snarling cougar that made Ryan's hand drop to the butt of his blaster, it looked so life-like. A wooden bar with a genuine brass-rail and spittoon underneath was in another small room of the main dining area. The aroma of cooking meat was redolent in the air, making Ryan's mouth water.

Doc and Mildred were the most appreciative of the place, pointing out different animals and comparing muttered notes over what each one might have seen or remembered in their own times gone by. The rest of the group was simply left to look at the place as a sort of snapshot of history, of a time they would never know, preserved and brought forward to the here and now, to serve as a backdrop for a meal the likes of which the place's founders could have never imagined.

The entire establishment was empty, except for two figures at the head of a long table. Dressed in a black suit jacket and matching pants over a white shirt and braided leather string tie fastened with a clip containing a rattlesnake head in amber, Josiah Carrington was engaged in a quiet yet heated conversation with his daughter. Rachel was dressed in blue jeans, a button-down shirt and black cowboy boots, her blond hair pulled back into a ponytail, exposing the strong lines of her cheekbone and jaw.

Upon seeing them, the two stood. The elder Carrington wore no visible weapons, but Rachel had a small revolver in a hand-tooled leather holster at her hip.

Josiah raised his arms in welcome. "Evening, friends, please, come and sit down! You are all honored guests of the Free City of Denver, so relax and enjoy yourselves tonight."

The six companions trooped over to the table, which was set with brightly colored plates decorated in geometric patterns of brown, blue and white, with silverware with stag horn handles next to them. Josiah pulled out the seat at his right hand. "Ryan, if you please."

"My pleasure." Ryan walked up to the chair and sat, with Krysty on his right side, Doc next to her. Jak took the chair at the opposite end of the table, and J.B. and Mildred took the ones on the other side, with the Armorer sitting next to Rachel—just in case. Carrington's daughter looked as if she might have been carved from stone, although her eyebrow raised when she saw the blaster on Ryan's hip.

"There was really no need to bring any blasters to dinner, Ryan."

The one-eyed man leaned back in his chair as a server appeared out of nowhere and filled his thick-walled glass with water. "I notice that didn't stop you from coming here strapped, either."

"We are always surrounded by our enemies, so it is best that we all be prepared, especially after the events of this afternoon."

"Well, I certainly hope that you do not consider us among that repellent group," Doc said as he lowered his tall frame into his chair.

"I couldn't possibly count such a well-dressed man among my enemies." Rachel smiled at the old man, making him blush and reach for his water glass, nearly knocking it over in his embarrassment.

Josiah smiled, the first real expression of delight Ryan had seen on his face. "I see that Doc Tanner has partaken of some of the things our city has to offer. I hope the rest of you have done the same."

"Your hotel is marvelous, and Trace at the bar makes the best White Russian I've ever had," Mildred said, earning a nod from Josiah.

"Good vids, too. Not seen anything like." This from Jak, slouched at the end of the long table.

"You'll find the beds most comfortable, as well, a far cry from sleeping on the open road, or on a hard cot in a bare ville." Josiah picked up a dark green bottle next to his wineglass on the table. "I've also taken the liberty of opening one of our rarer treasures, a few bottles of wine from Australia, bottled more than a century ago. It's held up rather well—much like myself, I might add." Josiah acknowledged the chuckles that came from Doc, Mildred and Krysty, and the smiles from Ryan and J.B., who, while maybe not quite as polished as the others, knew when to give their host his due. Only Jak missed the joke completely, staring around the room at the huge stuffed heads looking back at the party with their dark glass eyes.

"Everything's been great so far," Ryan said. So far, the experience had been much like many other villes he'd seen, only this one had been much cleaner. The local baron would show off his town and whatever treasures passed for wealth in them before trying to wheedle a favor or job out of Ryan and his crew, often resorting to ransoming needed parts or even kidnapping to enforce their "request." While Denver had amenities the likes of which Ryan and his group hadn't seen in a ville in a long time, it didn't hide the basic fact that the city had problems that seemed beyond their ability to handle—but a small group of the right people just might be "persuaded" to do whatever it was that needed handling for them.

Ryan picked up his wineglass and swirled the rich, dark red liquid around, raising the glass to his lips and sniffing it before taking a sip. He'd drunk enough pre-dark vintages to know what it should and shouldn't taste like—more or less. The wine was smooth and earthy, with hints of tobacco and chocolate as it slid down his throat. He'd noticed that Josiah's glass had contained the dregs of earlier indulgence, and wondered how many the man had downed before they had arrived.

His musings were interrupted by the arrival of several servants each bearing a covered dish that they set in front of each diner, along with baskets of warm, crusty bread. Josiah stood as the servers removed the covers and filed out of the room. "I hope you don't mind that we've planned the menu for the evening. It's better to give you a taste of what our lands have to offer."

Ryan and the others looked down at the small chunks

of pale meat swimming in a white sauce with an aroma that brought with it a hint of peppers.

"Anyone guess what it is?" Rachel asked, her fork already lifting to her mouth.

Ryan had a good idea, but J.B. beat him to it. "Rattler."

If she was disappointed, Rachel didn't show it. "Very good, Mr. Dix."

Ryan dug into his own plate, finding the meat tender, although a bit stringy, with the pungent sauce adding more than a bit of kick. Jak inhaled his, as usual, while the rest of the companions enjoyed theirs at a more leisurely pace. Grabbing a thick slice of bread to soak up some of the sauce, Ryan was pleased to bite into tangy, chewy sourdough.

"Quite the establishment you have here," he said after swallowing, letting another server remove the plate.

"From what we learned, the Buckhorn was the oldest established restaurant in Denver, and still is." Josiah refilled Ryan's and his glass as he talked. "Apparently about two centuries ago, give or take a decade or two, a buffalo scout named Shorty Zietz founded this place, and it's stood here ever since. Even the nuking didn't affect it much, so when we found it, it was like all it needed was a bit of cleaning and restocking, and its been serving the good people of Denver ever since."

"That is one thing I've been meaning to ask you, Mr. Carrington—"

"Josiah, if you don't mind."

"Not at all." Mildred's inquiry was interrupted by the next course, a salad of wild greens, including dandelion shoots mixed with lettuce, radish and wild onion, covered in a creamy dressing with chunks of a pungent cheese mixed in.

Doc's head popped up to stare at Josiah when the plate was set in front of him. "Blue cheese dressing?"

"Yes, although the milk is a mix of cow and buffalo. I'm afraid we just don't get enough pure cow's milk to make it straight. Still very good, however. Anyway, Mildred, you were saying?"

"Just a moment..." Mildred sampled the salad, her eyes closing in delight. "Just when I think the Deathlands are one long pit of despair, we come across somewhere like here, and I'm drinking a drink I haven't had in a—long time, and eating a delicious salad with dressing instead of munching dried meat or tasteless protein bars. For this alone you people deserve to prosper."

Ryan tried his own and found the cheese too sharp for his taste. Nevertheless, he made sure to clean his plate—after all, food was still food, no matter what plate it was served on, or with what liquid to drink.

Josiah sipped his wine and smiled. "Thank you for your kind words, however, all of this is due to a lot of hard work from a lot of very dedicated people."

"That reminds me—how did you find people to staff your hotel like that? I don't believe I've ever seen that level of hospitality anywhere before."

Josiah had only nibbled on his salad and moved the plate away from him. "It's simple, really. Every position at the Magnolia, from the front desk clerks to the people who prepare the various rooms, is a reward for dedicated service and exemplary behavior. The people there have to want to work in the hotel more than anything, and must demonstrate their loyalty to the city itself through various means before they can be placed in a position there. It is one of the highest careers in the city, and is aspired to by many."

J.B. cleared his throat. "I find it hard to believe a

hotel clerk holds a higher position than any of those men we saw on the wall this afternoon."

Rachel broke in. "Father's not saying that the staff of the Magnolia holds a higher social status here, simply that many wish to leave their jobs toiling in the fields or herding the cattle to work in a position that may suit them better. For as many that want to secure a job there, though, there's just as many who are comfortable herding buffalo or cattle—or defending our town on the wall. And everyone is educated to the same level at our school. Each position is just as important—there is no hierarchy."

"Indeed, except for the ones on top." This came from Doc in a loud voice, making all heads turn toward him. "No doubt a learned man such as yourself knows the phrase 'all animals are equal, but some are more equal than others.'"

Josiah set his wineglass on the table, ignoring his daughter's hand on his arm. "You did not mention that you had a scholar traveling with you, Ryan."

Ryan's eye flicked from one end of the table to the other. "I should've warned you that Doc's temperament can shift like the wind, particularly when wine is involved."

His attempted joke fell flat as the two men stared at each other. Josiah broke the suddenly heavy silence first. "I am familiar with the work of Orwell, Doc, indeed, I have seen the world he wrote of in his stories come to pass time and time again. When I struck out to try to create a new place to live, one free of the vice and hatred and bigotry and the strong always crushing the weak, I faced the most basic problem endemic to all societies—who should rule? For, mark my words, someone must. It cannot be a completely democratic society, for then each person thinks their voice should be listened to the most, and only the mob holds sway. Previous methods, from the vaunted Senate of Rome to the bicameral legislature of America in the late twentieth century, all were equally flawed in some way, subject to the will of weak and corrupt men who signed their souls away for power, money or influence. No, the only way to go in these dark times was to create a benevolent dictatorship, as distasteful as the term sounds. The moment I realized that, every decision made from that point on had a single goal at its base—how will this help the city? Everything I have done since arriving here has had that sole aim as its foundation—how will this improve the Free City of Denver? I like to think that the results speak for themselves."

Josiah stood at the head of the table, holding his wineglass as if he was about to salute an invisible honoree. "Over the years, we have attracted hundreds of like-minded individuals, people who wished to live their lives free of tyranny, to join in common cause of building a city out of the ashes of what had come before. Where every man, woman and child would be free to pursue a life of their own, not beholden to or under the thumb of some power-mad overlord. It is true, there are things that the city requires from all who dwell in it if it is to not only survive, but prosper. That's one thing that everyone who comes here must understand before they settle here, that being a citizen of this city carries weight, the weight of responsibility, to your neighbors, to your neighborhood, to your city itself. For those who accept and work within that requirement, the Free City of Denver is the result, one that everyone who participates in, benefits from."

As Josiah spoke, Ryan's expression changed from

neutral to interested to a puzzled frown. Previously he had only heard a certain, select group of people talk like this, and they usually wore white coats when they did. Other than his tendency toward long-winded oratory, Josiah didn't have any of the other hallmarks of a scientist, predark or otherwise. So where had he gotten the knowledge he was showing off at the moment?

Before anyone could reply, the silence was shattered by the sound of automatic rifle fire in the distance. Doc cocked an ear to listen, a sly smile creeping over his face. "You, good sir, are a magnificent orator. I now understand much of how you rose to your present position. You almost had me convinced—except for the barking of Tellen's wolves at your wall."

Josiah's expression curdled at the mention of his enemy. "That so-called freedom fighter is nothing more than a common thug who has brought together other low-minded individuals to rally under his cause, attempting to destroy everything I have worked to build here."

The tread of shoes on the polished wooden floor caught everyone's attention, and Josiah reverted from brooding to genial in an instant. Ryan caught the venomous look Rachel shot at Doc, who had already seemed to forget the current topic of conversation, and was busy munching on a last bite of salad before his plate was removed.

"And, to answer one of your companion's points, this food is not just for the 'men in charge.'" Josiah pointed out as the new plates were deposited in front of each person. "Right now hundreds of people across the city are enjoying meals similar to what we are about to dine on right now."

As if on cue, the servers whisked away the covers

to reveal thick slices of pink meat darkening to brown on the edges, swimming in gravy, flanked by a heap of mashed potatoes on the left side, and a neatly stacked pile of steaming green beans on the right.

"The finest buffalo prime rib you will ever have. Grass-fed on the plains outside the city and butchered at the peak of flavor. Go on, have a taste."

Although Ryan's appetite had been blunted by the turn the conversation had taken, he cut off a piece—the knife sliding through the meat like it was butter—and lifted a forkful to his mouth. The taste was, quite simply, unbelievable. The meat was lean, yet tender and rich nonetheless, almost melting in his mouth. Ryan chewed a few times, almost as an afterthought than due to any real need, and swallowed, the taste almost overwhelming his taste buds.

Josiah watched him finish the bite before taking any of his own. "Well?"

"It's damn good." Almost of their own volition, Ryan's hands moved to cut off more. Around him, the rest of the table was enjoying their main course, as well, from Jak sawing off huge chunks and stuffing them in his mouth, to Krysty, J.B. and Mildred enjoying their own meals with various degrees of pleasure. True to Josiah's word, it was a dish to be savored, with the conversation falling by the wayside in favor of relishing every last succulent morsel.

Scraping his plate clean, Ryan drained his wineglass and leaned back in his chair, feeling truly full for the first time in a long while, and what was more, enjoying it, as well. The servers brought out a selection of hand-cranked ice creams for dessert; mint, lemon sherbet, flavored with artificial flavoring, and even vanilla, made with rare, hoarded beans. There was also chicory coffee, port and a selection of various whiskeys for those so inclined. Krysty exchanged a glance with Ryan, nodding toward Doc as if to ask if he should indulge any more. Ryan shrugged, leaning over to whisper, "After a meal that big, a shot of whiskey should knock the old man right off his chair."

Sure enough, the rich food and wine were already conspiring to lull Doc into a drowse, his head drooping down to his chest as he labored in vain to stay awake. Ryan caught Josiah watching him with a small smile. "You attract the most interesting people to follow you, Ryan Cawdor."

Something in the other man's tone made Ryan's natural wariness stir under the torpor-inducing meal. "No more than the people who come to live here, I'd guess."

Josiah leaned forward, a smile playing around the corners of his mouth. "Perhaps, but then again, most of them don't know about places like Cheyenne Mountain."

Chapter Fifteen

The other man's words put Ryan on full alert, but his face betrayed nothing as he stared back at Josiah. He shifted in his chair, seeming to turn slightly toward the other man as if to hear him better, but in reality he was simply raising his hip so that his blaster was more readily accessible.

Only Krysty seemed to notice the dangerous direction the conversation was heading. J.B. and Mildred were occupied in keeping Doc from falling off his chair, and Jak already seemed inclined to sleep off the effects of the feast. Ryan kept his voice neutral as he replied, "Your major has better hearing than I expected."

"Major Kelor is a valued member of my sec force, and as such reports things he thinks may be of interest to me. Your man's comment this afternoon was one of those things."

"What's your point?"

"My point is that I would hazard a guess that the good doctor may know of other things—things that could greatly help our community continue to thrive."

"What, you want him to stay here and teach or something?"

Josiah waved off the question with a flick of his hand. "Nothing so mundane. As he so elegantly put it, we are beset by Tellen's army. The wall stops them for now, but he's determined, and I'm concerned that he'll find a way in sooner rather than later. Make no mistake, I mean to stop him, but a concerted attack against his headquarters would leave the city open to a counter-strike should we fail. Tellen is a devious enemy, willing to do whatever it takes to achieve his goals."

Ryan frowned. "You want us to chill him?"

Josiah shook his head. "I wouldn't ask that of you. I would have many volunteers of my own ready in an instant if I thought they could succeed at the task. No, what I'd request from you requires more than just simple skill with a blaster." He leaned back in his chair, regarding Ryan with a thoughtful expression. "Have you ever heard of Denver International Airport?"

"Can't say that I have." Mirroring his host's movements, Ryan also leaned back in his chair, figuring he might as well go along with this for the moment. "What is it?"

"Before skydark, the airport was built to be a major transportation hub for this half of what was then called the United States of America. It was constructed roughly twenty-five miles away from the city. Ever since, rumors have always circulated saying that far more earth was excavated than necessary to build an airport. That the government built a secret base under the structure to carry out some of their most top-secret experiments."

Josiah paused for a moment, as if letting the information he was imparting sink in. Ryan remained stone silent, unresponsive in any way. Another maxim of the Trader's surfaced in his memory: he who speaks first, loses. He simply remained still, staring at Josiah, waiting for the other man to continue. "Lately, some of our citizens have seen strange lights coming from that area, and had cattle either missing or killed in very strange ways. They've also reported strange sounds coming from the area, as well as seeing unusual wags there."

Josiah leaned forward, resting his elbows on the table and steepling his fingers. "If even half of what is rumored to be there is true, then the place could hold the key to stopping Tellen once and for all. And if there's someone trying to gain access, you would be in a position to evaluate them as a possible threat to the city."

Ryan drew in breath to reply, but Krysty beat him to it. "You want us to go out there because we're experienced and expendable."

The elder Carrington shook his head. "No, but I don't blame you for thinking that. As much as I would like to, I can't commit even the small force necessary to investigate, as we need every available man to repel Tellen's army. Also, I know he's watching us, constantly evaluating, probing for a weakness. The attack today was his largest to date, but it won't be his last. If he sees a unit from the city heading in that direction, he'll follow with a larger force to find out what they're doing, capture them and take the base for himself. My only ace in the hole is that he doesn't know I've found out about this yet. I have to move on it before word leaks out, and he begins searching for it himself."

Ryan stretched his arms up, then interlaced his fingers behind his head. "If it even exists."

"Look, you're the only ones I can ask to do this. You've proved yourselves more than capable. Hell, you brought my daughter back through hundreds of Tellen's men—you drove through practically his entire bastard army! If you could go and check out the place, see if the rumors are even close to true, then I could follow up on it, or perhaps even negotiate with whoever may be inside to create an alliance. I just need someone to open that door, and I think that someone is you."

Ryan poured the last of the wine into his glass as he thought about the situation. Normally, he'd dismiss the idea out of hand. It was bad enough that he knew redoubts existed in the first place, but self-contained whitecoat labs were something else entirely. Who knew what the crazy, inbred fuckers living in their artificial environments had been laboring on for the past century or so? Bioplague, sec robots, strange weapons capable of dealing death in an incredible variety of ways. They had come close to unleashing these things on the world a number of times before. He wasn't really interested in possibly unlocking another set of crackpots to spill their new poisons into the already overloaded Deathlands.

He glanced around the room, noticing that J.B. and Mildred had stopped their attempts at keeping Doc upright, and were now listening to the conversation, as well. Jak appeared asleep at the far end, but Ryan would have bet his blaster the albino teen was awake and listening to every word.

"Say we agreed to this, and, just for the sake of argument, let's say there actually is something down there. What would stop me from setting myself up first and cutting you out of the deal altogether?"

"Nothing at all, except I don't believe you would do that. When you had my daughter in your grasp, your first response was to return her here, when you could have played both Tellen and myself against each other and gotten whatever you wanted from either side."

Ryan considering pointing out that he hadn't had the slightest clue as to who she was when he'd found her, but decided not to bother. A quick glance across the table revealed that Rachel had a pretty good idea what he was thinking, and even now, she was probably wondering which way he was going to go. Turning back to her father, he said, "Go on."

"The fact that you didn't means you're not like those others out there." Josiah waved his hand in the general direction of the world outside the room they were sitting in. "In spite what you told Major Kelor, I don't believe you and your group are a band of wandering traders. Nor are you simpleminded raiders or bandits. In fact, while I'm not exactly sure who you are or what you're looking for—although I have a pretty good idea—I think if you agreed to do this, you would do it to the best of your ability. In return, I would be happy to offer you the first pick of any tech, wags or supplies found there."

Ryan pushed his chair back. "So all of this, the hotel, the dinner—it was all the prelude to your request?"

"Getting us in the mood to hear your proposal, so to speak." Mildred's voice was calm and quiet, an indication that the storm building behind her deep brown eyes was about to break.

Josiah held up his hands to placate them. "No, and yes. The hotel and this meal were the beginning of whatever meager thanks I could offer all of you for saving my daughter's life. If you'd like, I would be happy to outfit you all with whatever supplies and blasters you need, as well as a couple of gassed and ready vehicles to drive yourselves wherever you care to go, with my grateful thanks, and an open invite to return any time you're in the area."

Ryan cocked an eyebrow while he pretended to consider the idea. It certainly would help them get back to the redoubt in style. "You said you had a pretty good idea of who I am. Enlighten me."

Josiah leaned forward, speaking to Ryan as if they were the only two people in the room. "I think you are a cold-blooded chiller, but you only take life when it's necessary, culling the worst of the population. I think you're looking for something even you can't define right now, but you think it's out there somewhere, perhaps over the next horizon, and you're gonna keep looking for it until you find it."

Ryan blinked. He hadn't met a man who could size up another person like that since his time with the Trader. It was a bit unnerving, actually. Carrington had come close, but he wasn't about to give the man the satisfaction of knowing how accurate he'd been. "Still waters run deep. Other than getting lucky outside the wall, I think you're reading a bit too much into me."

"Am I, Cawdor?" Josiah pushed his chair back from the table and rose. "I know I can't order or attempt to force you to do this. I can only ask. I do want to leave you with one thought as you decide."

His blue steel gaze pinned everyone to his or her chair. "You've all had a chance to see what we've created here—the beginnings of a way out of the darkness. I can't speak for the rest of you, but I, for one, don't wish to go back to the savagery that was my formative years. I was educated, but I saw some dark times in my youth. You can choose to do this for whatever reason you wish—the possible tech you may find, the time you've spent here, helping to continue our way of life in whatever small way you can, whatever your reason may be. But I hope that you choose to undertake this because, like me, you don't want to see the ember of civilization extinguished before it has a chance to burst into flame."

Josiah stepped away from the table and pushed his

chair in. "Take the rest of the evening to think about it. We can talk more in the morning over breakfast. It's been a pleasure meeting you all, and I look forward to continuing our discussion tomorrow morning. Sergeant Caddeus will escort you back to the hotel. Until the morning, then. Rachel?"

Carrington's daughter rose and nodded to everyone, as well. "Thank you all for coming. It has been a most interesting evening."

The father and daughter strode out of the dining room, leaving Ryan and the others staring after them, the silence broken only by the explosive snort of Doc's snoring.

J.B. was the first to speak. "Certainly know how to make an exit."

"Yeah, and how to leave an impression, too." Mildred frowned. "He gives a very pretty speech, when it comes down to it. What did you make of all that, Ryan?"

"All I make of it at the moment is that we should follow their example and head back to the hotel. Don't know about you all, but after that meal, not to mention all the fireblasted talking, the night air'd do me some good. No discussion till we're back in our rooms." Ryan got up and headed for the front door, the others falling in behind him once they'd awakened Doc, who had been slouching in his chair, his finery only slightly blemished by a scattering of crumbs.

Outside, they were met by Sergeant Caddeus, who waved into the dusk to bring up another mil wag. Everyone climbed aboard, and they were driven back to the hotel through the quiet city streets. The staccato sounds of blasterfire were still coming from the wall, but more sporadically now. "Tellen's men coming back?" Ryan asked.

The sergeant shook his head once, his eyes never leaving the road. "Nope. Boys on the wall're stickie huntin'."

"How's that work?"

"Well, stickies love fire, so we been setting up little flashpots of gas and flammable materials and slingin' them over the wall. They come out to watch the flames—pop! Dead stickies."

"Doesn't that make it hard for your night snipers?" J.B. asked.

"Don't know what you're talking about. Nobody's shootin' anything without light. We tried keeping men in the dark, like they did long ago, but it messes with their heads, so we do this instead. Besides, you can't pull it off more than twice in a night before they get wise to it. But a few days later, it's like they forget, and you can do the same thing again. It's kinda led to a saying 'round here—you can't train a stickie."

Everyone chuckled at the joke, Ryan and J.B. exchanging glances. The Armorer had verified several things with his seemingly innocuous question—like the fact that Tellen's forces had somehow gotten their hands on better equipment than Carrington's men.

Mildred piped up. "How long's that been going on?"

"About a month or so, ever since that nest popped up in the ruins of the refinery."

"Any idea where they came from?" J.B. asked.

"Who the hell knows where those freakish bastards come from? As long as we keep popping them off, it shouldn't be long now before the nest dies out."

"How many do you get in a night?" Ryan asked.

"Depends. Used to be a half dozen easy, but now

we're lucky to get two or three. I figure that means there ain't as many of them to come out now."

Mebbe—else they're wising up to your little trap, Ryan thought, but kept that notion to himself.

The companions fell silent until they reached the hotel, the wag passing through the quiet streets without interference. Occasionally, they saw another vehicle go by, but even at this hour, there were hardly any pedestrians out. Caddeus brought the wag to a stop outside the hotel's front door. "End of the line, ladies and gentlemen."

Ryan and the rest of his group filed out. "Thanks for the ride, Sergeant."

Caddeus smiled, revealing surprisingly white teeth. "My pleasure—nice to get an easy duty night for a change. You folks have a good evening." With that, he drove away in a cloud of blue-black exhaust.

Everyone trooped into the lobby, which was also much quieter than it had been earlier in the evening. Carter seemed to have finally gone off duty, since a young woman, who greeted them with a smile and a nod, was now behind the desk. Ryan noticed the bar was also dark and silent. "Apparently, they do their drinking early in Denver."

"There are a variety of other places open if you care for more entertainment this evening, sir," the desk clerk said.

"Not tonight, thanks." They all headed for the elevator, a bleary-eyed Doc leaning against J.B., mumbling something incoherent as they waited for the doors.

"On an express elevator to hell…goin' down…"

"What the hell's he mumbling about?" Ryan asked.

J.B. grunted as he maneuvered Doc's nearly dead weight into the elevator. "Dunno—I'm just trying to make sure he doesn't drool on me before I can dump him in his room."

The trip up passed in relative quiet, with only Doc's loud breathing and muttering breaking the silence. Unfortunately, they hadn't yet reached their destination when a pungent stink assaulted everyone's nose.

"What in Gaia— Oh, who let go in here?" Krysty asked, covering her nose and mouth.

"Who think?" Jak said, waving at the offending air around him with his hand while trying to get as far away from Doc as possible.

"Call that a silent but deadly back on the war wags, eh, Ryan?" J.B., stuck as he was next to the old man, just did his best to grin and bear it.

"Can't talk—trying not to breathe." The sound of the elevator reaching its destination was the sweetest noise Ryan had heard all day.

Gasping, everyone spilled out as fast as they could. J.B. hustled the asleep-on-his-feet Doc to the door of his suite, then foisted him off on Jak. "Here—your problem now." Grabbing Mildred's hand, he towed her toward their room. "Suddenly feel like I have to wash up. See you in the morning."

"Yeah." Ryan fumbled with his key card, the light refusing to change from red to green. Muttering a curse, he swiped the card again, and the door clicked open. "Hmm, funny, door seemed to open on its own."

It might have been the drinks, or the dinner, or even Doc's gaseous emanation, but Ryan's normally razor-sharp reflexes were a bit dulled when he walked into the room to see an unfamiliar man dressed in khaki pants and a dark green shirt sitting on a chair in the middle of the room, each hand resting on the corresponding arm of the chair. Still, he retained enough presence of mind to reach for his blaster, actually getting his hand on it as he felt a prick in his back, right before his entire body was envelope d in a flood of searing pain.

Chapter Sixteen

The agony was like nothing Ryan had ever felt before. Every muscle, every nerve ending, every inch of his body was locked in tortured spasms. Even through the overwhelming pain, he tried to make his arm draw his Sig Sauer, but couldn't. It was as though his fingers—hell, his entire arm—was locked in place where it was, unable to do anything but clutch the butt of his blaster. He heard a strangled, incoherent noise, and was shocked to realize that the tortured grunt was coming from his own mouth. His jaw clenched, tears streaming from his squeezed-shut eyes, Ryan could do absolutely nothing but wait for death to come.

As suddenly as it had seized him, the pain stopped, except for a heavy, tingling feeling in his limbs and torso. Ryan cracked his eyes open to find himself staring at the carpet—he'd fallen over and hadn't even realized it. He felt like he had just run fifty miles, pulling a fully loaded war wag the entire way. He felt efficient hands on his body, expertly patting him down, taking his blaster and the knife at the back of his neck, and searching for any other hidden weapons. All the while, questions kept running through his scrambled mind: who the hell were these people? How did they get into their room?

"Well I'll be a son of a bitch—these crazy things really do work, don't they?"

Twisting his head, Ryan spotted Krysty standing a few feet away, arms up, a blaster aimed at her head by a masked man dressed in camouflage from head to toe. She moved her eyes left, right and back, indicating three men, then raised an eyebrow, her silent question clear.

Attack?

As he was being flipped over, Ryan managed to shake his head, telling her to hold off—for now. Although her Gaia power could probably reduce these three to a red, wet pulp, it took time for her to summon it, more than long enough for the gunman to put a round into her skull. Besides, if they'd wanted to kill them, they could have done it twice over already. The fact that they hadn't meant they wanted something.

Although, truth be told, Ryan much preferred the Carringtons' way of asking.

He turned his head to regard the leader, who was still sitting in the chair, watching him. In many ways he was the opposite of Carrington, short where the other man was tall, pale where the other was dark, with short, straw-blond hair and light blue eyes. They were both slim, but his gaze was as cold and dispassionate as the Denver leader's was fiery and ardent.

He opened his mouth to speak, but was stayed by a knock on the door of the suite. "Ryan, you okay in there?"

The man didn't move, but signaled the man holding the blaster on Krysty, who moved her forward with the pressure of the gun muzzle against the back of her neck. "Answer it and get him gone. You got one chance. No signals or funny business, or you both die before the cavalry comes. Nod if you understand."

Krysty's emerald-green gaze flicked to Ryan, still prone on the floor, as she nodded once, then reached for the door, opening it just wide enough for her face to appear.

"Hi, Krysty. Thought I heard a commotion in there. Everything all right?"

"Yeah, something Ryan ate at dinner isn't agreeing with him. He made for the bathroom the moment we got inside, and hasn't come out yet."

"Didn't seem bothered on the ride back."

"It hit him real sudden-like, but I think a good night's sleep will take care of it. Thanks for checking, though."

"Sure, well, if you're sure he's okay. See you tomorrow."

"Good night, J.B."

Ryan saw the sec man tense, but Krysty closed the door without incident and backed away from the door. The seated man waved her toward the bed. "Sit down and keep your hands when I can see them at all times."

"I suppose I should apologize for busting in here and bushwhacking you both, but I can't say I'm all that particularly sorry about it. I needed to make sure I had your attention, and since I have heard about the great and terrible Ryan Cawdor, it seemed that certain precautions were in order."

The last sentence got Ryan's full attention, even over the various twitches and aches from his body. "You know who I am?"

The man in the chair twitched one shoulder, which might have been a shrug or a simple deflection of the question. "Nowadays it seems I can't walk a mile without tripping over a one-eyed man, but a one-eyed man who's chilled as many people as folks say you have is a different story altogether."

Now Ryan was genuinely puzzled. "Have we met?"

"Nope, never set eyes on each other until about three minutes ago, but I imagine we both know whole lot about each other, mebbe some of it's even true. For example, I'm sure you both know who I am."

"You must be Tellen."

"Right in one, Cawdor. I knew you were smart. Course, a man has to be in this day and age, to see as many sunrises as you and your friends have."

Ryan gingerly rolled over and got on his hands and knees. His vision swam as he stared at the carpet and the rich meal he'd enjoyed earlier that evening now swam uneasily in his stomach like a huge, curdled pool of bile. He rose so he was kneeling on the carpet, his hands supporting him on his thighs. "I'm sure I'm not the only smart one around."

His captor nodded. "You'd be right. But even smart men don't know everything. Like I'll bet you didn't know that I used to be part of this little social experiment Carrington's running, did you?"

Ryan frowned, and Krysty also stared at him in disbelief. "Not only didn't I know that, but I have a bastard hard time believing it, given how chummy you two seem at the moment."

"Why would I bother telling you if it weren't true?"

"Oh, I'm sure you got a reason, but the question you should be asking yourself is whether or not I even give a flying fuck. Then your next question should be how long you think you're going to live once you leave this room."

That brought a smile to the blond-haired man's mouth. "I'd heard you had balls the size of boulders, and those rumors, at least, were correct. Both of those queries are very pertinent to the situation. Very well, I'll keep this short and to the point. I'm aware of why the illustrious leader of this city had dinner with you—and it wasn't to shine you on about how great he's made the place. No, he wants you to check out the lights to the east."

Ryan saw no point in lying. "That came up during the conversation."

Tellen shook his head. "Old fool. Does he really think he could keep that a secret? The ranchers I trade with on the outskirts have been talking about nothing else for the past few weeks."

"Then why don't you send your men to check it out? If there's anything there, you'd have first claim to it."

"No, once Carrington threw me out of here, I learned real quick to never go into a situation where you don't know the lay of the land. I learned even quicker that if you can convince someone else to go for you, so much the better."

"Well, you haven't done a very good job of convincing me to do shit for you, so I'm not even sure why you're still here flapping your gums."

"Because I have an offer for you, as well, one that I think would be very persuasive to a man of your talents."

"I'm listening."

"You play along as Carrington's lackey—just hear me out before you say anything," Tellen continued when Ryan's expression darkened even more. "You head out there, see what there is to see, and if it is anything remotely useful, you signal my men, who'll be waiting a couple miles away, and we come in and secure the area."

"Seems mighty one-sided to me."

"I wasn't quite finished. In return, once I take the city, you run it with me."

Ryan could hardly believe his ears. "I control Denver with you? Sort of a cobaronship?"

Tellen shook his head. "I'm not interested in lording over these people for petty power or domination. I doubt you'll believe this, but I want the same thing that Carrington wants—to spread the ideals of true civilization across this land."

"If you and Carrington agree on that, why the siege to take the city?" Krysty asked.

"Let's just say there's a large dispute between us about the correct method of operation," Tellen said. "But the fact is, he's dying—old bastard's just too stubborn to realize it—and handing the reins over to his daughter is like giving a stickie a lit torch and pointing it toward a barrel of gas. She's too hotheaded and impatient to run a place like this."

"But you're the guy the people will flock to when their leader is in the ground, is that it?" Ryan frowned at him like he was several bullets short of a full mag. "In case you hadn't noticed, you're the *invader* in this picture. You really think those people are going to welcome you with open arms, particularly after you've tried to take over the city by force?"

Now Tellen shook his head, staring at Ryan like he was the slow mutie. "You disappoint me, Cawdor. I'd've thought you'd knew how people fall in line under a strong leader. As long as their everyday existence isn't disrupted, they'll follow anyone who promises more of the same. Their lives are good here, and I'll bet they won't mind a change at the top, as long as they still get what's theirs. 'Sides, there's more people in this city who feel the way I do than you might think. Those folks—people who're smart enough to look to the future—are working toward my goals, not Carrington's."

Yeah, I figured that out already, Ryan thought. There was no way Tellen could have slipped through the perimeter and gotten here without inside help, and someone pretty high up in the chain of command to boot.

"Those goals include rape and pillage?" Krysty asked.

Her question seemed to throw Tellen off his stride for a moment. He glanced sidelong at her, his eyebrow raised. "Pray tell me just what you mean by that."

"I mean, if your men are following your lead, they're piss-poor examples of the kind of person you're attracting for your little army here." She went on to detail her experience at the hands of the sec men she had run into the night before.

Tellen stood, the top of his head barely coming level to her eyes. "Ma'am, on behalf of myself and all who follow me, I sincerely apologize for what you had to endure from those men. That sort of action is neither condoned nor encouraged. If you would give me a physical description of them, or their names if you happened to catch them, I will make sure they are arrested, tried and punished appropriately."

Now it was Krysty's turn to smile, her white teeth flashing in the lights like a satisfied animal. "You won't need to follow up on that promise. They're already dead."

Tellen nodded once, appraising both of them with a satisfied smile. "It seems you all live up to the stories, and then some. So, what's it gonna be, Cawdor? You've traveled all over this country, if the stories are true. What you looking for? Fame? Fortune? The land of plenty just over that next horizon? If it's any of the three, you could do a lot worse than here."

Ryan rose to his feet, mindful of the two blasters

tracking his every move. "Yeah, and I'm going to tell you the exact same thing I told Carrington—I'll think about it." He walked to the door, deliberately turning his back on Tellen and his sec men. Opening the door, he turned back to stare at the three of them. "Now get the fuck out of my room."

"Well, I'd hoped you'd be more of a conversationalist, but I also know when I'm coming close to overstaying my welcome. Think hard about my offer, Cawdor. I believe you'll find it's the best option around."

"How am I supposed to get hold of you when I've made up my mind?"

Tellen smiled. "Don't worry about it. I'll be in touch. I'm looking forward to working with you." He nodded at the man who had carefully moved to the other side of the door, and now scanned the hallway before nodding. The rebel leader walked to the exit, careful never to cross between his henchmen and either Ryan or Krysty. At the doorway, he paused to look back at both of them. "You both have a good evening now."

As soon as the three men were out of the room, Ryan locked the door and dragged a chair over, wedging it under the knob. Krysty had grabbed her blaster and held it at the ready while she retrieved Ryan's from under the bed where it had been tossed and handed it to him.

"You all right?"

He nodded, keeping his ear pressed to the door.

"What's the plan? We leaving?"

"Not yet. Soon as I'm sure they're gone, I want everyone together. It appears we're only getting half the story from both sides. Before we do anything, I want to go over what we know, don't know and need to know. Then we decide what to do about this city—and which side, if any, we come down on."

Chapter Seventeen

"Black dust! I knew something wasn't right when you answered the door. Should have gone back and made sure!" The Armorer smacked his fist into his leg. "I'm getting too bastard soft. Get a hot meal and a warm bed, and I start getting sloppy."

"No reason to beat yourself up, J.B.," Krysty replied. "There's nothing you could've done. If they'd thought you were on to them, Ryan and I would be dead, mebbe with you guys next. They were pros, they had help getting inside and they were ready for us. We're all good, but there's only so much you can do when you're staring down the wrong end of a blaster an inch from your head."

Once Ryan was sure Tellen and his men had left, he had gone to the other rooms and rousted everybody, herding them into J.B. and Mildred's room. After they had secured the area, Ryan explained about their unannounced visitors.

Mildred shook her head. "It just all seems so incredible. Tellen, the leader of the enemy at the gates, just waltzes in here like he owns the place to have a little fireside chat with you? Not only that, but he's comfortable enough to fill you in on how he used to be a part of the Free City, and that he's planning to take over, as well. The man's either got balls the size of grapefruits or he's certifiably crazy."

Ryan nodded. "Ace on the line with that, Mildred. Only problem is we don't know which one he is or how much to believe. The way he was talking, he plans on installing himself sooner rather than later. He figures the locals will bend the knee and welcome him as their new baron once he's gotten Carrington out of the way."

"He might be closer to accomplishing that than we think. Look how easily he got into the heart of the city." J.B. snorted, still disgusted with himself for his lapse of security. "Wonder if the major's on his side. He looked like the sneaky sort who'd sell out if he was assured of his piece of the pie. Course, if he is, I'm surprised they don't just head over to Carrington's house and put a bullet in his brain, as well. Save him the trouble of besieging the place."

"It seems both Tellen and Carrington have their own peculiar senses of honor. Either that, or neither of them are playing with a full deck," Mildred said. "The idea of assassinating Tellen was brought up at dinner, but Carrington dismissed it, as well. And however likely it is that Tellen could ambush Carrington and take him out, if he hasn't followed up on that option yet, he's not going to, either. You said Tellen also said Carrington is dying. How in the hell did he know that?"

Ryan shrugged. "Whoever his inside men are, like J.B. said, some are pretty high up. It would be easy enough to pass information, or the wrong information, to the other side. What we do know is that both these men want a third party to handle their problems—us. It gives them—what'd you call it, Doc?—'plausible deniability' if anything goes wrong."

"Nothin' sayin' we don't have 'accidents' when all's done," Jak piped up from his corner. "Whole place's stinkin' worse every minute."

Ryan rubbed his chin. "On the other hand, I'd say that makes our value to both sides appreciate considerably."

J.B. eyed him speculatively. "You're not going to play both ends against each other, are you? Even the Trader wasn't fool enough to attempt that twice."

"Nope. I think it's best we play this one by ear. It's obvious neither of these two can be trusted with finding out what's over there. The funny thing is, both of them think we're the best people to do it. I guess because of what you said, Mildred. We're supposedly disinterested parties. So I think the best thing to do is to give both sides what they want."

"And just how do you propose to do that?" Krysty asked.

"Simple—we scout the area for both sides, just like each one wants us to do."

J.B. rolled his eyes. "Dark night, you *are* going to play both of them against each other."

Ryan shook his head. "Did I stutter? Like I said, I'm going to give each of them what they want, nothing more, nothing less. Now let's all get some sleep. It's going to be a long day tomorrow, and I'm beat."

"You think it's safe to sleep in these rooms by ourselves?" Mildred asked.

"Hell, both Carrington and Tellen want us alive to do their work for them. I can't think of a safer place to be right now." With that, Ryan grabbed Krysty's hand and led her back to their room.

Once inside, he shoved a door under the handle again and inspected the windows. "Course, that doesn't mean I don't take stupid chances, either," he muttered, half to Krysty, half under his breath. Only when he was satisfied that the room was secure did he strip off his shirt, leaving his pants and boots on this time, crawl into bed beside Krysty and fall asleep almost before his head hit the pillow.

DESPITE THE COMFORTABLE BED, J.B. had spent a restless night tossing and turning, unable to get his lapse in concentration out of his mind. Beside him, Mildred slept peacefully, apparently taking refuge in Ryan's pronunciation of their safety.

The Armorer wasn't as confident, however, and his unanswered concerns had vexed him so that he'd finally gotten up from the plush bed and sat in a purple upholstered armchair, fingers tapping on the armrest while he stared out the window at the night-covered city. His mind whirled with unanswered questions. Since Tellen had men inside the city, were they watching the companions then? Had he given orders to take them out if they thought the friends posed a threat to him? Was the supposed mission just a wild-hare chance to get rid of them by one side or the other? Conspiracies and plots formed and reformed, with different sides playing each other, betraying each other. In the end, J.B. came to the only sensible conclusion there was—go along with whatever play Ryan had in mind, and back him to the last bullet if necessary.

At last he'd returned to bed, falling into fitful sleep as the sun started to creep over the horizon. The morning dawned bright and clear, with a yellow-white sun appearing in the eastern sky, and J.B. awoke to the smell of savory bacon, toasted bread and melted butter. His eyes snapped open, and still only half-awake, he groped for his mini-Uzi he'd placed near the side of the bed.

"What—" His eyes focused on Mildred, sitting up

next to him, and the large tray in front of her, full of covered dishes that steamed in the cool morning air.

"Relax, John, relax. I just wanted to surprise you, that's all." She passed over a mug full of dark, steaming liquid. "Chicory coffee?"

"Black dust, woman, you know surprises usually aren't a good thing." J.B. smiled as he accepted the cup and sipped the bitter brew. "In this case, however, I'll make an exception."

"You better. I'll probably never get the chance to have breakfast in bed with you again." She uncovered the plates, revealing scrambled eggs in butter, eight strips of bacon, a large grilled buffalo steak, and half a loaf of toasted sourdough bread next to small crocks of butter and a dark purple jam. "Well, stop staring and dig in. I got enough for three here."

The smile on his face growing wider, J.B. did just that. "Feel kind of bad having this without the others."

Mildred snorted. "They could do the same thing if they wanted. The instructions are on the nightstand for ordering room service—" She sat there, hands covering her mouth, staring at the bounty before her, tears trickling down her face.

"Mildred, what's wrong?" J.B. scooted close, taking her in his arms and holding her while she sobbed quietly. After a few moments, she drew away and wiped her eyes.

"Oh, you must think I'm a crazy woman to be crying over something like this."

"Well, since I'm not sure what 'this' is, why don't you tell me, and I'll let you know."

She socked him on the shoulder, but it was a playful blow. "Oh, John, it's just… All of this, it suddenly reminded me of what life used to be like, before the missiles blew everything to hell and gone. When you could get into a car or on a train or airplane and cross the country in a few hours, or go into any city and walk into a hotel like this, or a restaurant like where we ate last night, and… That was civilization, it was everyday, normal life, where the worst thing you had to worry about was losing your wallet or forgetting where you parked your car, or maybe even getting mugged—or for women, raped—on the street. Don't get me wrong, I'd rather be alive in this time than dead back then, but even when I had no idea I was going into the cryo-freeze, if they had told me, I would have thought I'd be coming out into a different world, sure, but a *better* one."

She sighed, stabbing a chunk of eggs on her fork and eating it. "I know this is the only one you've ever known, but if you only knew what the world was like back then… You just can't realize what's been lost forever. The culture of a people, the art, the literature, the history of thousands of years wiped out, looted or burned or destroyed by people who didn't know any better. Leaving us with a place where a night in an unspoiled hotel room is a luxury that hardly anyone will ever know, where might makes right, and the only law usually comes from the barrel of a gun. Where places that try to build something different are usually destroyed by two-legged vultures who exist only to destroy, never to build, always keeping civilization and the rest of the people down just to satisfy their greed and lust for power."

Still holding her, J.B. thought about that for a bit before replying. "No, I suppose I never have known that sort of a life. My time in Cripple Creek was about the best it could get growing up, till I started off on my own, eventually meeting up with the Trader. All I know is that we try to make the best of what we're given each day we have. If that means a peaceful day, then so be it, but if that means chilling someone before they chill us, well, that's part of life, too."

"I know, I know. I just wish that sometimes it wasn't, that's all. That there would be something better for all of us, not just you, me and the rest of our friends, but for everybody. Come on, the food's getting cold."

They both fell to, eating their fill. After a few blissful minutes, Mildred munched on the last piece of jam-smeared toast and turned to J.B. again. "Would you stay, John?"

"You mean here?" J.B. snatched the last piece of bacon and stuffed half of it into his mouth, chewing as he considered the question. "Can't say that I've given it much thought lately, given all our bouncing around all over the place. Even somewhere like Denver's got its problems, with Tellen and those stickies runnin' around." A thought struck in his head about the stickies—something about how neither leader had mentioned the problem—but it was gone before he could grasp it.

"There doesn't seem to be anywhere safe in the Deathlands. The coastal baronies are too busy squabbling and fighting, the west is scattered outposts of trouble like this one. Seems people are too busy taking as much as they can of what's left instead of trying to build something new."

"But doesn't that mean when someone like Carrington comes along and does the latter, we should try to make sure he gets a chance to succeed?"

J.B. shook his head. "That isn't always up to us, Millie. First rule is to always look out for yourselves and your friends, not stick your neck out for strangers, no matter how well they feed you. Anyone else we come across is way down on that list, you know that."

She rolled her eyes at him. "I'm no stupe, John, as you all so quaintly put it out here. But I know what life could be like again, if we could just pull the right people together, start carving a new country out of this fractured land, with everyone pulling together for a common goal."

J.B. covered a piece of buttered sourdough in jam and munched it. "Getting a ville together's one thing, but getting anything larger… When you find enough people for that, you let me know."

"Maybe I will, John, maybe I will."

THEY ALL ASSEMBLED in Ryan and Krysty's room that morning. Mildred and J.B. exchanged a knowing smile at the tray outside the door of the room. Jak and Doc were the last to arrive, both of them bleary-eyed and puffy-faced, as if neither had gotten a lot of sleep.

"By the Three Kennedys, if I ever imbibe like that again, I give any of you permission to put me down with a merciful bullet through my brainpan." He clapped his hands to his head. "I cannot even countenance the sound of my own voice ringing in my ears at the moment."

Krysty frowned as she examined the shorter of the bedraggled pair. "What about you, Jak? Didn't think you'd eaten or drank as much as the rest of us, but you look like you been run over—twice."

The albino teen began to reply, but Doc cut him off. "To make matters worse, this one insisted on playing those damn movies all night long, so I had to listen to spaceships flying and laser beams blasting and space worms doing…whatever it is space worms do. A more nonsensical plot I could not have come up with under the influence of absinthe and opium both, but this Lucas fellow apparently had no trouble with weaving his errant flights of fancy together for a gullible public."

"Lucas—you mean the director of the films?"

"Madam, I wouldn't know this good fellow if we were to bump into each other on the street, but yes, that is exactly who I mean."

Mildred shot a meaningful glance at J.B. before replying. "Doc, those movies were made in another time, before all this went down. Of course, now that I think about it, seems kind of tame now, all things considered."

Ryan had been leaning against the wall with his arms folded across his chest as he watched the group, but now he straightened and headed toward the door. "You both better be alert today, because we're going east to check out that supposedly hidden base. While I'm not happy about being in this situation, I also don't trust either of these two any farther than I can throw them, so I'm going to tell Carrington we'll take a look and let him know what we find out."

J.B. frowned. "What about Tellen?"

"He said I'd have a way to get in touch with him, so we'll deal with that when the time comes. Everyone get your stuff together and get down to the lobby in five minutes. Figure we'll get outfitted by noon or thereabouts, then drive out there and see what we can see."

Chapter Eighteen

Ryan had been right about the rest of the morning except one thing—Carrington had men, vehicles and equipment ready almost from the moment Ryan had agreed to go out and investigate the airport. It was all Ryan could do to convince him that they weren't heading out until later that morning.

"You bet much, Josiah? If you read men that well, we could make a fortune out east at the gambling halls."

The elder Carrington was overseeing the final preparations before they departed, and he flashed Ryan a wide smile. "I don't bet. I just try to cover as many angles as possible. If you'd said no, these men would have escorted you up to thirty miles outside of the city in any direction and sent you on your way. However, since they're here…" His manner was jovial this morning, a stark contrast to the alternating sly, bombastic and ingratiating facades he'd presented the night before.

They were taking three mil wags out to the site, one for Ryan's group and two to escort them. In order to fit all of Ryan's people into his vehicle, theirs didn't have a machine gun mount on it, but the other two did, an M-60 machine gun poking out of the top of each one. The Hummers appeared to be from the very top-of-the-line of the city's fleet, with well-treaded tires, almost no dents and hardly worn, comfortable seats.

Major Kelor was there, as well as Sergeant Caddeus,

who would apparently be leading the Denver units. This was over the major's objections, judging by his strained conversation with Josiah that Ryan had observed, but not heard, earlier. He kept his eye on the two sec men as they worked, but all he saw was efficient orders given and received between an officer and a subordinate.

That reminded Ryan of the fact that someone high up in the security chain of Denver was working with the enemy. He watched the two sec men as they instructed the men assigned to each outlying mil wag. Either one could be colluding with Tellen's men for the same plum he'd dangled in front of Ryan—a share of Denver itself. He'd seen it happen before in more villes than he cared to name. Either man was a likely candidate—Kelor if he was itching for a change of leadership, and found Tellen's more suited to his needs; and Caddeus if he wanted to get rid of both Carrington and Kelor in one bloody coup. Maybe the sergeant was going on this mission to feed information to Tellen's forces, as well. Ryan wouldn't put it past the man to have more than one plant in place, to verify that the intel he was receiving was correct. In his place, Ryan would have done the same thing.

At last everything and everyone was loaded up, and they were ready to head out. Ryan had just settled into the driver's seat and fired up the diesel engine when Josiah walked over to his door. "I won't waste your time with fancy speeches today, Ryan. It wouldn't make no difference anyway."

"Why's that?"

"Because you're gonna go out there and do what you think is best, regardless of anything I'd have to say about it."

"That's about the size of it. Now if you don't mind…"

Ryan pointed at the lead vehicle, which was already getting underway.

"Course not. Just wanted to wish you good luck before you left, that's all."

"Thanks, we'll be in touch." Ryan scanned the launch area for Rachel, but didn't see her. It was just as well. If she'd clamored to go with them, it would have made things a mite uncomfortable. Better that she was out of the way from the start. Nudging the accelerator, Ryan caught up to the lead wag, and the trio drove out of the city.

"See anything strange so far, J.B.?"

"Not outside. Just this brand-new radio in our ride, which doesn't match either of the ones in the other two vehicles." The Armorer held up the small, dark green box. "What do you want to bet it's preset to a freq that'll connect us right to your buddy on the other side of the wall?"

"I'll pass, thanks. When we get a little farther out, I'll try it and see who I raise. Meantime, everyone stay triple red, fingers on triggers. Since we have no idea of what we're driving into, it's best to be ready for anything."

They followed a northeasterly route first. Ryan thought to try to confuse any of Tellen's men that might be watching. The taller buildings rapidly fell away into rings of broken-down houses, many just a strong breeze away from collapsing into total ruins. After another ten minutes, they'd left the ville behind, and were on a battered highway that seemed to lead into endless, parched plains. The heat was already climbing inside the cab of the vehicle, and the dust thrown up from the passage of the first wag created a dry cloud that settled over everything and everyone in a fine layer of tan.

"Sure we not want peel off head to redoubt?" Jak asked after a violent bit of sneezing from the specks that had turned his white hair a mottled, creamy brown and covered his canvas jacket, as well. "Seems like fool's run."

"Mebbe so, but we're already out this far. Might as well see what's here. If anything. Although at the moment, I'm starting to think you may be right. What the hell—"

Ryan interrupted himself as they came over a rise to see one of the oddest sights he'd come across—a statue of a large, bright blue horse, rearing up on its hind legs, front hooves pawing at the sky. He started to slow down just as the rear of the lead wag seemed to tilt up and disappear in a large cloud of dust.

"Lead vehicle is gone! Repeat, lead vehicle is gone!" Ryan said over the radio as he slammed on the brakes. "Rear guard, keep your eyes open for ambushers! Everyone keep a watch all around. J.B., on me!"

Leaving the engine running, he opened the door and got out, trying to see past the thick dust cloud ahead. He heard cursing and shouting a few yards away, however, verifying that someone was alive in the mil wag. "Hey, down there, what happened?"

"Bastard pit dug in the road!" a voice shouted back. "Whole wag went in. We aren't gonna get it out without a couple Hummers pullin' on it! Hey, who's— What the hell!"

Blasterfire suddenly erupted from the bottom, the sharp barks of blasters interspersed with some kind of loud whoops. Ryan tried to see what was happening, but the plume of dust kicked up by the SUV still hadn't dissipated, and he wasn't about to slide into whatever was going on down there without seeing where he was going first.

The heavy chatter of the M-60 on the rear Hummer suddenly overwhelmed the fight that had broken out in the pit. Ryan turned to see the turret gunner firing short bursts at groups of raiders mounted on…blue horses?

Ryan resisted the urge to rub his eye to see if his was hallucinating, but a blink or two cleared the last of the errant dust away, letting him see the figures astride their painted horses clearly.

As if they had headed back down to the hell-roasted southwestern desert, Ryan and his convoy were being set upon by a large group of Native Americans on horses streaked with blue paint, obviously in homage to their crazy dark blue effigy on the desert plain. These raiders were armed with automatic longblasters, and, Ryan had to admit, insane courage, guiding their mounts with their knees while using both hands to aim and shoot their weapons. Bursts of fire were coming from both wags on the road now, aimed in all directions, as the raiders seemed to flow in and out of the dust cloud their galloping horses raised like desert ghosts.

The dust had settled enough in the pit for Ryan to finally be able to see enough to try to descend into it to help the men down there. He had just taken his first step when a woman's shout was heard, followed by three shots, then the sounds of a scuffle.

"J.B., take the right side!" Ryan hissed as he tested the rear bumper of the wag, which was resting on the lip of the square hole. Satisfied that it would hold, he stepped up onto the back of the vehicle and started making his way across the roof, intending to reach the hood of the vehicle and use that as a way to reach the floor. His attempt was interrupted, however, when a dark brown hand striped with blue reached out from inside the Hummer and grabbed his ankle.

Surprised, Ryan tried to wrench his foot free while keeping his balance on the metal rooftop, and failed to do both. Pitching headlong over the side, he vanished into the black space between the wag and the dirt wall.

"WHAT FUCK!" JAK HAD DRAWN his .357 Magnum Colt Python and was watching the horde of perhaps thirty to forty riding bandits approach. "Bein' attacked by Indians!"

"The correct term would be 'Native Americans,' since they had roamed this land long before either your or my ancestors had come along." Doc peered out of his side of the wag at the approaching raiders, readying his LeMat for action.

"At least we aren't in a covered wagon on this prairie." Mildred had also drawn her target pistol at the first sign of trouble, and was watching the riders gallop toward them along with everyone else. "I take it we're staying here?"

"Can't leave Ryan and J.B. out there unprotected," Krysty said from the front seat. "Besides, these wags are armored enough to protect us from whatever they're carrying. We just have to make sure they don't get too close to us."

Just then the gunner from the rear Hummer shouted in surprise. Mildred and Doc in the backseat both looked back to see something shiny and flaming arc through the air from one side and land in the turret with the tinkle of glass. A moment later, a burst of flame made the sec man leap out, screaming as he beat at the fire consuming his clothes. A shot cracked, and he fell to the ground, the fire hungrily consuming his body.

The return fire increased from the third mil wag, but more burning bottles seemed to come from nowhere, and soon the entire top of the vehicle was covered in flames.

"Shit, Ryan and J.B.'ll take care selves. If not get out here, we dead!" Jak scrambled into the driver's seat and pulled the start button.

"Jak, we can't leave without them—" she began when the tinkling of glass was heard nearby as a bottle smashed to pieces on the hood of their wag. It was followed by the familiar whoosh of flames as flammable liquid covered the hood.

"Fuck! Not leavin' them. Evenin' odds to come get 'em later!" Jak pushed the button again, letting the engine roar into life while he twisted the wheel and stomped on the accelerator. The wag surged forward—directly into the running line of men and horses. As they moved, Krysty saw bursts of flame erupt in the dry prairie grass as more Molotovs exploded nearby. "Head west! The fire's going to spread east." She glanced over at the rear end of the mil wag that had fallen into the pit, but couldn't see anyone moving there. Ryan, she knew, would be all right. He'd been in worse situations than this.

"Goddamn! The sec men getting out of the other one are being cut down right and left!" Mildred shouted as she watched. "Looks like Jak had the right idea."

"Mebbe. Hang on!" Jak pushed the Hummer up as fast as he dared, playing a deadly game of chicken with a group of six riders coming right at him. Most of them shied away, but one, his face and upper body painted bright blue, was determined to face down the four-wheeled menace, and kept his horse charging right at them while he aimed his M-16 at the windshield, snapping off shots as fast as he could pull the trigger, his bullets starring the windshield as he drew closer and closer.

It was no contest. The armored three-ton vehicle, traveling at almost forty-five miles per hour, pulverized the horse and rider, snapping off the animal's front legs and disintegrating its rib cage into fragmented shards of bone. The horse didn't even have time to scream before its internal organs were pulped into mush by the battering ram of the mil wag's front bumper and grille. Its body tumbled across the hood, smothering most of the fire before sliding off as Jak whipped the steering wheel hard right to dislodge the great bloody mess. The firing warrior was thrown from his mount and sailed twenty more yards through the air before crashing to the ground, dead upon impact.

Jak powered over the dead horse's body, the wheels snapping more bones as they passed over the corpse, and turned back again toward the ambush site.

"Gotta provide distraction for Ryan, J.B.," he grunted, sticking his blaster out the side window and firing at the remaining warriors.

"By the three Kennedys, I think that ought to turn their heads!" Doc took aim with his LeMat, dropping another rider in a cloud of smoke and pellets.

Their ambush only partially successful, the raiders had swiftly reformed into four smaller parties, and were now charging at the wag from four different directions. The companions' smaller blasters were outmatched by both the caliber and number of weapons carried by their attackers, as well as the incoming volume of fire. They were reduced to sniping when they could as Jak labored to keep the groups scattered while not setting themselves up for too much concentrated return fire.

The best way to do this, he accidentally discovered, was to charge straight at one of the groups, forcing it to scatter as Krysty, Mildred and Doc took out riders or their mounts. Doc's LeMat scattergun barrel was particularly effective, the balls crashing into the legs of horses and their riders, often sending the raiders crashing to the ground in a screaming, tangled heap of horse and human. Often Krysty or Mildred were able to take out at least a couple of the blue-painted warriors as they passed, as well. Although the horses were able to change directions more nimbly, the faster, more powerful wag had the edge in outpacing its attackers, and after several passes, the remains of the large group of raiders were broken and demoralized, with lone riders peeling off to retreat and fight another day.

Doc blew smoke out of the barrel of his ancient revolver. "Verily, I declare that we have driven off the raiders without injury to ourselves, and thus I declare us victorious."

Krysty's sweat and dust-covered face was grim. "Yeah, but we haven't won the day just yet. Let's get back to Ryan and J.B., and make sure they're all right."

Jak executed a neat 180-degree turn and headed back to the ambush site, clearly marked by the column of greasy, black smoke rising into the sky. A few minutes driving brought them back to the road, where the bodies of sec men and painted warriors littered the ground.

But there was no sign of Ryan and J.B. at all.

Chapter Nineteen

Ryan hit the ground with a bone-jarring thud, his attempt to roll with the impact thwarted by the narrow space he found himself in, trapped upside down between the dry earthen wall and the wag's front fender. Tasting acrid dust, he spit to clear his mouth. He knew his ambusher was still nearby, but couldn't tell exactly where he was, and that was the second largest problem he had.

On the wag's other side, he heard the short burst of an automatic weapon—J.B.'s mini-Uzi. He'd bet his life on it. He tried to call to the Armorer for help, but he could only manage a pitiful wheeze. The awkward way he'd landed was compressing his lungs so that he could only suck in enough air to survive, but not to call for help.

His right arm was pinned against the ground, making drawing his blaster impossible. Reaching out with his left hand, he felt empty space, then warm rubber—the tire of the wag! Just then he felt a stinging blow on his leg, as if someone had whacked him with a thick stick. He didn't know if his enemy was checking to see if he was still alive or just torturing him, although judging by his throbbing shin, Ryan suspected the latter. He reached around the tire just as the stick came down again, this time on his other leg, making him grunt with pain. He lashed out with his left foot and felt it graze something, but before he could connect with it a second time, his shin was struck again, the pain jolting all the way up his leg.

Gonna grab that fuckin' stick and shove it up his ass, Ryan thought. Grabbing the tire again, he pulled himself forward with all his might. At first he didn't move, but then his body shifted an inch, then another. All the while more blows rained down on his legs, the pain radiating from each strike almost overwhelming. Ryan grit his teeth and remained silent, not wanting to give his tormentor the satisfaction of knowing he was doing damage. At last, his other arm was free, and he scrambled underneath the mil wag, narrowly avoiding another flurry of blows.

Ryan groped for his Sig Sauer just as a face out of nightmare appeared, glaring at him from the side of the Hummer. With wide, wild eyes, a snarling mouth filled with rotting teeth, and his entire face painted in diagonal stripes of blue, the warrior brought the other end of his stick around—this one ending in a razor-sharp metal spearhead—as Ryan was trying to line up his blaster with a tingling, partially numb hand.

Both men attacked at the same time. Ryan was forced to scoot backward to avoid being stabbed by the spear, which threw off his aim, making his shot go wide. The Native American saw the blaster but apparently didn't care, since his only reaction was to crouch near the rear tire and advance under the Hummer, jabbing with the spear as he did so. As he shuffled forward, chanting an incomprehensible language, Ryan saw he was mostly naked, with only a leather breechcloth covering his genitals. His face was broad and flat, with narrow, dark brown eyes and a protruding forehead and jaw that made the rest of his face look like it had been pushed in. He was also fairly short, at least a foot shorter than Ryan's own rangy frame.

Hot, sweaty and furious at being stymied by his stone-age attacker, Ryan rolled toward the front of the vehicle, giving him enough time to aim properly and fire three times. The trio of bullets pierced the man's chest and carved through his heart, killing him almost instantly. He stumbled backward, leaning against the rear tire for a second before it shifted under his weight and sent him sprawling to the ground.

J.B.'s face appeared on the far side of the Hummer. "You okay?"

Ryan tried to speak again, but only expelled a small cloud of dust. He nodded, hawking up saliva for his parched throat and spitting out more brown dust. "Fine, thanks..." He took J.B.'s extended hand and slid out from underneath the wag, narrowly avoiding stepping on four more breechcloth-wearing, brown-skinned bodies. "Busy over here?"

"Only took out two. Other two were dead when I got here. There's a wounded man, too, one of Carrington's. Not for too much longer, looks like." J.B. shook his head as he regarded the man sprawled half out of the passenger seat, the front of his fatigues covered in dark red blood. The man's face was growing paler as he bled out, but he lifted a soaked hand and beckoned the two men closer.

"Hell, it's a wonder he's still living now." Ryan leaned over to hear what he had to say.

"Rachel...Carr...ington...stowaway...taken prisoner...taken..." He tried to say something else, but his voice was cut off by a bright red bubble of blood, and when it burst on his lips, his last breath hissed out with it.

Ryan turned to stare at J.B. "You've got to be kidding me. We have to go after her again?"

"Apparently so. But where the hell'd they take her? Didn't see anyone come out on my side."

"Me neither. And if these guys were waiting to attack anyone in the vehicle, that means..." Ryan grabbed a flashlight from its holder under the dash, switched it on and played the beam around the interior of the pit. Underneath the rear wheels he saw what he was looking for, but hoped he wouldn't find—a low, narrow tunnel leading away from the trap.

"Still thinking this was a good idea?" J.B. asked as he stared at the black opening.

"Less every minute." Ryan coughed as he replaced the low magazine in his blaster with a full one. Climbing up on the fender of the wag, he peered into the passenger compartment until he found a heavy, plastic canteen. After draining half the bottle and splashing the rest over his head, he walked to the entrance to play his light down the tight corridor. "That woman's going to be the death of me yet."

"Tell the others?"

"No time. If we're only a few minutes behind, we got a better chance of taking them by surprise and getting her back now than if we regroup and come back later. Come on."

Ducking, he entered the passageway, almost stumbling over another body as he did so. A third warrior lay before him, his bulging eyes and protruding tongue making it fairly clear how he'd died. "Looks like someone took out another one here."

J.B. didn't waste words on the body's condition. "Yup."

Ryan shuffled down the tight passageway, breathing

shallowly with each step. As hot as it had been in the pit itself, the tunnel had to have been at least twenty degrees warmer, making sweat bead all over his body. The air was also thick and foul, smelling of earth, unwashed bodies and smoke. The top of Ryan's head brushed the ceiling, and there was just enough room for him to advance if he turned his shoulders so they were at an angle to the walls. Blaster in his right hand, crank flashlight in his left, he duckwalked farther in, ready to chill anything that moved in front of him. He thought he might be on a downward slope, but it was hard to tell. He heard J.B.'s stealthy movement behind him, so Ryan had no worries as far as his back was concerned.

The tunnel continued straight for several dozen yards, then doglegged left. Ryan paused at the bend, keeping the light low so as not to make himself a target. He flashed the light around the corner first, trying to flush out any ambushers. When no spears or bullets came his way, Ryan leaned out long enough to glance down the tunnel, seeing nothing but empty corridor.

He reached behind to signal J.B. to move out, then crept into the passageway. After the noise of the fight both in and out of the pit, the silence was disconcerting. Ryan expected to hear movement at least, maybe conversation, screaming, some sign of life, but although he strained as hard as he could, he heard nothing at all up ahead.

Where the fuck did everyone go? he wondered. He hadn't passed any side tunnels, and there hadn't been any forks yet, either. The passageway just seemed to keep on going, deeper and deeper. Squaring his shoulders, Ryan followed, trying not to think too much about the tons of dirt and stones above his head, or what would happen if a section of tunnel were to suddenly collapse on him.

After another hundred feet, he saw that the tunnel seemed to open into a larger room, almost big enough to stand in. Ryan still approached cautiously, leading with his blaster. He could make out at least two other tunnels branching off from the intersection, and stopped just before the entrance, concealing his light again. With J.B. still and ready right behind him, Ryan listened for any sign of life in the area ahead. Just because he couldn't see anyone didn't mean the area was clear.

After a slow thirty-count, he was satisfied the area was empty. Edging into the doorway, he swept the entire area with the muzzle of his blaster one last time. Straightening, Ryan stepped inside—and was shoved to the ground as a large weight fell on him from above, his blaster flying from his grasp as a dirty arm snaked around his throat.

Ryan felt another hand tear at his face, and he grabbed it and bent the fingers back at an impossible angle, feeling two snap under the pressure. His opponent didn't make a sound in response, but the forearm around his throat constricted more tightly, cutting off Ryan's air. Grabbing the man's arm with his left hand, he wrenched it off his windpipe and back around while reaching for his blaster, just out of grasp, with his right hand. His adversary wriggled out of his grasp and tried to choke him again, but Ryan jammed his chin into his chest, preventing the warrior from securing his stranglehold again. Feeling hot, fetid breath on his ear, he dipped his head even lower and snapped it back, feeling a crack as his skull smacked the other man's jaw. He head butted him a second time, this one landing more solidly, making the man rear back.

Giving up on reaching his blaster, Ryan went for the panga on his left hip, drawing it as he rolled onto his back to try to dislodge the man. As he did, he saw J.B. locked in combat with another of the short men, both of them shuffling around as if in a deadly, clumsy dance.

Ryan's enemy tried to grab him again, but he sat up out of the guy's reach and turned, swinging the heavy panga at the man's head as he did so. The warrior threw up his right arm to block the blow, and the thick blade chopped into his forearm, breaking both bones with an audible crack that Ryan felt through the knife's handle.

The serious wound didn't stop the warrior in the least. Instead, he pushed off the ground with his good arm and came at Ryan again, his teeth bared and spittle flying from his mouth. Ryan brought the panga around again, this time in a savage chop to his enemy's throat. The keen edge sank in, cutting through skin, muscle and the major blood vessels. He pulled the blade down and out, slicing through even more flesh, so deep he felt the metal grate against the bones of the spine.

The man halted in his tracks, his outstretched hand falling to his side as the knife nearly cut off his head. When Ryan finished pulling the blade out, a huge gush of blood followed, splattering on the dusty floor. The Native American put his uninjured hand to the gaping slash, but his eyes rolled back in his head even as he fell to one knee, then onto his side, the fountain of blood already subsiding.

Glancing over at J.B., Ryan saw the smaller, wiry man standing over the body of his fallen enemy, wiping blood off his knife, still watching the other tunnel entrances. His eyes suddenly widening, he flipped the knife end-over-end to throw.

Ryan hurled his panga in the general direction the

Armorer was staring at as he dived for his Sig Sauer. Even as he hit the dirt, his fingers closed around the blaster's grip, a part of his mind screamed that it was probably already too late, but he figured he'd rather die with a blaster in his hand than with nothing.

Raising the dusty Sig Sauer, he saw another of the squat Native Americans, this one armed with an ancient-looking AK-47, aiming directly at his face, his finger about to squeeze the trigger.

Chapter Twenty

Realizing he was a heartbeat away from dying, Ryan lined up his blaster's sights on the man's chest and squeezed the trigger, knowing he'd at least be able to take the fucker who'd chilled him along on the last train to the coast.

As he fired, the man spasmed and arched his back, raising his head as if to scream, but no sound came out. The automatic rifle slipped from his fingers, landing on the floor without a shot fired. The man bucked once more, a trickle of blood leaking from the corner of his mouth before easing limply from the ground—almost as if he was being set down by someone. Ryan didn't lower his focus for a moment, but kept his blaster's sights aimed at the middle of the darkness, ready to shoot again if necessary.

A moment later, a human shape appeared in the tunnel's black mouth. Sergeant Caddeus knelt and wiped his crimson blade on the dead Native American's loincloth before sheathing it, then picked up J.B.'s knife and Ryan's panga and held them out to the two men, handle first. "Dropped your knives, boys."

Ryan stood and accepted his, brushing as much dirt and blood off as he could. "I had him, but thanks for the help."

"Doesn't matter who takes 'em down, long as they go down for good." Caddeus was dressed in his full web harness, and had a short-barreled Colt Commando 5.56 mm carbine slung over one shoulder. "Damn warriors have been a thorn in our side for years. Always hittin' and runnin', then vanishing when we try to follow. Thought they were hidin' out in the hills, but looks like they did the opposite—went underground."

"Where did you come from?" J.B. asked as he snatched his knife out of the sec man's hand. "We were in the tunnel two minutes after the wag hit bottom, and didn't see you there."

Caddeus smiled. "My momma told me, 'always be faster than everyone else thinks you are.' Those raiders were all over us. My driver collapsed his sternum when he hit the steering wheel—always told that crazy mother to wear his seat belt. I tapped two, then saw Carrington get snatched—"

Ryan raised a finger. "Hold up. You knew she was in your wag?"

Caddeus shook his head. "Keep your voices down. No, I didn't know. She was in the back and kept her cap low the whole time, at least till she was grabbed. I heard her yell and started after them. She took out one at the tunnel entrance. She's a tough girl."

"Didn't stop them from taking her, though."

Caddeus nodded. "That it didn't. I followed them to their main quarters, then headed back to get reinforcements when I heard fighting here, and figured I'd better lend a hand—just in case, you understand."

"Yeah. Guess we're it, far as I know. How're you seeing down here, anyway?" Ryan asked.

Caddeus turned on the small LED flashlight tucked into the epaulet on his shoulder. The light it emitted was red, enough to see the immediate surroundings without giving the wielder's position away.

Ryan grinned. "Slick. You're on point, then."

The black man smiled back. "Well, I *am* the only one who knows where we're going, so turn off that big, white target and let's move out." He spun on his heel and headed down the passage he'd come out of at a fast clip.

Grabbing the AK-47 and slinging it, Ryan looked at J.B. and shrugged. "With him in front, at least I'll be able to chill him if necessary." He followed Caddeus down the black tunnel, with J.B. right behind him.

They traveled another couple hundred feet, passing several side tunnels that Ryan marked with slashes from his panga so they could find their way back. Caddeus slowed, then came to a stop, motioning the other two to come closer. Ryan and J.B. did, their eyes widening as they saw what lay ahead.

"How far below the surface are we?" J.B. asked, adjusting his glasses to better view what they had found.

The tunnel led to a huge room, easily a hundred feet across and several stories high. Every surface was smooth here, as if many hands had created walls and the ceiling out of wet clay that had been allowed to bake in the constant dry heat. A large fire down in the middle of open space gave off enough light to see at the bottom, along with a haze of smoke that filled the upper third of the complex, drifting out of strategically placed holes and let in more light and also let smoke escape. The walls were covered with an intricate system of cave openings, with steps carved into the walls leading up and down.

"She's in here? How in the hell do you expect us to find her? Or get past everyone here?"

"Relax, the warriors must have had a run of bad luck

lately. There doesn't seem to be a lot of them left. Look closely."

Now Ryan and J.B. saw that a lot of the caves seemed abandoned, with only a few lit from within. Perhaps two dozen people moved about, all in roughly the same area on the other side of the gigantic cavern.

Caddeus pointed at a cave opening near the bottom. "I saw them take her in there. All we have to do is sneak in, get her and sneak out."

"That's all, huh? And here I thought it might be difficult." Ryan exchanged a dour glance with J.B. "Remember what the Trader said about planning?"

"Yeah—no battle plan survives contact with the enemy."

Caddeus's eyebrows raised at this. "Your Trader knew his military history. That was written in the nineteenth century by a guy named Helmuth von Moltke the Elder, a German army commander."

Now it was Ryan's turn to be impressed. "How'd you know that?"

"The Free City library has a pretty good collection of books, some on war. Carrington has all the men on active duty in the militia read and report on one a month, no exceptions." He turned back to the strange ville ahead. "Anyway, it's a good thing we're not plannin' on doin' any fightin, ain' it?"

Ryan frowned. "Yeah. Let's hope they aren't planning on doing any, either."

Caddeus unslung his Colt Commando and carefully pulled the bolt back to chamber a round. "Even if they do, we should have the edge on firepower. Follow me, and remember, up is a threat direction here, as well." He crept out, looking everywhere as he headed for the nearest stairway, a steep, narrow group of steps that could easily be cut off at both ends, trapping anyone on it to be cut down at the attackers' leisure.

J.B. let air leak from between his lips. "Don't know about you, but I got a bad feeling about this."

"Not much choice. We go back for reinforcements, and most likely we'll find her dead. Come on." Ryan made sure his newly acquired automatic longblaster was secure, then headed after the sergeant, trying to creep inconspicuously, if such a thing was possible. J.B. was right behind him, trying not to make a wrong step on the tight flight of stairs.

Caddeus snuck around on the hard-packed staircases as if he'd been doing it all his life. Ryan and J.B. were more cautious, but as they made it farther down with no one seeming to notice them, they started to think they might actually pull off what had seemed like a suicide mission at first but what Ryan had now downgraded to merely crazy.

They had only one bit of trouble on the descent. Caddeus was just about to start down the last staircase that would take them to the cave Rachel was being held in when two men appeared at the bottom and began to climb toward them. The sergeant signaled Ryan and J.B. to take cover in the nearest cave opening, which was pitch-black. The two men entered, hoping they wouldn't stumble over a sleeping person and raise an alarm before they could chill him or her. Caddeus edged into the shadows right behind them just as the pair of men crested the top of the stairs, talking low between themselves in a language Ryan didn't understand.

Caddeus drew his combat blade, but froze at a light touch from Ryan, who had his own panga out, as well. J.B. had melded into the deep shadows on the other side, and all three men waited for the pair to pass. The smell of sweat, stale or uncooked food, and the general stench of too many bodies living too close together here was almost overwhelming.

The snort that erupted behind them was so close that Ryan was hard-pressed not to whirl and bury his blade into whoever had made the noise. His eyes had adjusted to the dimness enough to see a banked fire at the back of the room, making him wonder where all the smoke went from each cave. Ryan also saw huddled forms sleeping next to the fire, including a small one who had just gotten up and was stumbling toward them.

Caddeus tensed, readying himself to reach out and cover the boy's mouth and nose while cutting his throat with one slash of his blade. Again, Ryan stopped him. While he wouldn't hesitate to kill any one of these people if he had to, he wasn't going to chill a child who, as of yet, hadn't done anything to warrant death.

The boy headed out of the cave, rubbing his eyes as he went. Caddeus put his lips to Ryan's ear. "Why the hell did you stop me?"

"Kill the boy, mebbe he's discovered before we're gone. Only if he sees us do we chill him, got it?"

"Long as you're willin' to take that chance."

"I am. Shh. Listen." Ryan nodded toward the entrance, where the sound of splashing liquid could be heard. Caddeus's smile was quick, but he nodded, and moved back against the wall again.

Having finished relieving himself, the boy trudged back into the stifling sleeping room, again not looking left or right, but heading with single-minded determination to his sleeping area, collapsing on it and curling into a tight ball, where he immediately fell asleep.

Caddeus nodded. "Let's go." He checked the small landing, then crept out to the stairway. At the top, he motioned the other two to follow as he began his descent.

Ryan and J.B. quickly came up behind him, the three men creeping down to where they thought Rachel was being held. Unlike the rest, this cave opening was covered by a rough-cured hide from some unrecognizable animal. As they drew closer, Ryan heard noises, movement of some kind. They better not be doing anything to her, he thought, not because it wasn't a possibility, but because he thought Caddeus might go crazy and want to kill everyone in the place if he found Carrington's daughter being raped or tortured.

The sergeant was at the hide now, and was easing it aside with the blade of his knife just enough to see inside. Ryan signaled to J.B. to watch the far half of the ville caves while he kept his eye on the near ones.

Caddeus pulled back far enough to catch Ryan's eye and held up three fingers, then made a *C* with his hand, indicating Rachel, Ryan guessed, then stuck two fingers above his head to mimic feathers, indicating two men with her. Ryan pointed at him, held up the two fingers, then drew his finger across his throat in the universal gesture. Caddeus's answering smile was as ice-cold as Ryan had ever seen on a man. He nodded and disappeared into the cave before the one-eyed man could say anything else. There was a loud crack, followed by a strangled gurgle, then silence. Caddeus stuck his head back out. "Inside. Now!"

Ryan and J.B. wasted no time. In the small room, they found Rachel, gagged and bound hand and foot, and sporting a nasty welt under one eye, but otherwise apparently unharmed. The bodies of two long-haired, lifeless warriors were sprawled on the floor, one with his head twisted at an odd angle, the other leaking blood from a slit throat. Caddeus had gone to Rachel and was untying her, rubbing her ankles and wrists to restore circulation.

As soon as her hands were free, Rachel tore off the filthy hunk of hide that had bound her mouth. "Give me a blaster."

Ryan wasn't about to surrender one to her, but Caddeus drew his Beretta M9 blaster, chambered a round and handed it to her butt first. "Can you walk?"

"Hell, yes! I can run right the fuck out of here. Let's go before those other two come back. It sounded like they were bringing the chief, or whoever runs the show around here."

"That's just great. J.B., keep an eye on the door." Ryan rifled through the rest of the room, finding nothing but threadbare blankets and broken tools. "Just the ammo we have on us. Time to go."

J.B. was peeking out under the hide, and pulled back quickly. "Company's coming. The two warriors and an old guy, all at the top of the stairs."

"Fireblast!" Ryan looked at the small space, realizing that the other three men wouldn't be able to pack into the small room.

"Rachel, stay where you are and put your hands behind your back again. Caddeus, on my side again. J.B., right there. Try to let all of them get inside before we start chilling. Knives only. A ricochet in here could kill any one of us."

"They're here!" J.B. whispered.

Everyone fell silent as they waited for the men to walk into the trap. Ryan was counting on the moment of surprise when they walked in to find their guards dead. During that valuable one or two seconds, the three men would join their deceased brethren.

The footsteps came closer to the hide covering, murmuring voices carrying to the group inside. There was a pausc, as if someone was arguing their point to the others, then another voice raised in what sounded like disagreement.

Ryan took a moment to assess the other three. J.B. was his calm, phlegmatic self, ready to chill at a moment's notice. Caddeus seemed a bit distracted by his concern for Rachel, but looked ready to go, as well. He was a bit unsure about Rachel. Her face was flushed, and her chest rose and fell rapidly. Her head moved in quick jerks, like a bird's, and Ryan could have sworn her pupils had contracted when he'd seen her up close. He wasn't sure, but from conversations with Mildred, she looked like she was in mild shock. Nothing to be done about it now but get her out of here as quickly as possible.

Ryan turned back to the opening just as the hide was swept aside, and one of the men stooped to enter the hut. He walked in, his eyes alighting on Rachel first, then falling on his bodies of the dead guards. He stopped, causing the second man to bump into him, and opened his mouth to shout a warning when Rachel brought her Beretta out from behind her back and shot him three times.

Chapter Twenty-One

As soon as he sensed motion from behind him, Ryan knew what was about to happen, and cursed himself for not taking the blaster away from her when he'd had the chance. He pushed away from the men in the doorway, dropping to the ground and drawing his own weapon, in spite of his standing orders. The Beretta's reports were thunderously loud in the confines of the small room, making him grimace as the sound buffeted his eardrums.

One thing he couldn't fault—Rachel had certainly aimed well, not that it was all that difficult from a range of less than ten feet. Her trio of 9 mm bullets punched into the man's upper chest, at least one piercing the heart, judging by how he lurched to a stop before falling over, one hand clutching the pulped, bloody hole where his heart used to beat.

The second man looked like a chief, given the tattered buffalo robe on his scrawny shoulders and the threadbare hawk feather headdress atop his head. Having just entered the small chamber, he was now trapped between his suddenly dead guard and the warrior behind him, who was of no use there. He had just managed to turn and begin to shout an alarm when his throat was seized by Caddeus, cutting off his shout in midcry. Before the chief could raise his staff in defense, the sec man casually flicked out his dagger, stabbing the old man in the heart. He sagged at the attack, held up only by the black man's strong arm. He tried to form a last sentence, whether it was a curse or a cry for mercy, Ryan would never know, particularly since he couldn't understand a word these people said. But before he could speak, his head drooped to one side as he died in Caddeus's hand.

The third man had backed out of the entryway, and was shouting for help as he sprinted for the nearest stairway. J.B. stepped out of the cave, leveled his mini-Uzi, and squeezed off a short burst, which punched through the man's chest and sent him tumbling out of sight down the stairway. J.B. stuck his head back in the cave. "Time to go," he said over the shouts of alarm that were sounding in other areas of the cave complex.

Rolling to his feet, Ryan grabbed Rachel by the arm, snatching the blaster out of her hand as he pulled her up. "What bastard part of no shooting did you not understand?"

"I thought I saw a blaster in his hand—"

"We had everything under control." Ryan's head snapped up at a light pressure from Caddeus, and he fixed the other man with his intense, ice-blue glare.

"She made a mistake, but now ain't the time to discuss it."

"Hey, you all coming or what?" J.B.'s question was punctuated by rapid shots from his mini-Uzi.

Ryan released her and unslung his AK-47, unfolding the stiff stock and setting the burst selector to single shot to conserve ammunition. "She's your responsibility now, Sergeant, and know this—if she endangers any of us like that again, I'll take her out myself."

"That may cause a bit of a problem between us." His Colt Commando held in one hand, Caddeus went to the door and peeked out, then edged outside, keeping Rachel close to him. "Again, something we can discuss later. Let's move, Cawdor."

Still fuming over the incident, Ryan tamped his rage down and concentrated on one of the things he did best—getting out of a lethal situation in one piece. Readying the AK, he came out to back up J.B., who was scouting the ascending stairway that would take them up to the next level. Caddeus exited the cave after him, hugging the wall, keeping Rachel behind him as he also moved toward the stairs.

Sensing movement from above, Ryan looked up to see a figure aiming a longblaster at them from about twenty yards away. Snugging the weapon's stock to his shoulder, he snap-aimed and fired two rounds. The figure jerked, then pitched forward and fell soundlessly to the rock floor, almost at Ryan's feet, his ancient carbine shattering to pieces upon impact. His head was still intact, enough for Ryan to make out the neat hole in his lower jaw, the slug having bored through his head and blown off the top of his skull.

"Ought to make them think twice before rushing at us anytime soon." Waving J.B. forward, Ryan took the rear guard position, figuring they'd have more trouble from that side than above, judging by the frantic motion he saw around the main fire. He snapped off three more shots in that direction, and was gratified to see several of the figures duck for cover. What he really wished for was his Steyr, which had been left in the wag back on the surface—but who'd have thought he'd need a long-range weapon a couple hundred feet underground?

The loud chatter of J.B.'s mini-Uzi and Caddeus's carbine above him made Ryan take the stairs in four giant bounds. As he leaped, he started taking fire from across the chamber, the bullets sending up fragments of hard clay as they smashed into the wall and floor next to him. Ryan reached the next plateau and ducked around the wall. Sticking his AK back around the corner, he fired several shots in the general direction of where the enemy fire had been coming from, the longblaster bucking in his hands. Glancing over, he saw J.B. on the opposite side of the semicircular bowl they were in, with Caddeus firing from the doorway of the cave they had hidden in earlier.

Caddeus let off a 3-round burst, then another. "Move, Cawdor!"

Ryan bolted across the clearing under the other man's cover fire. Hitting the wall next to J.B., he turned and aimed at the muzzle-flashes across the way. "Go! I'll cover you!"

The Armorer nodded and began creeping up the stairs again, firing single shots both above him and ahead as he went. The return fire was more organized now, with shots coming from at least four different directions. He did his best to keep their heads down, but was aware of his dwindling ammunition supply. "Caddeus, get her out!"

The sergeant led Rachel along the wall, firing his carbine one-handed at the enemy shooters as he stepped along the wall. As they passed, Ryan handed Rachel the Beretta. "Don't shoot any of us!"

The glare she gave him was pure hatred. "If we're trapped, I sure as hell won't save a bullet for you, either." She shrugged off Caddeus's hand and aimed the blaster above them as they began climbing the next stairway.

Ryan fired twice more, then followed, watching for movement on the stairs at the other end of the landing.

Seeing shadows, he waited until the head and upper body of a man appeared, then leaned around the curving wall and fired twice, watching him drop, and the rest of the men fall back. He scurried to cover with the rest, almost slipping on the thin layer of what seemed to be dried horse shit all over the floor.

There were at least three more flights to go, and Ryan was starting to doubt whether any of them were going to make it to the tunnel alive. The incoming fire was withering now, a sustained hail of bullets that seemed to be coming from all directions. They chipped off fragments of rock that proved to be almost as dangerous, as J.B. found out when one flying piece gashed his cheek, only about a quarter-inch from his eye.

"If we stay here, we're dead!" he said, wiping blood off his cheek.

Ryan poked his head and longblaster out long enough to squeeze off three shots, then ducked back as a curtain of lead rained down on them. "Tell me something I don't know. We need some kind of diversion!"

"How about some cover?" Caddeus shouted.

"Sure, but what?"

The sergeant nodded at the cave entrance behind them. "Might be something burnable in there, could make a smoke screen."

Ryan and J.B. exchanged glances, and the Armorer shrugged. "Better than nothing."

Caddeus waved them forward. "I'll cover you—got the most ammo left. Go! Go!"

He changed magazines with quick, efficient movements, then leaned out and fired short bursts at each of the places showing muzzle-flashes. "Move it!"

Ryan and J.B. shot out from the wall and ran to the cave, bullets pinging off the rocks around them. The

Armorer had just reached the opening when he stumbled, grunting as he grabbed the back of his right leg. "Damn! I'm hit!"

Ryan almost bowled him over as he pushed the smaller man inside. "Fireblast, don't give them a second chance. Here, let me see." He switched on the flashlight and played the beam on J.B.'s leg. "Hell, it's barely a scratch."

He was downplaying the wound's seriousness. The bullet had punched through the other man's calf, a neat hole that steadily leaked blood with each movement. "Hold still." Ryan tore off a strip from J.B. shirt and wrapped the wound tightly. "Can you walk?"

J.B. put weight on the injured leg briefly, his sallow features tightening as the pain hit. "I can limp, but not fast."

"Still better than carryin' you out." Ryan moved the flashlight to illuminate the room. "This looks promising—I think."

The room was filled with stacked piles of what looked like large bricks of dried horse dung, carrying with them that unmistakable smell. Ryan poked one, finding it solid under his hard tap. "If we had more time, we could build a whole wall of this."

"Yeah, only one problem—this shit is hard to light, and I don't think any of us want to stick around out there any longer than necessary."

"Mebbe—" Ryan's thought was interrupted by Caddeus's shout.

"Cawdor, if you're doing something in there, you better do it fast!"

Ryan panned the light around one last time, thinking he'd caught a glimpse of something shiny in one corner. The gleam of glass reflecting his flashlight beam caught his eye, and he stooped to pick up a jar half-full of a pale yellow liquid. Opening the rusty screw-top, he sniffed it. "Kerosene."

"But not enough to light all this."

"Mebbe it is. Take off your shirt." Ryan stripped his off as well, and tore it into narrow strips. "Soak each one in the kerosene, then wrap it around a brick."

J.B. took his off, exposing a chest as pale as the rest of him. "I liked this shirt, you know."

"Just be glad I'm not suggesting we use your pants, too." Ryan had created three of his homemade smoke pots and was working on the fourth when J.B. raised an eyebrow.

"How we going to ignite these? My butane is empty."

"You've got a flint and steel, right? You spark them, and once they've caught, I toss them out the door. They'll break up, which is more or less what we want, to spread the fire around—"

"You hope." J.B. had finished making his four and stood ready to go. "Let's do it."

"Caddeus, we're ready!"

"About bastard time. It's getting thick out here!"

"Okay, here it comes!" Ryan held the first brick while J.B. created a shower of sparks with his knife blade and magnesium fire starter. The wick caught almost immediately, and Ryan tossed it out into the middle of the clearing, where it broke into several large pieces upon hitting the ground. The flaming cloth was still going, however, and soon the pieces were smoldering, as well. Ryan followed suit with the other ones, tossing them as soon as the cloth caught. He tried to angle them closer to the stairs, so the produced smoke would cover them as they climbed, but the enemy shooters caught on to their plan sooner than he'd expected, and began shooting at the dung bricks as soon as they were tossed out, succeeding in blowing one apart in midair.

When they were finished, there was a smoky pall over the area, but it wasn't nearly as thick as Ryan would have liked. "Better than nothing, I guess," he said. "You ready?"

J.B.'s mouth was a grim, thin line as he favored his leg, but he nodded, raising his mini-Uzi. "Let's do it."

Ryan led the way, ducking out the door and heading for the stairs. He'd only taken three steps when he felt a stabbing pain lance through his left shoulder, followed by another one near his neck, and a third stabbing through his right collarbone. The air filled with a chattering sound, and he realized he was being shot from above. Whirling, his arms felt like they were on fire, yet he raised his AK-47 using only his elbows, screaming with the pain as he unloaded the rest of the magazine into his attacker, who was standing on the roof of the cave. Hit by several of the bullets, the man jerked under the impacts, then fell backward as Ryan did the same.

Chapter Twenty-Two

"Ryan!" Heedless of his own injuries, J.B. bolted to his side, firing his Uzi through the veil of smoke at the shooters on the far side of the cave. Grabbing Ryan by the legs, he dragged him back to the wall. "How bad is it?"

Ryan was having a hard time keeping his head straight; it suddenly wanted to wobble all over the place. "Not good. I know that much." He brought his trembling neck muscles under control to look down at his shoulders, seeing a lot of blood, and the jagged end of bone poking up through his skin on his right shoulder. "It doesn't hurt much, though." That was strange, but true. At the moment, the upper portion of his body felt oddly stiff and almost numb.

"Enjoy that while you can, because it won't last." J.B. gingerly explored the wound. "This is going to hurt a lot." J.B. eased himself under Ryan's right arm, eliciting a groan of pain from his old friend as he gripped his hand tight to keep him in place. "You're going to want to die in the next few minutes, but you hang on, you hear me?" When he stood, Ryan nearly threw up from the agony shooting through his injured shoulders.

The room was swimming now, and Ryan's vision kept telescoping in and out. First gray, then spots of black, then back to normal. "J.B., if it comes down to it, you won't let them get me—"

"Don't talk like that. No one's dying in this shit hole, you hear me? Your legs still work, now use them!" J.B. snapped off a long burst through the smoke, which was growing thicker now, providing a good wall of cover. "Just hang on. We'll be out of here in no time."

"If you say so..." Ryan was finding it hard to put one foot in front of the other, but he did his best to focus through the fog of pain and listen to J.B.'s commands. They were moving now, and he dimly heard the smaller man cursing him out in between exhorting him to climb the steps they were on. To Ryan, it felt like they were floating. He tasted blood at the back of his mouth and swallowed it, aware he was closer to boarding that last train to the coast than he'd been in a long time. He tried shaking his head to clear it, but the movement only gave him vertigo, making the room sway and spin around him.

They'd obviously met up with Caddeus and Rachel, who were both still shooting as they progressed farther up the vertical labyrinth of stairs and caves. Ryan heard only part of the conversation, but he caught J.B.'s strained voice saying "—I'll step over both your dead bodies before I leave Ryan here. Now keep shooting and get the fuck moving!"

The rest of the trip out came to him in a haze—climbing, running and more climbing, a scream from someone—Caddeus, mebbe?—and more arguing between a thin man in glasses that Ryan should have recognized, and a woman he knew he couldn't stand, although he couldn't remember why. All he knew was that his arms and shoulders ached like a son of a bitch, and maybe the smaller man should do what the woman was saying and leave him here to rest a bit.

"If I get some rest, I'll be all right. Just let me rest a bit..."

"Fuck you, Ryan. I haven't carried your ass all this way to leave you now. Fuck you, too, Carrington. Mention dumping anyone again, and I'll kneecap you myself and leave you for the shooters. Now pick up the sergeant and move your—"

Ryan didn't hear the rest. He was drifting in and out of consciousness, awakened only by bright flashes of pain every time he took a step. The good thing was that they had stopped climbing, but now every time he opened his eyes, he saw crazy strobes of bright light, interspersed with an eerie red glow. There were more blasters firing around him now, the bright flashes illuminating the thin wearing man's face, his teeth gritted as he shot at figures that seemed to be staying just beyond the light. Next to him was a blond-haired woman supporting a black man whose face was tight with pain, yet who still held a carbine that he fired every so often as she hauled him down a dark corridor.

"Almost there. Keep that eye open, Ryan. I didn't haul you this far to have you fuckin' die on me now!" Ryan pried his eyelid open and glared at the thin man. If he could just move his arms, he'd pop that tough-talking bastard right in the mouth.

"Wait'll I get my hands on you, asshole."

"If we get out of here, Ryan, you can beat me to your heart's content, but until then you stay awake, dammit!"

Ryan did his best to listen, but the prospect of sleep was just too tempting to stave off. The tunnel they were in seemed to go on forever, and it was warm here, so warm. His head lolled, and he slumped forward, only to be awakened by a stinging slap across his cheek.

"I'm not gonna tell you again—stay awake!"

"Tryin' to. Gotta beat the piss out of you when we—get outta here, remember?" Ryan lifted his head, which felt as if it weighed a thousand pounds, to see a bright square of light ahead. "Hey! I see…light ahead."

The glasses-wearing man—J.B.! His name is John Barrymore, or J.B. for short, Ryan suddenly remembered—was panting as he wrestled Ryan's stumbling body forward. "Yup, and we're heading right for it. Gonna have Mildred patch you up and you'll be back slinging lead and walking tall in no time. Just…a little farther…now."

They staggered forward another few yards, with both J.B. and the woman yelling as they walked. "Help! We got wounded down here! Help! Anyone out there?" They entered the light, which was so bright it hurt Ryan's eye, making it squeeze closed.

An oddly modulated, artificial-sounding voice answered. "All humans in the pit, we have your companions in our custody. You have ten seconds to surrender and throw your weapons up here, or we will open fire on you. This warning will not be repeated."

"What the hell—?" The woman and the man conferred for a moment, then the man shouted back. "Okay, we're tossing everything out. But send someone down to help us, please!"

They threw every weapon they had out of the pit, even the Sig Sauer holstered at Ryan's waist, which he would have held on to, if not for the curious fact that he couldn't move his arms. One was being held by J.B., causing a dull agony to burn across his entire arm and shoulder. His other arm dangled at his side, and even thinking about moving it made his upper body hurt.

His entire chest and back felt wet and sticky, and while Ryan hoped it was sweat making him uncomfortable, the tang of warm copper in his nostrils—and his increasingly common spells of light-headedness—made him think otherwise.

J.B. shouted to their unseen antagonists again. "Come on. We got two men hurt bad here. If they don't get some attention, they're gonna die!"

"Stand by to remove vehicle from the pit. All humans inside may wish to take cover."

The artificially modulated voice was drowned out by the roar of a large engine as a wag approached. Whatever it was, it kicked up a lot of sand and dust, bringing a cloud that swirled around in the pit, reducing visibility to zero.

"Back into the tunnel. It's our only chance!" J.B. shouted.

Nearly unconscious, Ryan tried to resist being dragged into the darkness again, but he couldn't stop a mouse right now, much less his determined friend. No sooner had they reached the tunnel entrance than something slammed down on the roof of the wag with a loud bang, making the whole vehicle shake. The trapped wag started to rise, slowly at first, then faster as the machine pulled it out of the trap. It rose into the air and disappeared from view.

"Humans, come out, and you will receive assistance," the voice called again.

"Come on, Ryan. I'm gonna get you some help." J.B. pulled him back out again, moving much more slowly now. Before they could see anyone above them, two small devices fell into the hole, releasing streams of white gas as they hit the ground.

"Knockout gas…cheatin' bastards." J.B. tried to let

his friend down easy, but he fell over suddenly, and Ryan slipped from his grasp, collapsing to the ground and unable to break his fall. He landed on his face, scraping his cheek in the rough dirt, and lay there, unable to move.

If that is knockout gas, I sure wish it'd work faster, he thought. He saw J.B. slumped over next to him, out cold, and the blond woman seemed to be unconscious, as well. Ryan wasn't sure about the black man. He couldn't see what had happened to him.

He heard someone calling his name from very far away, a woman's voice shouting, "Ryan!" He tried to answer, but his mouth was bone-dry, and he couldn't even make a sound, no matter how hard he tried. Next came an odd scraping noise of boots on dirt, as if someone had jumped down into the pit. Ryan heard approaching footsteps, then he was rolled onto his back, the afternoon sunlight burning into his eye before it was blocked out by a figure bending over him.

Ryan felt himself being examined, but his eye was on the mirrored faceplate that hovered over him, concealing the person's features. It was attached to some kind of full helmet that protected the wearer, and was attached to a suit that seemed to be composed of equal parts heavy cloth and hard armor plates covering the person's upper chest and shoulders. The person seemed to ripple as he or she knelt over him, and Ryan swore he saw the suit's color shimmer and change to a light tan that blended with the walls and floor of the pit.

The hands were gentle as they examined his injuries, and he heard a hiss and one final command before his vision tunneled out, turning gray, then fading to black.

"Subject is seriously injured, multiple gunshots, trauma level three. Request immediate evac to the ICU ward, stat."

Chapter Twenty-Three

Ryan's eye fluttered open, and he stared at the pristine white ceiling above his head. He lay perfectly still, letting his senses and body come awake, gathering as much information about where he was without giving away his current condition.

A cursory glance around the room revealed he was lying on a bed with rails on either side, in an antiseptically clean room with walls the color of pale peaches. A blinking red light in the corner probably indicated a sec camera, confirming that he was being watched. As his awareness sharpened, he realized there were things attached to his body; what felt like a needle was sticking into his right forearm, and sticky electrodes were on his chest and temple.

That was another thing he realized—he was dressed in a clean hospital gown, and he had been washed.

My arms! he thought.

Heedless of whoever might be watching, Ryan turned his head to look at his shoulders as the memory of what had happened flooded over him, ignoring the stab of pain that flashed up his neck to the base of his skull. Both arms ended in their normal accoutrements—two hands, ten fingers, he saw with relief. His shoulders, however, were trapped in a strange cage made of metal rods that kept him immobile on the bed.

"It's to help your bones mend, Ryan," a familiar voice said from a few feet away.

"J.B.?" Ryan slowly turned his head toward the other bed in the room, where the Armorer's familiar, steady eyes stared back at him.

"None other." J.B. winced, presumably at the contraption holding Ryan. "That thing hurt much?"

Ryan's gaze flicked around the strange cage, and was a bit surprised. "Actually, it feels okay. I've got an itch on the back of my neck I'd like to scratch that's drivin' me loco, but otherwise I can't complain. Where are we?"

J.B. swung his legs off the bed, giving Ryan a glimpse of a strange, smooth plastic cast with some kind of nozzle sticking out near the calf, and walked over to Ryan's without a trace of a limp. "In the hospital section of a redoubt called the Bunker, underneath the Denver International Airport." He leaned over and scratched Ryan's neck. "That do it?"

"Bit lower…that's got it." Ryan eyed J.B.'s new toy. "You seem to be doing all right."

J.B. mouth quirked up, and he nodded. "They got some things here that even you probably wouldn't believe till you see them."

"How long have I been out?"

"About two and a half days. Got no gear, nothing except what they gave us, which, besides this breeze-flapper, isn't much. What do you remember?"

Ryan didn't have to think back too far. "Last thing was a whole lot of fuckin' pain, then you hauling me all over creation like a bastard meat puppet." Ryan grinned. "Think I still owe you for some of the stuff you said down there."

J.B.'s smile was genuine this time. "If you think

you can lift those arms anytime soon, you're welcome to try." His expression turned serious again. "Ryan, I haven't been as afraid since that time you went into that river, or mebbe when you ate that poisoned food on account of what a stubborn stupe you can be..."

Ryan rolled his eye. "Spare me the compliments and fill me in on what went down."

"Like I said, you were hit bad. Broken collarbone, bleeding like a fountain, even more muscle damage. One of the docs said they removed a bullet that had nestled up against your carotid artery." J.B. massaged his lower back. "Couple more millimeters, and I wouldn't have had to strain myself hauling your ass out of there."

"But you did."

"Yeah, didn't feel like burying you just yet. Those fuckin' raiders were out for blood, our balls on a necklace, you name it. Caddeus nearly lost his lower leg to a double-barreled shotgun blast just as we reached the tunnel entrance. I made Rachel take him, and the four of us gimped out, fighting off the whole crazy tribe all the way. Still not entirely sure how we got out of there. When we got back to the pit, I was down to my last magazine. That'll teach us not to leave the shotgun behind next time. Later found I had five bullets left."

"Just enough—one for each of us, and a spare in case you fucked one up." Ryan didn't smile at his gallows humor.

J.B. didn't, either. "We reach the pit again, and these strange suited figures tell us to surrender or die, so we take the first option. They hauled out the wag using a vehicle I've never seen before. Even lookin' like something the cat dragged all over the place, they knocked us out for transport."

"Yeah, I remember seeing one of them, all covered in a faceplate and helmet and some kind of armor suit."

"Yeah, probably one of the sec personnel. Next thing I know, I'm in this bed, wearing a gown similar to yours, my leg's been treated by this 'adaptable limb cast' and I'm being fed half-decent food, but not a scrap of information yet. They wheeled you in yesterday afternoon, and other than check-ups—always accompanied by an armed guard—no one's told me jack-shit so far."

Ryan indicated the unblinking camera eye with a slight motion of his head. "They're probably watching us talk right now, so I'd expect someone to show up any second."

Both men looked at the formidable steel door, which remained silent and shut. "Okay, might be a bit longer then. You said the food's good?"

"It'll do. Had worse, had better. You must be starving by now."

"Damn near, considering the last time I ate was what, two days ago? Since then—"

The door cycling open interrupted Ryan, and a heavyset man strode into the room, dressed in a white biohazard suit that covered him from head to toe. A smooth leather belt encircled his waist, carrying a holstered blaster, along with several other small pouches and a set of handcuffs. His faceplate was transparent, revealing a broad face with a heavy brow and thick, black eyebrows over bright blue eyes. He took a position to the right of the door.

"Patient Dix, you are advised to return to your bed, otherwise we will be forced to sedate you—again." The man's hands dangled loosely at his sides, but Ryan spotted the look in his eye immediately. This man was a chiller, pure and simple.

J.B. grimaced as he walked back to his bed. "Almost forgot to tell you that part, Ryan. They busted me examining the door last night and knocked me out. They like to use gas."

"The sedation was for your own good, as well as for ours. I'm afraid that we must keep you all under quarantine until we can confirm that none of you pose any kind of threat to our environment." This came from another white-suited man who had come into the room, this one shorter and wearing glasses behind his faceplate.

"Who are you and where are we?" Ryan asked.

"I am Dr. Stephen Agathem, and I head the medical division of this compound. You are guests of a place called the Bunker—" Ryan and J.B. exchanged knowing glances at the pause, but said nothing "—and your injuries will be attended to until it is decided what will be done with you. In the meantime, I suggest that you rest as much as possible. Your wounds were very serious, and even with the treatment, it will be some time before you regain full function of your limbs again." He came around to the side of the bed and regarded Ryan. "Hold still, please." He checked the framework around him, tightening a screw here, loosening one there. Then he shone the beam of a small penlight into Ryan's eye. "Pupil reaction seems normal. How do you feel?"

Ryan stared at the cage around him. "Good overall. I feel a vague itching in my shoulders."

"That's the muscles and bones coming back together. It's mostly psychosomatic, but it should diminish in the next day or so."

"What exactly did you do to me?"

"There was extensive trauma from three bullet wounds to your shoulders, aggravated by what I would call the exact opposite way to properly move someone to safety." Agathem stared hard at J.B., who only shrugged. "You were very fortunate there wasn't any spinal cord or vertebra damage. We repaired the tissue and ligament damage, replaced the 2.3 pints of blood lost and reset your broken collarbone, using nanograftors to ensure that the bones set properly. I'm afraid you'll have to be in the immobilization frame for at least another twenty-four to forty-eight hours to allow the bones to mend cleanly."

"When can we see our friends?" Ryan asked.

"Possibly as early as tomorrow afternoon, pending the results of the last tests. You were all cleansed thoroughly before admittance, and as long as nothing dangerous is detected, it would be possible to allow supervised visitation within the next twenty-four hours. A base administrator will also want to speak with you, but I imagine you're probably hungry, and it is mealtime, so…"

Without another word, the door opened again, this time allowing Ryan to see that it was an airlock, with another outer door at the end of a small corridor. Another white-suited person pushing a wheeled cart walked in and stopped it between the two beds. He swung out individual tables for Ryan and J.B., revealing trays filled with what looked like meat loaf and gravy, mashed potatoes, diced carrots and peas, two slices of wheat bread, a dark brown lump of something that might have been a brownie, along with a glass of water and a sealed plastic cup of orange-red liquid. The smells weren't quite right. The food had been either freeze-dried or reconstituted, but at the moment neither Ryan's nose or stomach really cared.

"Regular nutrition will enable to you recover your health faster, Patient Cawdor. Eat now, and I'll see about advancing those appointments and letting you see your companions."

"Want to see the administrator soon as possible," Ryan said around a giant mouthful of meat and bread. It was awkward eating without moving his shoulders, but he soon adapted, mindful of the sharp flares of pain when he moved too fast.

"They are busy men, but I'll see what can be done. In the meantime, rest and let us know if there are any sudden changes in your condition, pain flare-ups and-or fever, nausea, or light headedness."

Still shoveling food into his mouth, Ryan nodded. Without another word, the man turned and left, followed by the sec guard.

J.B. didn't say anything until Ryan was almost done, but gave him another slice of meat loaf and all his bread. Ryan assembled them into a sloppy sandwich and devoured it in three large bites, drained the last of his water and frowned at the plastic sealed cup.

"Server said it's something called pink grapefruit juice. Not bad," J.B. said.

Tearing open the foil top, Ryan sniffed it, then sipped. The tart-sweetness washed away the meal's bland, processed taste, and he drained the cup in one long gulp. With a satisfied belch, he set it on the tray and pushed it back toward the cart as far as he could without straining his arm. "You were right—had better, had worse."

"So what now?"

"Not much happening till I get out of this thing."

Ryan eyed the camera in the corner, wondering if they had the room wired for sound, too. He turned his head as far as he could, trying to keep whoever was watching from seeing his lips move as he pitched his voice low.

"Got to find out what they know. Do they know about the ville? What firepower do they have? How many personnel? Place like this can unbalance the entire region, particularly if they start heading out and visiting the neighbors."

"How do you want to play it?"

"Same as when we came into Denver at first—mouths shut and eyes open. Stick to the 'traveling traders' story. It should buy us some time so we can figure out how to handle these people."

"What about Caddeus? He's liable to spill the whole story."

"Not if they really run the militia in Denver as tight as it seems. He probably considers himself a prisoner of war, so he won't say anything to them. Whatever happens, just follow my lead."

"Always do." J.B. leaned back in his bed as the door cycled open again. Ryan turned his head with some effort to see another white-suited man enter the room, this one taller and more slender than the others. He was armed with a blaster at his side, and was carrying a small, gray case. He was followed by another thickly built sec man, not the same as the first one, Ryan noticed.

"It's good to see you both doing well," he began. "I am Captain Daryn Waltrop, commander of security of this facility. I'd like to ask you both a few questions."

Ryan and J.B. exchanged glances again. It was rare enough for any sec man to request an interview, much less do it politely. Ryan nodded carefully. "Go ahead."

"What brought you and your group to this area?"

Ryan tried to keep it short and simple. "Me and my friends're traders—or we were till a small town tried to double-cross us about a week south of here. We had to fight our way out, left most of our wares behind. We were heading north till our steamer gave out a couple days ago. Thought we heard about a ville in the area, so we kept going until those men in the vehicles picked us up as mercs. We were heading back to their ville when the Indians attacked. You probably know the rest."

For a sec man, Waltrop seemed very relaxed, even leaning against the wall as he listened to the story. Ryan wasn't quite sure what to make of that. Usually sec men had a chip on their shoulder, a stick up their ass, or both, each the size of a tree trunk. "All I know right now is that your convoy of three vehicles was spotted approaching our perimeter when you were attacked by those damn Indians which have been a thorn in our side for a long time. However, it seems you managed to uncover how they were able to strike and disappear so quickly. Although we've been trying to track their travel paths for—well, for a while now, we hadn't thought they were using underground tunnels. This will help immensely in our future operations against them."

Ryan's eyebrow rose. Was this guy thanking them for inadvertently uncovering the Indians' hiding place? "You're welcome, I guess. Are you one of the administrators we're supposed to be seeing?"

Daryn shook his head. "No, but as head of security, I keep tabs on any visitors to our facility, particularly ones as capable as you all seem to be. I may sit in on that interview, however."

J.B. spoke up. "Is there anything you can tell us about this facility?"

Daryn shook his head again. "No. Any questions you have can be asked of Administrator Carr. Most likely he'll be the one to interview you."

"What about the rest of our friends? We'd like to see them and make sure they're all right."

"Until an administrator sees you and you've been cleared for leaving the room, I'm afraid that isn't possible. However..." He set the small case on the bed and opened it up, revealing a monitor screen that flickered into life. Daryn came over to Ryan's bed and held the device so he could see it, then pressed a button. A color picture of a room similar to theirs appeared, with two beds. Doc lay on one of them, shaking his head, while Jak paced the room, waving his hands at the old man while his lips moved soundlessly.

"Your white-haired companion is very interesting. He does not like being confined."

Ryan shrugged. "Yeah, I could have warned you about that if I'd been awake."

"It doesn't matter. They can't be let out until the testing is complete. He'll simply have to make do. If he doesn't, there's always the gas."

Ryan examined the grainy image, seeing the tension in the teen's thin shoulders. "It'd probably help if I talked to him, even through a telephone or walkie-talkie."

Daryn slowly nodded. "I'll see what can be arranged. Here are others." He pressed the button again, and the picture changed to show Sergeant Caddeus in his own room, sleeping.

"Your other man went through quite a lot. The doctors were unable to save his lower leg, but they should be able to fix him up with an excellent prosthetic."

"Yeah, he looks all right. How about the others?"

The sec man changed the picture again, this one showing Krysty and Mildred, each sitting on her own bed across from each other, talking.

"To be a fly on the wall for that conversation, eh, Ryan?" J.B. asked with a smile.

"Mebbe. Women have their own way of discussing things that men shouldn't have any part of sometimes." Ryan noticed that both Daryn and the other sec man had taken a particular interest in the picture of the two women, with the second man even leaving his post by the door, edging closer to get a better look. "There was a blond woman with us. Can you show her, too?"

Now Daryn exchanged a glance with his henchman. "Ah, yes, the feisty one." He switched pictures again, showing Rachel in a room alone, doing push-ups on the floor. She had stripped down to her panties and an undershirt, revealing long, lean legs, well-developed arms and a lithe, toned body. Ryan glanced out of the corner of his eye to see the sec man's attention focused completely on the screen. "Now that's a sight I could watch all day."

Ryan reached out and closed the screen, making Daryn straighten hurriedly. "Well, they all seem to be all right. If you can arrange a way for me to talk with Jak and Doc, I'd appreciate it."

"I can't promise anything, but I'll see what I can do. Thank you for your time." With that, Daryn left the room, the other sec man following close behind.

"What do you make of that?" Ryan asked J.B. as soon as the airlock doors closed.

"They certainly seemed mighty interested in our women," the Armorer observed.

"Yeah, and we haven't seen a single one here yet. Everyone who's come in here has been male. Wonder what that's all about, if anything." Ryan's gaze returned to the red dot of the camera in the ceiling. "We've certainly seen our share of polite motherfuckers hiding blasters and blades behind those nice smiles. Be interesting to see what this administrator has to say when he arrives."

Chapter Twenty-Four

The rest of the day passed in slowness that was at first boring, then irritating, then painful and finally agonizing. Unable to move, Ryan found the enforced immobility to be one of the worst things he'd ever experienced—worse than torture, because that was something that could be actively resisted, even if only in the mind. Worse than combat, because you were so busy staying alive you didn't have time to consider the possibility of dying.

Being trapped in this cage of metal bars, however, with every minute ticking by with the slowness of cold molasses flowing, was just about worse than anything he could imagine. He'd tried to sleep, but the cage made it impossible to change his position, much less get comfortable. After figuring out their plan, neither Ryan nor J.B. were given to desultory conversation, so he'd been stuck staring at the thick airlock door straight ahead of him. And above it, the clock, which silently counted out the minutes in cool blue digital numbers that changed every second.

At first, Ryan had tried to look away, letting his eyes roam around the room, and eventually turning his head away. But the discomfort it caused had rapidly turned to pain, which forced him to turn his head back to looking forward again. He had then looked at his body lying on the bed, raising his knees to block his view of the ever-changing numbers that weren't changing fast enough. A sideways glance confirmed that J.B. had slipped back into sleep.

Thinking about Krysty, Doc, Jak or Mildred didn't help, either. Ryan hadn't discounted the thought that what Waltrop had shown him may have been previously recorded, and that even now the rest of his friends might be undergoing experiments, torture or already be dead. He'd immediately banished such thoughts from his mind, leaving him back at square one—stuck in bed, staring at the clock on the wall, watching the seconds slowly count in circles up and then resetting, the minutes ticking by like drops of water wearing at a rock throughout infinity.

When another meal had come after a few hours, Ryan was grateful enough for the distraction. The food was similar to before—mushy, processed fish fillets in a soggy crust, accompanied by peas that had the strange aftertaste of mint, limp sticks of what were supposed to be fried potatoes, and the same slices of bread with white, flavorless butter. Ryan was still hungry enough to eat it all without comment. Questioning the server—yet another man—yielded either a polite brush-off or a blank stare.

Dr. Agathem came in thirty minutes after the meal tray had been cleared away, accompanied by Daryn Waltrop. The doctor checked both Ryan and J.B. before speaking. "There is one series of tests still to be run, however, it would appear you'll be taken off the quarantine list tomorrow morning. That is also when Administrator Carr will see you, as well." Again, he turned and left, leaving the sec commander in the room alone this time.

Once the door had cycled shut, Waltrop took his

hand out from behind his back, revealing a small, two-way radio. "I was able to work out a way for you to talk to your friend before he does something he's going to end up regretting."

Ryan was fairly confident that it would more likely be the sec men who would regret trying anything on Jak, but if they gassed him first, the albino youth would be easy pickings. He nodded and lifted his own hand. "Grateful for this."

A peculiar expression crossed the sec man's face, although it was hard to tell through the faceplate. Waltrop handed over the device. "The other handset is in their room, so you should be able to contact him right now."

Ryan lifted it to his mouth, his lips tightening at the pain shooting through his shoulders, and pressed the transmission button, noticing as he did that Waltrop stood so that his body obscured the camera's view of the bed. "Jak? Can you hear me?"

"Ryan?" The teen's voice sounded tinny and far away. "Not like place. Want out."

"I know, but you've got to listen to me. They're going to let us all out real soon, so you have to wait a little longer, okay?"

"Can wait a bit more." There was a strange note in Jak's voice, and it took Ryan a moment to place it. He was trying to mask it, but the kid was scared.

"They said we'd probably see you tomorrow morning, so just wait it out, and you'll be out of there before you know it, all right?"

"Yeah. Can't wait get out whole bastard place."

"Soon enough, Jak, it won't be long now. Give this thing to Doc, will you?"

He heard rustling as the walkie-talkie was passed,

then snippets of conversation. "Hold that—button—no, that one, talk."

"Ryan, is that you on the other end of this infernal squawking thing? You sound like your head's in an iron box underwater or something."

Ryan resisted shaking his head. Even after all the time he'd spent with Doc, he still didn't know where the man was coming from day to day. "Good to hear you, Doc, how you doing?"

"My nerves are somewhat tremulous at the moment. Our snow-haired companion is ready to either climb the walls or try to break through them, and I fear that I will not be able to contain him for much longer. Do you have any news as to when we will be released from our present captivity?"

"They said we should be out of quarantine by tomorrow morning. Just do your best to keep Jak from doing anything foolish, and we'll see you before you know it."

"That is my fervent hope indeed, Ryan. To be honest, I do wish we were back sipping drinks at that hotel in the cit—"

Ryan cut him off with his own transmit button. "Yeah, Doc, we'll see you real soon. Meantime, keep an eye on Jak, okay?" He turned off the device and held it out to Waltrop with an embarrassed smile. "He's a bit touched in the head. Gets like that sometimes, rambling on about people and places we saw a long time ago. Thanks for letting us talk to them."

The sec man accepted the walkie-talkie and carefully concealed it in his palm. The expression on his face was similar to the one Major Kelor had when Doc had slipped up during the ride to the hotel, and Ryan didn't like it one bit. "No problem. With luck you'll see them all tomorrow. Why don't you get some rest, and we'll get a bright and early start tomorrow morning?"

"Yeah, I think we'll do that." Ryan tried a smile, hoping it didn't seem too forced.

Waltrop headed for the door, Ryan's gaze following him the entire way until the closing door cut him off from view. "Fireblast! Think we can get a muzzle for Doc one of these days?"

"Ten to one says we aren't going to see him or Jak tomorrow," J.B. said.

"I'm not taking those odds, 'specially since you're probably right." The only thing Ryan hated more than captivity was being unable to do a thing about it—like right now. He flexed his shoulders slightly. Was he imagining it, or did the muscles hurt less as he moved? "Let's get some rest, be ready for what comes tomorrow."

RYAN'S EYE BLINKED OPEN. The room was still pitch-dark, the blue numbers of the clock seeming to float in the air above the door. He had been checked on every few hours by a silent, efficient orderly who adjusted the metal frame. This latest visitor had come more quickly than he should have, the first inkling that something wasn't right.

"J.B.—" was all he got out before a gloved hand clamped down on his mouth, just below his nose, allowing him to breath, but not to do anything else. Another hand clamped down on his left wrist, squeezing with bone-creaking power. He heard slow breathing by his head, and thought he also sensed a high-pitched whine, almost at the edge of his hearing, as if the person in the room was using night-vision goggles.

A harsh whisper, distorted even more by the

biohazard mask, assaulted his ear. "Your friend is out of it for the time being. Listen up, Cawdor. You and your friends are in danger. The scientists are planning to kill you and keep your women for breeding stock. However, there are allies here inside the Bunker who will reveal themselves when the time is right. They won't right now, in case you don't believe them, but they wanted to warn you. Don't believe anything the scientists say. They'll do anything to win you over to their side before they betray you."

The twin pressures on his hand and mouth disappeared, and a few seconds later, the door cycled open, although no lights came on either in the airlock or the hallway outside. Ryan counted to thirty under his breath before breaking the silence with a hiss. "J.B.? J.B.!" No response came from the other bed.

"Nuking hell! I'm not staying in this contraption another second." Bringing his hand up to grab the metal bar nearest it, he tried to pull it up and off his shoulder, regardless of the stab of pain that knifed through his arm. He heard a shrill beeping sound from somewhere in the room, followed by a hissing noise that came from somewhere above his head. Ryan looked up, seeing only darkness, but he felt air moving across his face, followed by the scent of lilacs or maybe peaches, he couldn't tell.

The blackness grew more intense as Ryan tried to free himself from the framework, but everything suddenly blurred around him, the glowing blue numbers on the wall clock stretching into meaningless blue smears as they changed from one to another. Ryan pulled at the metal again, but his fingers plucked uselessly at the bar, unable to grasp it, much less pull it away.

Gas! The realization didn't bring with it a sudden

burst of strength to free himself, nor did it prevent Ryan from slowly falling into the long tunnel of darkness that rose all around him, as the room and everything in it faded away.

RYAN RETURNED TO CONSCIOUSNESS again more slowly this time, his head foggy, his mouth tasting of bitter metal and a dull headache pounding in his forehead right above his empty eye socket.

"He's coming around."

The nearby voice focused his attention, and Ryan blinked his eye several times in an effort to recover his equilibrium. "Who's there?"

"Stay still, Patient Cawdor, there's some work to be done before you can move." The vague blurs around him sharpened into three humans: Dr. Agathem, Daryn Waltrop and another man. None of them were wearing biohazard suits. Ryan saw thick glasses and wide, pale blue eyes and strands of gray, balding hair combed in a thick wave over his pink scalp.

"All right. The graftors have done their work, and we can now remove the stabilization frame." Agathem leaned over and fiddled with the framework, and Ryan suddenly got a distinct feeling of pressure removed, that he was no longer connected to anything on the bed. Even better, the framework retracted from around him, rising to disappear into the wall or ceiling somewhere. Ryan didn't notice, as he was busy testing his arms and shoulders, feeling the occasional twinge of pain, but overall, he had regained nearly full function of his upper limbs. A glance down at his shoulders revealed hardly any evidence of injury at all; just a strange row of white dots along both shoulders, where the framework had held him still.

"And how do you feel?"

Ryan planted his hands on the bed and pushed himself into a sitting position, exulting in the simple act of moving as he desired. "Not bad."

"The readouts are fine, Doctor." This came from the third man—Administrator Carr, Ryan assumed. "What does he know about last night?"

"Administrator, Doctor, perhaps I should handle this." Waltrop stepped forward, fixing Ryan with a neutral stare. "Patient Cawdor, there was an unauthorized person in your room last night, someone who wasn't a doctor or an attendant. We'd like to know if you remember anything out of the ordinary regarding this incident?"

Ryan stared levelly back at him, wondering if Waltrop was the one who had snuck in last night. He waited a moment or two for some kind of signal, not knowing what to expect—was the sec man suddenly going to wink at him or something? Give him the secret underground revolution high sign? When nothing happened, except for the man's steady blinking, Ryan spoke. "I didn't notice anything last night—I think I might have had a nightmare. I remember trying to move the frame thing, and smelling flowers or fruit, and the next thing I know you're all here. What happened exactly?"

"Apparently, someone entered your room, gassed Patient Dix, then began doing something to your framework, as well. They left shortly thereafter, and then you began trying to interfere with the frame, at which point the automatic monitors prescribed a mild sedative for you. You don't remember anything else?"

"No."

The three men exchanged glances, then stared back at Ryan, who looked at all of them with the same blank expression on his face. "When do we get to see the rest of our friends?"

The glasses-wearing man regarded Ryan with no fear, just a calculating, unnerving intelligence. "As you have proved to no longer be a threat to the integrity of this habitat, we can take you both to your friends right now."

"Mind if we get dressed first?" J.B. said from his bed, stifling a yawn as he glanced over at Ryan.

"We've taken the liberty of preparing clothes for both of you." Carr nodded, and Waltrop held out a neatly folded bundle to each man. "They should fit you both well."

The clothes were simple—undershirts, underwear, slippers and plain, dark yellow jumpsuits that covered them from neck to ankles. Ryan slipped his on carefully, mindful of stretching the muscles and bones in his shoulders. J.B. didn't look the same without his fedora, but there was nothing to be done about it now.

Zipping up the one-piece uniform, Ryan turned to face the men. "Let's go."

Chapter Twenty-Five

"A moment, if you please, Mr. Cawdor." Carr's voice stopped him in his tracks.

Fingers flexing, Ryan's teeth ground together behind his lips, but he kept his expression cool as he faced the facility's leader. Of them, only Waltrop was armed, and Ryan figured J.B. or he could probably take him out and subdue the rest before an alarm could be tripped. However, even if they took the others as hostages, what was the point? They had no idea where Krysty and the others were being held, and the guards outside would simply gas them all before they could kill anybody. They'd wake up right back where they started, only this time, treated as true captives. Ryan had already had enough of the framework that had held him. He had no desire to find out what their real prisoner cells might be like.

"Yes?"

"You seem like an intelligent man, so I'm sure you'll hear me out," Carr said, his tone indicating that he'd known exactly what Ryan had been thinking about. "I have a question or two for you and your friend—" he nodded at J.B., who leaned against the wall, arms folded against his chest as he yawned again "—before we let you see your other companions."

Ryan assumed an air of nonchalance as he sat on the

bed. "It doesn't look like we're going anywhere fast, so fire away."

"What is your association with the group of men and women currently living in the city of Denver?"

The frank query took him by surprise, but Ryan tried to bull through anyway. "Didn't you read the report from your sec man? We're traders, from the south—"

Carr held up his hand, brushing away Ryan's words. "Please, do not try to mislead me with whatever story you've created during your recovery here. Our reconnaissance drones spotted your convoy leaving the city from its northeastern quadrant, and tracked the heat signature of your vehicles' exhaust back to their headquarters, so we know you are involved with them in some way. We also know that they are under siege from an opposing force that is quite large, although given their enemies' recent lack of success, there is no telling just how long that force will stay together before internal friction begins to tear it apart. The bottom line is that you aren't who you say you are, and therefore the obvious conclusion is that you have been sent out here to spy on us. The only questions to be answered now is for whom and why?"

Ryan had also folded his arms across his chest while the small man spoke, and he sensed rather than saw J.B. subtly tense a few feet away, ready to spring into action should Ryan give the signal. Instead, he lifted the index finger of his left arm up an inch, telling the Armorer to hold his ground—for now.

"Sounds like you've got this all figured out, so I don't know how answering any of your questions is going to help me any."

The administrator's chest rose and fell in what might have been a sigh of annoyance, only Ryan couldn't hear anything, since he was so damn quiet. "I'm not going to try to bully or threaten you, Mr. Cawdor. Such crude tactics are better suited to the ill-dressed barbarians outside our gates, such as those deluded Indians that you revealed to us."

"And whom you plan on eradicating from the earth, if possible, right?" J.B. asked, not moving a muscle other than his lips.

"Regrettably, yes. Although we have tried to work out a peaceful settlement with them before, the negotiations have always devolved into violence before anything meaningful could be worked out. I'm afraid that, since we cannot seem to live peacefully alongside them, and since their ambush tactics seem to be improving, they have left us with no choice but to eliminate them once and for all. I hope this won't be the case with any other indigenous groups we may encounter. However, be that as it may, it is my hope that you and I can have a civilized conversation, wherein I can learn what I'd like to know without resorting to any sort of—" his lips twitched, as if he had just tasted something unpleasant "—physical coercion."

The not-so-subtle message wasn't lost on Ryan, either, and he shrugged. There was nothing in the deal he'd made with each leader that said he had to keep quiet about either of them. "I can tell you what I know about both of them, which isn't much." He laid out what he had discovered about both sides—Carrington and his vision of a free city, and Tellen leading his ragtag but well-armed army of revolution. He talked about what he had seen in Denver, both the good and the bad, and even speculated about where the rebuilt city's power was coming from. The only thing he didn't mention was that the people of the Bunker had Carrington's daughter among their guests. He didn't want them to have that much leverage.

When he had finished, he leaned back in the bed and fixed Carr with his steady stare. "Okay, I've given you about all I care to at the moment. Now take us to our friends."

"Fair enough, Mr. Cawdor. After all, I'm sure there will be plenty of time to talk later. Commander Waltrop, if you would escort both of these men to their friends so they can catch up."

"Certainly, sir. Mr. Cawdor, Mr. Dix." Waltrop gestured at the door, indicating both men should precede him through the exit.

As J.B. fell in step beside him, and they passed through the thick door, he muttered out of the side of his mouth, "That what you call mouths shut and eyes open?"

"When the other side already knows you're slinging bullshit, throwing more usually doesn't help."

J.B. accepted the Trader's wisdom with a nod. "So what are we doing?"

"Going along, for now." This was the third time Ryan had been surprised by a potential adversary, and it was a feeling he liked less and less every time it happened. Also, he needed to learn more about this place before he formulated any kind of plan, and what he had seen so far—the formidable security, the incredibly high level of tech—hadn't filled him with confidence regarding their ability to escape. But first things first. He wanted to see that the rest of his group was unharmed, and find out if they could add anything to what he'd seen so far.

Once in the corridor, Ryan was unsurprised to find two other well-muscled sec men in armor and carrying submachine guns flanking the entrance to their room.

The two men fell into step a pace behind and to each side of each man, while Waltrop stayed a few paces away, outside easy reach.

"Just follow the blue line, gentlemen, and it will take you to your destination."

Ryan looked down to see a glowing blue line on the floor. He trailed it through the spotless white hallways, broken only by several more of the large airlock doors. They passed medical staff intent on their own duties, pushing small carts laden with equipment of reading some kind of electronic touch pads, every few seconds. The line led to an elevator, which opened when Ryan pushed the button. They entered, and saw that the button for one floor was also glowing blue. "I assume this is the one."

"Correct."

Ryan pushed it, and found he could barely tell that the elevator was moving. A few seconds later, the double doors opened, and he faced a nearly identical hallway, this one carpeted, with walls painted a soothing pale beige. The doors were more normal, as well, opening on hinges instead of the complicated airlocks in the hospital wing. The blue line led to two doors halfway down the corridor, one on either side of the hall.

"Krysty Wroth and Mildred Wyeth are in the room to the left, and Jak Lauren and Theophilus Tanner are in the room to the right."

"Where are Caddeus and Rachel?" Ryan asked.

"They are being held in a separate facility," was the only reply.

Ryan shrugged. That was something they would deal with when the time came, if possible. He went to the left door and waited for Waltrop, who spoke into a small earpiece. After a moment, the door clicked open, revealing the two women inside.

"Ryan!" Krysty rose to her feet in a single fluid motion, but before she could reach him, he stepped aside to reveal the men in the doorway, holding his hand up in front of him, out of their sight, to warn her from showing any obvious affection for him.

"Good to see you, Krysty."

Mildred had managed to repress her similar reaction upon seeing J.B., and had sat on the bed again, her right hand twisting the bedclothes the only sign of her nervousness.

"You folks probably want to talk, so we'll leave you alone for now."

"Any chance we can see Jak and Doc, as well?"

"The administrators are not comfortable with letting all of you congregate in one place at the moment. Perhaps something can be arranged later."

"At the very least, can you get Jak outside for a bit? The kid gets a little stir-crazy if he's confined for too long." Ryan caught the sec man's gaze and held it with his own. "Something like that might be remembered later on."

Waltrop's expression didn't change one bit. "I'll see if anything can be done." He let the door close in front of him, his eyes never leaving Ryan.

Krysty waited until the door closed, then came up on Ryan fast, pushing him into the corner next to the door underneath the camera's ever-watching eye. Her arms wrapped around him as she kissed him long and hard, then buried her face in the juncture of his chest and neck. Her whispered words carried up to his ear. "Saw you out on the ground when J.B. pulled you out of the tunnel, with blood everywhere, and your face so pale… I thought I'd lost you for good."

Ryan took her chin and lifted her face so he could stare into those emerald-green eyes, thinking like as not that he might drown in their depths someday, and that it would be a damn fine way to go. "I'm still here, walking and talking, so don't you go putting me in the ground just yet."

Near the other bed, J.B. and Mildred had enjoyed their own quiet reunion, and now Mildred turned back to the other two. "You see Doc or Jak yet?"

"No, but I spoke to both of them by walkie-talkie yesterday. Jak's getting a bit wild, so I'm trying to get him outside for a while before he does something permanently bad to someone in here. How about Caddeus or Rachel?"

Mildred shook her head. "Nope, haven't seen hide nor hair of either since we arrived. From what I gather, she's also been kind of a handful during her stay here."

Ryan frowned. "Yeah, that's what I heard, too. I assume you two haven't tried anything yet."

"No, and neither have they—other than getting the distinct feeling that the guys around here haven't seen a woman in a while, we've been treated very well." Krysty's eyebrows narrowed. "Any idea what they plan to do with us?"

Ryan shrugged as he exchanged a puzzled glance with J.B. "That's the thing. We're not quite sure yet. Why don't you tell us what happened while we were in the caves first."

"Not that much to tell." Krysty recounted their encounter with the Native Americans, and how Jak's inspired driving had helped them fight off the warriors. "Just when we were done and coming back to the ambush hole, we saw this big old flying machine drop out of the sky in front of us. It was either stop or crash into it, so we chose the former. As soon as we come to a stop, these other vehicles seemed to come out of nowhere and surround us—and I don't mean they drove up to us, they appeared out of nowhere, like they had been invisible and decided to appear around us. They were also armed with things we haven't seen in a long time—like the stuff we saw at Crater Lake, only theirs worked a lot better."

Ryan nodded as he listened, remembering the isolated compound of insane whitecoats that had been working to finish the job skydark had begun all those years ago. They had put an end to the whitecoats' madness.

Mildred broke in. "They chased off the rest of the riders and shot them out of their saddles. The vehicle-mounted weapons had to be some kind of laser—just point and shoot, a blink of light flashed, and people were dying left and right."

Ryan held up his hand to stop her. "You don't think these guys are linked with Major Burroughs and his people, do you?"

Krysty shook her head. "Not from what we've seen. This seems to be a self-contained facility with no contact with anywhere else—at least, not that we know of. Anyway, don't you think if they'd told Burroughs they had us, he'd be making tracks up here?"

Ryan conceded the point. They'd left Burroughs in a pretty high state the last time their paths had crossed. No doubt he'd love to get his hands on them again. "Yeah."

Krysty continued, "Anyway, everything we saw was a pretty strong inducement to surrender when they asked, and it's not like we had much of a choice. Jak was for trying to fight our way out, but the cooler heads prevailed."

Mildred sat on the bed now as she warmed to their tale. "All of the men were dressed in those armored enviro-suits like the ones they used when we were in quarantine, only bulkier. They could probably stop a rifle bullet, maybe even a .30-caliber shell. They asked us if we were allied with the men in the vehicles near the city, and Krysty and I just looked at each other, 'cause neither of us knew what the hell they were talking about."

"So one of them shows us a picture on a small monitor of a few mil wags taken from an aerial position. It seems either Carrington or Tellen sent another convoy to shadow us and see exactly what we would find out here. We both say—"

"That we've never seen them before in our lives. The man nods and tells us to keep watching the monitor. The picture continues for a few moments, then boom! The group is vaporized, just like that." Mildred snapped her fingers. "That's why they wanted us to keep watching. They were looking for any kind of reaction to those guys getting killed. Damn, I'm getting slow in my old age."

Krysty grinned at the other woman's flash of insight. "There's a whole lot about these people we don't understand. We see the fireball in the distance, and a second later, we hear the report of the bomb they used. These people have some heavy-duty tech. That came from what they called a remote-piloted drone vehicle, if I heard them correctly."

"And their medical equipment, too… Ryan, do you mind if I look at that shoulder?" At his nod, Mildred waved him over. "Sit on the bed, please. It's easier to examine their work." He did so, and unzipped his jumpsuit enough so she could examine his healed injuries. "If I hadn't seen it, I wouldn't believe it. I'd have thought you'd be on your back for at least four to six weeks, maybe even immobilized in an upper-body cast while your bone knit back together. Instead, you were out how long?"

"J.B., you said I was out two days, then another one in the bed—it wasn't fun, let me tell you—and this morning they let me out of the frame that had been holding me in place and said I could walk around."

"And you feel fine?"

Ryan raised both arms above his head, then lowered them, then stretched them both out to either side. "Occasional twinge now and then, but otherwise I feel fine."

"That's unbelievable, is what it is. Okay, so they have incredible weaponry and medical tech that's beyond anything we know. Anything else we've found out about them?"

"Yeah." Ryan motioned everyone closer around him. "Apparently, they need women." He detailed the encounter he'd had in the middle of the night with the mysterious person who had warned him about the whitecoats and their true goals.

"Did you believe him?" Krysty asked when he'd finished.

"I'm not sure. The administrator isn't coming off like a guy who's keeping us prisoner so they can impregnate both of you and Rachel, although mebbe he's trying to get on our good side to lull us into a false sense of security."

"Doubtful," J.B. chimed in. "If that was the case,

why heal us? Could have chilled us, tossed our bodies in the desert and had you women all to themselves."

"Exactly. They want us alive for a reason. I'm just not sure what that is right now."

"So what do we do?" Mildred asked.

Ryan stroked his chin as he thought about what could happen next. "No doubt Administrator Carr took what I told him about Denver, Carrington and Tellen to the rest of his buddies, and they're figuring out what to do with this information. Once they've chewed it over for a while, I figure they'll probably come back to us and inform us if and how we fit into their plans. If we do fit in somehow, that doesn't involve being kept here for some kind of experimentation, then we'll go along until we decide otherwise. If not, then we've got to figure out a way out of here, which isn't going to be easy from what we've seen so far."

"Yeah," J.B. said, "the sec here is some of the best I've ever seen, almost airtight, with well-trained men armed and ready at a moment's notice." He lowered his voice to a near whisper. "Our only choice may be allying with this rebel group, assuming it actually exists, and using its force to fight our way out."

Ryan frowned. "Let's see if it actually comes to that first. I can't believe I'm saying this, but Carr seems to be on the level, and until he makes a move, I don't see a lot we can do except keep our ears and eyes open and mouths shut. Try to find out as much as you can about the base and the people in it.

"We don't have much choice. They've had the upper hand from the start, stripping us of our gear and keeping us separated so we can't plan. They know what they're doing. Carr and Waltrop know we won't leave here, assuming we could find our way out of this maze in the first place, without the others. The main thing we have to do right now is to keep them from figuring out who Rachel is. If they learn that, all the leverage goes to them." Ryan stretched again and headed to the door. "Let's see if I can talk to Doc and Jak, then we'll try to get an audience with the administrator."

As he finished talking, the door opened, and Waltrop appeared in the entryway. "Mr. Cawdor, Administrator Carr would like a word with you—privately."

Chapter Twenty-Six

Ryan rose slowly off the bed, squeezing Krysty's hand as he did. "Will anything be done about Jak?"

"The best I could arrange was to let your friends see him, in hopes of calming him down. An escort is ready to take them to him, so if you would accompany me..."

"What about the other two members of our group—Rachel and Sergeant Caddeus?" Mildred interrupted. "We'd like to see them, as well."

"I cannot speak to that right now, but perhaps after you talk with Administrator Carr and the others, something can be arranged."

That sounded familiar—the exchange of a favor for a favor. Behind his back, Ryan released Krysty's hand, then gave everyone the signal to stay alert, but not to try anything against their captors until he returned. The understanding was that the rest of the group would give him twenty-four hours, then, if he didn't come back in that time, they were to try to escape any way they could. If they could find him along the way, great, but they all knew they weren't supposed to make any effort that would put them in danger. Ryan hoped it wouldn't come to that. They had all been through so much together that to lose anyone would be like losing his own limb.

"Lead the way." He followed Waltrop into the corridor, where the sec man motioned for him to walk in front. "Any progress on finding out who broke into my room last night?"

Waltrop grunted. "Not yet."

Ryan glanced at the sec man out of the corner of his eye. "Whoever it was had to have a pretty high sec clearance to get inside. My jack's on one of the men in your department."

"Plenty of doctors in the wing with access, as well. Don't worry about it, we'll find out who's responsible soon enough."

Ryan considered upping his interrogation in the elevator, but decided against it. Waltrop could stonewall him all day, and if the sec leader wasn't part of the rebel group, saying anything about it would just put him on guard.

They walked down the corridor to the elevator. Ryan tried to figure out if they were ascending or descending, but the metal box traveled so smoothly that he couldn't tell. After a thirty-count, the elevator stopped and the doors slid open, revealing another hallway, this one featureless except for the lone door at the other end.

"Only one way to go."

Ryan twitched his shoulders, then his biceps, then his wrists and hands, listening all the while for the telltale sound of Waltrop's blaster clearing its holster. This would be the perfect spot for an execution, but he wasn't about to give the other man the satisfaction, or the chance. When he checked the sec man out of the corner of his eye again, he saw him relaxed and walking a pace back, his arms loose at his sides.

This whole thing just gets weirder and weirder, he thought as they reached the door, which slid open when he was a step away. The room inside was brightly lit and held a long table at the far end, with places for six men sitting behind it. Five of those places were occupied, with Dr. Agathem and Administrator Carr in two seats, next to three men Ryan didn't recognize. Upon his entry, the murmur of conversation between the men died away.

Waltrop passed Ryan, walked over to the sixth seat and sat down. Carr closed a manila folder in front of him and regarded Ryan with that same scrutinizing, magnified stare. "Mr. Cawdor, thank you for joining us. No doubt you're wondering why I've asked you here."

"It crossed my mind." Ryan noticed the empty chair in front of the table, and sat in it.

"Let me introduce the rest of the administrators who oversee the Bunker. You already know Dr. Agathem and Commander Waltrop. The man to my far right is Kenneth Galbrait, head of research and development, the man next to him is Arnold Mayweather, chief of internal operations, and the man on my far left is Charles Kilenny, head of agriculture and food production."

Ryan eyed the last man, a tall, thin redhead with a prominent Adam's apple. "Should have a word with you. Your menu needs some work."

"We do the best we can with what we have, Mr. Cawdor," Kilenny replied. "Although I would be open to hearing any suggestions you may have on the matter." His tone straddled the line between subtle sarcasm and outright dismissal, but Ryan let it go. That wasn't why he was here. Instead, he focused on Carr as the small man ended the subtle hostility simply by clearing his throat.

"By now I expect you have a lot of questions about this facility and its overall purpose. Yet, at the same time, I get the distinct impression that this place isn't all that unfamiliar to you. Neither you nor any of your group has reacted even remotely similarly to other people who have stumbled upon us. To what do you attribute this indifferent response?"

Ryan leaned back in the chair and stretched out his legs, crossing them as he replied. "I've been almost everywhere on this rad-blasted continent ever since I could walk. I've seen everything from mutie animals and people of every size and stripe to even weirder things, from the mountains to the deserts and everywhere in between. Not much surprises me anymore. The point is, I'm not a slack-jawed dirt farmer who shits his pants when he first sees something he doesn't understand, so if this little get-together has a point, I'd prefer you get to it right quick, otherwise, we're just wasting each other's time."

As Ryan spoke, the expressions on some of the men's faces shifted from neutral to surprised or angry. Carr's, Agathem's and Waltrop's, however, didn't change; the administrator even cracked a brief smile. "Very well, I can appreciate that."

He leaned back in his chair. "I won't go into the history of this site in any great detail. Suffice it to say that before what you people living on the outside call 'skydark,' this facility, along with several others created at various points around the continent, were created as fallback points in the event of a nuclear or other worldwide disaster. Our instructions were explicit and precise—stay concealed until the original staff, or its descendents, felt the time was right to reemerge and begin rebuilding civilization."

Ryan's expression and posture didn't change. He'd heard this speech many times before, most often out of the mouths of crazed psychotics whose idea of rebuilding meant bringing everyone they could conquer under their iron-shod heel. Other times it was from even-crazier muties with delusions of grandeur who felt that the age of humankind had passed, and a new era was emerging, with them—no matter what kind of freak they were—now being the rightful inheritors of the blasted planet. Whenever anyone began talking like this within his earshot, he figured sooner or later there was only one thing to do—put a bullet between their eyes, sparing both them and the land whatever insane plan they had concocted to ensure their domination. He resisted an urge to blow air through his teeth as he waited for the small man to finish.

"I must say that, according to the records of the first generation, it was very doubtful that this point would ever be reached. Exposing ourselves too soon could lead to outside forces attempting to overwhelm us for the technology and skills we possess. In that regard, the Indian tribe that took up residence in the nearby area served as excellent cover for many years, since they would keep anyone who might be interested in the ruins of the airport above us away. We also needed to make sure that we knew how to survive in this new world ourselves. It wouldn't do to open our doors and be laid low by a new pathogen or mutated virus."

"No, I suppose not, although it seems to me that you all took your sweet time if it took more than a hundred years for you to start looking past the ends of your noses."

Ryan's verbal barb didn't ruffle Carr one bit. "I won't overstate the hazards of premature exposure. Suffice it to say that previous generations took the precautions they thought necessary, and so did we. Those few outsiders who did stumble upon our perimeter were either taken in for interrogation, then mind-wiped—just so any memory of us was gone, not making them a drooling vegetable, you understand—and released, or, if they had promise, were invited to stay. The latter, sadly, have been few and far between."

Even as he prepared to dismiss Carr's words as the usual overblown rhetoric, Ryan found himself actually listening to the man, since his talk wasn't filled with the typical inflated boasts and threats so many others had made. Instead, this man's speech seemed to be governed by something that often seemed to be in short supply in the Deathlands—logic.

"However, there have been glimmerings of progress on the horizon, most notably in the city that has been created out of the ruins of suburban Denver to the west of here. We have been keeping the area under surveillance for the past four years, and have seen much to be hopeful about. On the other hand, recently the city has come under siege by an outside force, and our intelligence operatives have told us that the man leading the attacking force used to be a member of the city itself."

Ryan kept his eyebrow down with an effort; so Tellen *had* been telling the truth about that. "Okay, I'm still not seeing where me and my people fit into all of this." He was fibbing. He had a very good idea of what Carr was about to say, but Ryan had found that playing dumb often got better information than busting fingers with a hammer.

"I doubt that very much, however, it is of no consequence. You and your people are, quite simply, the perfect go-betweens for us to make our presence known. You have managed to ingratiate yourself with leaders on both sides of the conflict in short order, despite—or perhaps because of—your outsider status. I don't know what sort of bargain you've made with either group, nor do I care. However, since they apparently trust you, that makes you the perfect person to introduce us to the principals on both sides of the conflict."

"And what's the plan once that happens?" Ryan asked.

"We invite both sides to sit down and take stock of the situation. A third player in the area, particularly one with the resources that we have to offer, changes the dynamics considerably. It is our hope that we can bring both sides to the negotiating table to work out a compromise that will benefit everyone. Denver's location—relatively isolated, yet the gateway to both sides of what remains of the nation—makes it a perfect place to begin rebuilding a society that stands a chance of establishing law and order as it once existed."

Ryan frowned. "With your group reigning over everyone else? I've seen far too many places where that sort of power corrupted anyone who tried to wield it for too long."

Administrator Mayweather spoke for the first time. "Sadly, history is filled with those who attempted to force change upon a world that wasn't ready for it, or, having done so, were loath to give up the power that allowed them to enact that change. One of the first things an effective system of government needs is a system of checks and balances, like an advisory panel that ensures the single leader doesn't gain too much power. This would be addressed if—and when—a cease-fire agreement is brokered."

Ryan's mouth quirked in what might have passed for a brief smile. "Yeah, you realize that there's a strong chance that one or both sides would use this meeting to try and blow you all straight to hell, just on general principle."

Carr's genial expression vanished, replaced by a cool look of complete, almost ruthless efficiency. "I think they'll be willing to talk when they see what we bring to the table. So, will you set up a meeting between the various sides?"

Ryan's gaze swept the six men as he drew out the silence before replying. "On the other hand, why do I have any reason to trust you, either? I've already heard rumors that you folks are short on women, and plan on obtaining them by any means necessary. What would stop you all from chilling the leaders once they arrived, then rolling in and taking over the entire city yourself?" He'd been watching all of them as he spoke, particularly Carr, and wasn't surprised to see the head whitecoat evince absolutely no trace of a reaction to the accusation.

In fact, the man smiled again, while Dr. Agathem spoke up. "Tales of our gender imbalance, while somewhat accurate, are also a misnomer. Certain elements of our personnel aren't altogether happy either with the situation as it has evolved or the steps we have taken to correct the problem, and are advocating a more immediate remedy. However, if that situation were in effect, why would we have kept you here, treated your injuries, fed you, housed you, clothed you, when there was no guarantee that you would be of any use to us? If that were the case, we would have simply terminated you and left you in the hole where we first found you."

Carr leaned forward, steepling his hands on the table. "While we believe in the sanctity of human life, we'll take whatever measures necessary to defend our way of living. Past experience has taught us that, if nothing else. You aren't a threat to us, but you have something that we can use here. Therefore, we treated you in the hopes that you would be able to help us in turn. Now, will you do this for us?"

Ryan rose from his chair and slowly paced the room, aware of the six pairs of eyes on him. "Do I have a choice?"

"There are always choices, Mr. Cawdor. An intelligent man evaluates the ones open to him at any time and selects the best option available. In this situation, it is you who has the power here, not us. We need you to broker this introduction, rather than us risking a, shall we say, overzealous reaction from the other parties."

Ryan turned to stare him directly in the eyes. "Sounds like a polite way of saying no to me. I don't appreciate being forced into making my decision. We 'outsiders' call that a baron's choice—one that looks like you have a decision to make on your own, but he's really making it for you."

"It is possible that other members of your group may feel differently when presented with this opportunity. Besides, are we really asking that much of you? In return, as the person who made this all possible, you would have a high position in the new government, or we could outfit you with just about anything you may need, and see you on your way to wherever you wish."

Ryan certainly had his doubts about that. After all, Carr had just said they'd mind-wiped the others before releasing them. But for now…

"All right, I'll do what I can. But our part in this is only to get you all to the table. Anything that happens afterward is up to you."

"Fair enough. No time like the present to get started."

"That's what I always say," Ryan replied, mimicking the food administrator's tone perfectly. He suspected the man knew he was being mocked, and he saw the man glare at him as he got up to leave the room. However, at the moment, he didn't much care.

Chapter Twenty-Seven

Of course, Ryan didn't let his help go unrewarded. Within short order he'd gotten all of his friends into their own suite of rooms, with separate but adjoining bedrooms, and their own bathroom and shower.

Once everyone had cleaned up, Ryan called them together in Krysty and his room, shaking his head as they assembled. "Fireblast, this looks familiar. Didn't we just do this exact same thing a few days ago?"

"Fer pretty much same fuckin' reason," Jak said from the corner. He'd been happy to see the rest of the group, but had stayed quiet ever since they'd all been reunited. Even his hair, normally a wild mane sticking up in all directions, now fell lank and subdued around his face. "Seems like all been doin' since leavin' redoubt is comin' and goin'. When we get fuck out here?"

"Soon enough, Jak, that's a promise." Ryan quickly filled in everyone on the agreement he had reached with the Bunker overseers, eliciting a variety of surprised looks, with Doc even bolting to his feet in shock.

"Ryan, I thought you knew better. You cannot trust these whitecoats for a single moment! Even you said someone broke into your room and threatened Krysty and Mildred—"

Ryan raised his hands and motioned for Doc to sit back down. "Whoa, whoa, Doc, just hold on. First, no one came out and 'threatened' Krysty and Mildred.

They just warned us that people in the lab here might be after any women they found. But if that were true, then, as J.B. said earlier, they certainly wouldn't have kept him or me around—or you two, either." His gaze included Jak and Doc. "We'd all be buzzard food on the plains this very minute."

"So they plan to keep us for the Lord knows what kind of experimentation. We cannot wait for them to come and find us, cowering and helpless—"

"Doc! You aren't helping anything right now. Sit back down and listen, okay?" Pulling out a chair from the desk, Ryan sat. "They do have a task for us, and that's to bring the two sides together for a meeting with them so everyone can work out some kind of treaty."

Doc threw up his hands in helpless anger and got up to pace the room, muttering, "I would rather die than have to work alongside those steel-hearted whitecoats. They cause nothing but pain and suffering under their so-called 'science to aid humanity.' A pox on all their houses!"

Ryan stood again, jabbing a finger at the skinny, white-haired man. "Doc, if you don't shut that lip of yours, I'm going to have to shut it for you!"

"Please accept my humblest apologies, my dear Ryan, I did not mean to offend...." Doc retreated to another corner of the room and sat on the bed, his wide eyes wandering back and forth between the rest of the group and the walls themselves.

"Sorry about that. I guess we're all a bit on edge from being shut up in here. I don't like it any more than any of you, but it's the best way to get us all out of here in one piece. That's the deal I made—we get them all to the table, and our obligation is done. The sooner we blow out of here, the better. Between Carrington, Tellen and the sec boys in here, that meet's gonna be a bastard powder keg any way you look at it."

"Any chance we can get a head start before the lead starts flying?" J.B. asked.

"Doubtful. Carr'll be looking to me to make the introductions, but there's no telling what either of those crazy SOBs'll do when I present the idea in the first place. Granted, I'm not telling either one the other's going to be there, but I'm sure they'll all come packing serious hardware. All it'll take is one twitchy trigger finger, and we'll be in the middle of an all-out war."

"Yeah, and one of those a week is enough already," Krysty remarked drily. Ryan threw her a stern look, but she didn't give an inch, just thrust out her chin in defiance.

"So, we don't have anything to lose except our freedom, and mebbe what's left of Doc's sanity. And if we help out these whitecoats, they're gonna send us on our way with a wag, gas and food, and just wave goodbye as we drive off into the sunset?" J.B. snorted. "I've heard plans with a better chance of succeeding out of hardcore jolt addicts. You sure this is the way you want to play it?"

Ryan shook his head. "No, but unless you got a plan that involves defeating these mag-locks with your fingernails, and making it more than five steps down a corridor before begin gassed to the floor, I don't see any other way."

Krysty lowered her voice. "You said they were lookin' for women. We could use that to get a guard down, take his clothes and sec gear and 'escort' us to the surface."

"Yeah, except none of us know any way out of here. It'd be pretty suspicious to see a guard with no idea where he's going." Ryan jerked a thumb at the camera in the corner. "Besides, I haven't seen a room in here yet that didn't have extra eyeballs. Where you going to do this and not be seen?"

"Just a thought, lover, that's all. If this is the way you say to go, I'll back you every step."

Ryan looked at Krysty a moment, feeling that surge of love, and simply nodded. "All right, then."

Mildred's expression turned dreamy. "Man, I sure would have liked to see their medical facilities. Any place that can heal a person as fast as they did Ryan has got to have some incredible equipment." She shook her head. "Ah, well, maybe next time we pass through. I'm in."

Krysty said nothing, but simply nodded again, with Jak right behind her.

His mouth set in a thin line, J.B.'s head bobbed curtly, leaving only one. Walking over to Doc, Ryan knelt next to him. "Doc, we've all got to be in this together, you understand? I know you've got a powerful hate for the whitecoats, but just this once, let's give it a try and work with them. What do you say?"

The old man turned his rheumy, reddened eyes to Ryan. "You know that I am always your faithful man, come hell or high water, sir."

Ryan nodded. "Okay, Doc's in. Let's get this bastard thing set up and over with so we can all get the hell out of here."

Chapter Twenty-Eight

Ryan stood under the shade of a large, tan canopy, its sides open to let the hot plains wind push the sweat around on the back of his neck. He scanned the horizon and hills all around with a pair of powerful binoculars, looking for the slightest movement, anything larger than a jackrabbit, but seeing nothing.

"While I appreciate your vigilance, Mr. Cawdor, I wouldn't be too concerned with any trap either side may attempt to spring on us. I assure you, we're well prepared to handle any contingency." Administrator Carr was dressed in plain fatigues and a t-shirt under his constant white lab coat, which was slowly being speckled a light brown by the dusty wind swirling around them. Yellow-tinted aviator sunglasses protected his eyes, and he held a metal canister filled with cold water that he sipped from every few minutes.

Ryan had to admit the other man might have a good point. There were four heavily armed and armored guards, one at each corner of the canopy. More were posted at the corner of the second large canopy where the rest of his friends, including Rachel and Sergeant Caddeus, sat or stood. Behind them were three armored personnel carriers the likes of which Ryan had never seen before—squat, wide-bodied vehicles with huge tires that lifted the body at least five feet off the ground. The entire body was made of some kind of dull gray metal, with bulbous, closed pods on the top and sides that held a variety of weapons, including missiles and at least one chain gun, and no exposed windows. Waltrop had told him everyone inside saw out using cameras. Each vehicle held twenty men, half of which were arrayed in neat lines in front of each APC, the other half of which were manning stations inside the wag itself. While Ryan would have loved to get a look at the innards—J.B. even more so—he hadn't expressed a whit of interest in it, but had simply nodded.

He also knew that the Bunker had sent its wondrous drone aircraft aloft since the time and location of the meeting had been set, in order to keep tabs on the surrounding area and make sure that nothing out of the ordinary happened at the site. No doubt he also had reserves he could call on in an emergency, too, probably waiting at the base or a mile away, ready to rush in if needed. All in all, it looked like they had the place sewn up tighter than a gnat's ass just before it hit a windshield.

As for Ryan and his companions, they'd been given their weapons, but not the clothes they'd been captured in. Compared to the firepower around them, his group was toting the equivalent of slingshots, but Ryan knew just how much damage one shot in the right place could do.

Despite all the precautions, Ryan couldn't help poking the administrator a bit. "Just like your guys were able to take care of that Indian problem you had before we showed up."

Carr choked on the sip of water he had taken, and tapped his chest to ease it away. "That was fighting a guerrilla insurgency. This is gaining the upper hand through a show of formidable strength."

"Well, having been around these kinds of folks all my life, I wouldn't put too much stock into your little show here. People like Carrington and Tellen don't get to where they are by spooking easy."

"I don't wish for them to 'spook,' as you so quaintly put it, I wish for them to recognize that a superior force has entered the equation, and that they should adjust their plans accordingly. They should realize how that changes things, and be willing to come to the table to discuss how we might be all able to work toward a common goal."

It was these last words that had Ryan a bit worried. It was all well and good for Carr to want to make a place of safety in the Deathlands, he just wasn't sure how the other two would react to the idea, particularly since, if taken wrong, it could smack of "let us help you fix your problems," only to find that the "helpers" were suddenly running the show before you knew it.

And in the Deathlands, the surest way to stop this progression was to cut it off before it really got started—preferably with a lot of bullets.

Waltrop raised a hand to his headset. "Sir, we have a dust trail from due west coming toward us, fast. Drone reads heat signatures of four vehicles. Image coming onscreen now." He hit a button on the portable monitor, which flickered into life to reveal an overhead view of a four-vehicle convoy, two Hummers, one at the front and one behind two large olive-green trucks, their framed cargo areas concealed by heavy canvas tarps.

"Looks like someone else had the same idea you have," Ryan said. He still couldn't believe that both men had agreed to meet with Carr in the first place. Of course, the fact that each one didn't know the other was attending probably had something to do with it. No doubt both Carrington and Tellen each had the same idea—enlist the new group to wipe out their enemy.

Someone's gonna be very surprised when this all goes down—the only problem is, I haven no bastard idea who that's gonna be, Ryan thought, his eye glued to the screen.

"Commander Waltrop, please send out a vehicle to escort our guests into the perimeter."

The sec man spoke into his mouthpiece, and one of the APCs roared into life, accelerating away in a spurt of dust.

Once it was gone, Ryan nodded at the other tent. "Before they get here, I want to check on my friends, make sure they're doing all right in this heat."

"By all means." Carr dismissed him with a wave of his hand as he sipped water and regarded the screen. Ryan left the comparative comfort of the canopy, feeling the heat beat down on him for the few steps between the tents, and entered the shadow of the second one, smiling tightly at the group. His people feigned being relaxed very well, with Jak and J.B. sitting against different tent poles, Krysty conversing with Doc, and Mildred watching the dust cloud grow larger as it approached.

Rachel and Caddeus were another matter. Carrington's daughter, wearing a frown, had earned her very own personal sec man. Caddeus was right at her side, looking none the worse for wear, considering the injury he'd suffered three days ago.

"How's everyone doing?" Ryan asked as he walked under the protective covering.

A ragged chorus of replies greeted him, but Ryan made sure that all his people's eyes were on him when he made the brief signal that told them when the shooting started, to get out any way they could. He saw the understanding in everyone's eyes or a brief nod of assent, then went to Caddeus and Rachel, plopping down beside them and rubbing his right foot. "How are you guys holding up?"

"What the hell is going on, Cawdor? Have you and the runt over there—" she pointed at Carr with her chin "—made a deal to sell me to Tellen?"

"Fireblast, you just don't let up, do you?" Ryan shook his head. "I'm actually trying to prevent a bloodbath out here. Carr wants to meet with your father and Tellen and make them agree to a truce so they can all begin working together."

She stared at him, incredulous, then chuckled, the bitter laugh escaping through clenched teeth. "Surely you told him that would be impossible, especially after what Tellen tried on me."

Ryan leaned close to her and lowered his voice. "Actually, I never told them who you were. I assume you didn't, either."

"Hell, no. I'm not about to give them that kind of bargaining tool. But thanks for not telling them, either."

Ryan's eyebrow quirked at the unexpected gratitude, but he immediately regained his composure. "You're welcome. Would you speak for the idea? You know, try to convince your father."

"It wouldn't do any good. Carr there thinks he's so bastard smart. He has no idea just how much of a hornet's nest he's about to stir up."

Ryan nodded. "Yeah, I was afraid something like that might happen." He rubbed his foot more, wincing. "Hey, there's something you could do for me."

"What?"

Ryan pointed at the table of water bottles and covered platters of food on the other side of the tent. "Damn sprain is acting up from when I fell in that fireblasted pit. Could you get me a bottle of water? I'm parched."

She stared at him, her brows lowering, and Ryan swore he saw the wheels turning in her head as she tried to figure out his angle. But he just licked his dry lips and stared at her until she rose to her feet and stalked across the dirt floor.

"Not the smoothest move I ever saw, but it did the trick." Ryan turned to see Caddeus regarding him, the black man's face expressionless. "I bet your foot suddenly heals very nicely once we're done talking."

"Only got a few seconds, so listen up. You know what's happening here?" Ryan barely waited for the other man's nod before continuing. "You need to stick with her like stink on shit, understand? Get her out of here and back to the city in one piece."

"Already one step ahead of you." Caddeus shrugged his jumpsuit leg up to reveal the end of what looked like a pipe hidden inside, along with the smooth metal and plastic of a prosthetic leg where it went down into his boot. "Don't worry about us. We'll make it out all right."

"Okay. How's the new foot?"

Now Caddeus grinned. "Better than my old one. It's only been three days, but I'm walking on it like it was my own flesh and blood."

A shadow fell across him, and Ryan looked up to see Rachel holding out a container of water just as Carr called out to him.

"Ryan, we need you!"

"Thanks, Rachel." Ryan stood and accepted the water, pouring half of it down his throat in one long, satisfying gulp. He looked at the plastic cover she held in her other hand, then took it and screwed it on the top. He hefted the metal cylinder in his hand, feeling the liquid inside slosh back and forth, then walked back over to Carr and Waltrop under the tent.

"Looks like Tellen's the first to arrive," Carr said, still watching the overhead view from the drone. Ryan wasn't surprised at that, although he'd tried to get Carrington on-site first, figuring him for the slightly more sane of the two—he'd expected Tellen to show up as soon as he could. He watched as the convoy was brought in and stopped about a hundred yards away from the Bunker's people. The two trucks came to a halt, still in a line, and the mil wag began driving toward the tent, covering about twenty yards before the APC flanking it sprouted a half dozen weapons as missiles and machine guns appeared from the various pods on its roof and sides, all aimed at the wag, which quickly came to a stop. A door opened, and several sec men spilled out in uniform precision, taking up positions in a semicircle around the stopped off-roader.

"That certainly got his attention." A thin smile played around Carr's lips. "Waltrop, bring them to me."

A strange noise, like a sandy hiss, caught Ryan's attention as he watched the squad escort the men out of the Hummer, relieving them of weapons and patting them all down. He looked around, but nothing had changed—only a puff of dust from the rear wheel of the large APC, as if the tire had broken through a sinkhole or something. With a frown, he turned back to the group now entering the tent.

Tellen was dressed immaculately in clean, but not pressed fatigues. His blond crew cut stuck straight up, giving him the barest hint of another inch on his small frame. His men had been relieved of their weapons, but flanked him protectively, as if they were still armed. Tellen's gaze picked out Ryan first, then went to Administrator Carr, who was still watching the monitor, and finally passed over Waltrop dismissively.

"Ryan, you've done all I expected and more. Care to make the introductions?"

Ryan bared his teeth in what could loosely be called a smile. "You got the 'and more' part right." Before Tellen could ask what he meant, Ryan charged on. "This is Administrator Carr, who helps to run the Bunker, the compound located underneath the Denver Airport. He's the one who suggested this little meeting." Ryan glanced at Carr. "We're just waiting for the last person to arrive."

Carr nodded, his eyes flicking to the monitor. "He's approaching now." He finally looked up at Tellen. "An old friend of yours, I believe."

The shot was perfect. Tellen's mask of composure slipped just enough as he grabbed the monitor, causing all four guards at the corners of the canopy to turn and aim their drawn sidearms at him, regardless of the bodyguards that interposed themselves between the sec men and their leader.

Tellen was oblivious to the threat, his icy-blue eyes locked on the monitor, which showed an overhead view of another convoy heading their way, this one composed of four mil wags, each one armed with a man in a turret. Another APC came at them from the east, stopping in front of them and signaling the small procession to follow it.

When Tellen looked up again, his face was composed, and he even sketched a mocking bow toward the whitecoat. "Well played, sir. It would seem that I have underestimated you."

"Oh, I can't take all the credit. After all, it was Ryan's idea not to tell each of you that the other was coming." Carr turned to Waltrop, leaving Ryan and Tellen to exchange pointed glares. "Bring the girl and her escort to us, please."

"You wanted in, well, here's your chance," Ryan said.

"Like I said, you did all I expected and more." Tellen's smile as he pulled out a chair and sat was equally discomfiting, like he knew something no one else did. Again Ryan looked around, not seeing anything out of the ordinary. His gaze met Krysty's in the other tent, and even across the distance the question was asked.

Trouble?

His brief nod was all she needed. A nudge to J.B., and they were immediately deep in whispered conversation. Meanwhile, Ryan glanced past the diminutive would-be dictator to his mil wag, which was still being guarded by two of his men, and ten of the Bunker's security force.

A commotion from the other side accompanied Rachel and Caddeus's arrival, making the space under the canopy even more crowded. "You!" Rachel spit upon seeing Tellen, who flourished his hand at her.

"The same. Don't tell me you're also trying to work out some kind of deal here?"

"I'd rather eat glass and throw it up in your face than have anything to do with you, traitor!"

Tellen turned to the other men with an injured look. "And this is who the Free City of Denver is pinning their hopes for the future on?"

Tensing, Rachel would have gone for him right then and there, but was restrained by Caddeus's hand on her arm. Carr regarded the conversation with a slight frown.

"We'll wait for our other guests to arrive and then begin. Can I offer anyone anything, water, food?"

"A table in the presence of my enemies?" Tellen answered with a bright smile. "Some water for my men, if you can spare it."

"Of course." Carr motioned to the table. "They are free to help themselves."

The two sec men didn't move until Tellen nodded at them, then they each walked to the table and took a bottle one at a time. Ryan watched every step each one took, all the while wishing that Carrington would hurry up and get his ass over here.

He arrived a few minutes later, trailed by Major Kelor, Carrington's smile at seeing his daughter again—Ryan had managed to let him know she was safe in his radio message—collapsing when he saw his enemy seated at the table. "What the hell is he doing here?" Carrington spit, his eyes flashing. "Cawdor, what have you done—"

Carr held up his hand to forestall any further outburst. "I'm afraid the deception was necessary, Mr. Carrington, to bring both of you together in one place. But first, I imagine you'd like to make sure that your daughter in uninjured while in our care."

As Ryan frowned at the admission that Carr knew Rachel's identity, Carr motioned to Waltrop, who stood aside, letting Rachel go to her father, Caddeus following a step behind. Ryan tensed as the two met, sure that Tellen would spring any trap or surprise he might have planned at that moment. But as they came together, Tellen lounged in his chair, drinking from the water container handed to him by one of his men.

Josiah and Rachel exchanged a brief conversation, then the elder Carrington turned back to the assembled group, inserting himself between his daughter and the rest of the men. "So, you have us here. Now, what's this all about?"

Carr was about to reply when Tellen beat him to it. "While Mr.—Carr, is it?—thinks he's running the show, the *real* reason you are both here is so that I can receive your complete and total surrender to my forces."

Chapter Twenty-Nine

Tellen's calm statement certainly got everyone's attention. Carrington and Carr both stared at the small man in disbelief before they both starting talking at once, with Rachel chiming in a moment later.

"Are you serious, man? Do you not see the force that surrounds you and your men—"

"I always knew you were insane, Tellen, but this proves it—"

"You can't possibly be asking for—"

"Enough!" Tellen slammed both fists on the table, making the monitor fall over, the chorus of voices quiet, and Ryan edged his hand even closer toward the butt of his blaster. Once he had restored order, the small man leaned back in his chair. "I meant every word. As commander of the Free Army of Denver, I hereby demand your immediate and unconditional surrender, both of yourselves and all of the forces under your jurisdiction. Once the official transfer of power has occurred, we can begin assimilating the various men from the city and your complex into the already existing units. All I require is that you both make the necessary announcements to your men and women, and we'll begin making the arrangements immediately afterward."

Carr and Carrington glanced at each other, suddenly allied against their common enemy. Carr spoke first, before Carrington gave himself a stroke trying to force a conversation with his adversary. "Let's say, for the sake of argument, that you are serious—"

Tellen simply nodded.

"Look around you." Carr swept the area with his arm, taking in the looming APCs, the armed and armored men, the overwhelming numbers on his side. "Surely you don't possibly think you can force us to capitulate with just the men you've brought?"

"Yes, I do. Although you may not realize it, even at this moment you're all surrounded by my own people," Tellen replied.

Frowning, Carr shot a look at Waltrop, who muttered into his headset mike, then spoke louder a few seconds later. "Sentries report no hostiles within view."

With a nod, Carr turned back to Tellen. "If you are a madman, sir, you are a clever one, but mad nonetheless. I think we should dismiss your nonsensical talk about surrender, and perhaps discuss a more rational way forward—"

Josiah broke in. "You're wasting your breath, Carr. He's a mad dog in human guise. You'll never reason with him."

"It does take one to know one, doesn't it, Josiah?" Tellen smiled that strange smile once again. "I have spoken nothing but the truth here today, but obviously you all need more proof, therefore…"

He raised his hand into the air, drawing more attention from the corner sec men, but Tellen only shook his head. "Carr, tell your men to stand down. I'm hardly going to call a strike on the position where I'm sitting."

After a tense few moments, Carr nodded at Waltrop, who signaled his men to put up their weapons. The moment they did that, Tellen dropped his hand.

The canvas covering the backs of the two cargo

trucks dropped away, revealing the beds of both vehicles in the bright sunlight. Each cargo area was packed with what looked like people, but as Ryan squinted to see better, the horrific realization of what he was looking at became clear.

Loaded into each cage were at least two dozen stickies, maybe more, all milling around uncertainly. Each one had a familiar black band around its neck, the mysterious collars that Ryan had found on the ones he had encountered in the ruins to the south. When their eyes had adjusted to the light, the muties noticed the group of people nearby and rushed at the bars, suckered hands outstretched to attempt to grab and rend human flesh. Their sudden movement was so fierce it rocked the truck's suspension as all of them crowded onto one side, making those strange snuffling noises as they sighted fresh meat.

Ryan, along with Carr, the Carringtons and the rest of the men present stared at the sudden imbalance with mouths agape. Carr recovered first. "So you have enslaved those primitive mutants to serve as your own personal suicide troops. I can't think of anything more repellant than forcing mindless creatures to die for something they can't even understand."

Tellen glanced back, almost as an afterthought. "Every creature under the sun serves its purpose, even those creatures. When fighting a war, one must use every weapon in one's arsenal to ensure a victory."

Rachel followed, almost on his heels. "So that's what they are—just another weapon in your arsenal. And you're the person who's going to keep order in the Free City? Not once we let everyone know what we've seen here."

"Ah, but that would presume that you are going to

survive this little meeting. I expect to be hailed as the city's savior once I come back to tell them that you and your father were tragically killed by the deviant people in the Bunker, who lured you out under false pretenses to try and control you so they could take over the city themselves. Of course, if you abdicate in my favor now, there would be no need for further violence."

Waltrop stepped in front of Carr, shielding him as he spoke. "I can stop any further possibility of violence right now. Unit One, prepare to target the two cargo trucks approximately one hundred yards southwest of your position." He stared at Tellen with a frown. "If you don't want the drivers of those trucks killed in three seconds, I suggest you tell them to stand down and surrender to us immediately."

Tellen remained amazingly unperturbed. "In order to issue demands from a position of force, you must be able to back up those demands with consequences. But if you are unable to, your demands are just empty threats." With that, he pushed off the floor with his foot, tipping his chair backward.

Ryan's combat-honed senses were already shrieking, and he dived to the ground, shouting "Get down!" before clapping his hands over his ears and opening his mouth. He had a momentary glimpse of Krysty and the others doing the same before he squeezed his eye shut.

"What the hell is he—" was all Waltrop had time to say before the APC twenty yards away erupted in a thunderous explosion that launched the large machine into the air, the flaming wreckage crashing back to earth a few seconds later, a fiery pyre of destroyed tech. The sec men in front of it had literally disappeared, immolated in the blast. Ryan shielded his head as a gory rain of bloody, flaming body parts fell to earth around them, several landing on the canopied tent with wet thuds.

Ryan opened his eye to see Tellen pulling Rachel away with him toward the two trucks while his pair of bodyguards covered his retreat. Glancing back, he saw the other force under Tellen's control begin their attack. Groups of blue-painted Indians swarmed out of more tunnel openings and moving to kill the stunned or wounded Bunker guards. The pincer movement had been executed almost perfectly, with the majority of Carr's force caught between the two improvised but effective armies.

Hefting the water bottle in his left hand, Ryan hurled it at the head of Tellen's nearest sec man while drawing his blaster with his right. The metal bottle smacked into the man's forehead, making him stagger back from the dead Bunker guard's weapon he'd been reaching for. Ryan brought up his Sig Sauer and triggered it twice, sending two bullets into the chest of the second bodyguard. The man, who had been coming at him, slowed to a stop as the 9 mm slugs mangled his heart and lungs. Unable to breathe, he fell to the ground, his face slowly turning red as he drowned in his own blood. Ryan switched his aim to the second man, who was going for the other weapon again, and shot him in the head, blood and brains flying as he fell over the body of the dead guard.

Glancing at the men around him, Ryan saw both Waltrop and Kelor lying motionless a few feet away, and Carr sitting against the overturned table, breathing heavily, his face pale where it wasn't streaked with blood. Ryan crawled to him, his ears were still ringing with the incredible force of the blast.

When he reached the whitecoat, he saw why the

other man wasn't moving. Carr had been impaled by a metal shaft, most likely from the APC's engine, that had punched straight through his abdomen, pinning him to the table. Each breath was labored, but he motioned Ryan closer. Straining to hear, Ryan pressed his ear to the small man's lips.

"Don't…let…Tellen…win…" Carr's head lolled, his eyes glazing into the sightlessness of death.

"Fireblast!" Ryan swore, just as Josiah Carrington sat upright from beneath a pile of papers, spitting dirt and blood out of his mouth.

"Rachel!" He clapped his hands to his ears and hunched over as the aftereffects of the blast hit him, his fingers coming away bloody. Spotting Ryan, he shouted, "Where's Rachel?"

"Tellen's got her!" Ryan pointed at the two trucks where two figures struggled while the caged stickies watched.

"No!" Josiah pulled himself to his feet, leaning against the overturned table, grimacing in pain. Despite that, he staggered forward, apparently intent on attacking Tellen with his bare hands.

"Damn it, stop!" Ryan lunged for the other man, his fingers just grazing his leg as the leader of Denver stumbled out into the harsh sunlight. Torn between going after the man and getting to his friends so they could all get the hell out of there, Ryan glanced back to see the rest of his people fighting off a wave of blue Indians that had appeared out of the smoke. Looking back the other way, he saw Carrington, his mouth open and screaming incoherently, staggering toward Tellen. The rebel leader ignored him, his attention fixed on Rachel, or more specifically, her hands, as he struggled to fasten something around them. She was resisting as best as she could, her balled fists trying to connect with his head, but he hauled off and slapped her across the face with a roundhouse open hand. Rachel sagged against the truck for a moment, stunned.

"Oh, shit." As if he was going to unleash it himself, Ryan knew what was coming next. And all he could do was watch.

The collar fastened, Tellen shouted a command, and the back door of the cages of both trucks swung open.

The stickies saw the open door. They paused for a moment, as if enjoying the appearance of their freedom from captivity.

Then, in a massive, slobbering, hooting mass, they surged for the exit, spilling to the ground and coming right at the lone man in their path—Josiah Carrington.

Chapter Thirty

From the moment her gaze locked with Ryan's, Krysty felt that small, cold ball of dread at the base of her neck grow to envelop her entire mind with the dull, red throb of approaching trouble—a lot of trouble.

Krysty's latent doomie power had warned her early that morning, the dull throb just behind her temples foreshadowing a stronger indication of danger to come. When Tellen's men had appeared at the meeting location, her feeling of impending destruction had spiked, but she hadn't needed any psychic powers to understand that the most dangerous man in sight had just arrived.

So, when Ryan had caught her eye and given that silent warning, the first thing she had done was whisper, "J.B."

"What's going on?" He was squinting at the other tent, but apparently hadn't made out Ryan's warning.

"Trouble coming. Ryan wants everyone to be ready to move." Krysty shaded her eyes with one hand as she watched another small group crowd into the tent, the press of people making it hard to discern exactly what was happening. "Looks like Carrington's arrived. This isn't going to go well."

"Old man got crazy eyes." Jak's voice surprised Krysty. He'd spent the morning slumped against one of the tent poles, not looking any better, despite the change in surroundings. "Hate all this—get fuck out here soonest."

"Our snow-headed friend's suggestion is looking more and more appealing the longer we sit here while dark men plan dark deeds," Doc said, casting suspicious glances at the armored men stationed nearby in their helmets and longblasters. "I'm inclined to believe that no good will come of our strange host's misguided intentions, no matter how noble they may be."

"Yeah, Doc's right-on about that one," Mildred said, straightening so that she could try to see what was going on at the other tent just as a loud bang came from under the canopy, making the guards start and glance over in case they were needed. "What the hell is going on over there? Everyone seems to be talking at once."

"Best think about how we get out once the shit starts raining down." J.B. patted his waist for his knife.

Krysty leaned close to J.B. "What's the plan?"

"Depends on the direction trouble comes from first. We need to break through the perimeter, steal a vehicle. The big ones—" he jabbed a thumb at the massive APCs that loomed nearby "—are far too dangerous. Too many sec men inside. Best to try and hook up with Carrington's forces, if possible, but we don't know if they'll even recognize us."

"So it'd probably be best to have Carrington or Rachel with us when we left." Krysty mused. "How the hell are we going to do that?"

"Got me—" J.B. began before he was cut off by a shout from Ryan that spurred everyone to action.

"Get down!"

Immediately, everyone under the tent flattened themselves to the floor, shielding their faces and ears. A moment later, a gigantic blast muted the world, followed by a concussive shock wave that blew the tent away and sent the guards flying.

Krysty opened her eyes to find the world aflame. Both APCs that had been parked nearby had been destroyed, the once-deadly vehicles now hulks of burning wreckage spewing thick, black plumes of smoke. Her head felt like it was stuffed with cotton, and what should have been a cacophony of noises around her all sounded like they were very far away. She pushed herself up to her knees, then to her feet, swaying a bit, but managing to draw her blaster. Feeling a hand on her arm, she pulled away, her blaster hand poised to slam the Smith & Wesson's butt into her attacker's face, but arrested the blow when she saw J.B.'s face.

"We've got to evac! That ammo could cook off any second! Get Doc and Jak up and moving!" he called as he moved off into the haze again.

Mildred was already standing, grimacing either at the pain stabbing through her head or the sudden destruction around her. She looked up at Krysty, her expression turning to one of horror as she raised her Czech-made target pistol. "Duck!"

Krysty obeyed without thought, whirling as she did to see a figure charging straight at her. Naked except for a breechclout, the man's face was painted a dark blue. His wide, white eyes and black hole of a mouth as he screamed while holding a thick war club over his head made him a vision out of a nightmare. Before he could come any closer, Krysty heard a dull clap, and the man fell on his face and skidded to a stop a few feet away, the back of his head blown out by Mildred's single bullet.

Krysty didn't pause to thank her—she was already aiming at the next blue-painted warrior rushing out of the smoke near the burning APCs. Steadying her right hand with her left, she aimed and took three down in quick succession. Mildred had stepped up beside her, and for a few moments, the two women were the calm eye of the storm, taking out anyone wearing a hint of blue that came near. However, another wave of warriors was gathering. Their war cries could be heard through the black haze obscuring the landscape, and as Krysty and Mildred reloaded, they glanced at each other, then around, looking for the rest of their friends.

"Come on, this way!" J.B. appeared again behind them, toting one of the Bunker weapons, a strange-looking blaster with two thick, hexagonal tubes mounted above the barrel. Jak and Doc were with him, Doc holding his smoking LeMat in one hand and his bloody rapier blade in the other. Jak flanked him, his .357 Magnum Cold Python in one hand, and the old man's sword scabbard in the other.

"What's that do?" Mildred asked.

"Not sure, but we're about to find out. Let's go." J.B. led them away from the burning wags, out toward the plains.

"What about Ryan?"

"If we see him and can get to him, great, otherwise we get some wheels, then try and find him. Everyone ready? Let's go."

With J.B. in the lead, they had taken only a few steps before another wave of blue warriors swarmed them from the smoke. Bracing his new weapon against his hip, J.B. pulled the trigger, playing the muzzle across the nearest group of five attackers. The device sprayed a thick stream of bright red, gelatinous goo across their bodies, making them howl in pain and begin trying to wipe off the thick sludge. One of the men took a shot directly in the face and fell to the ground, screaming not in rage but agony as he clawed at his irritated skin with both hands.

"Fuck, not point at me!" Jak skittered away, aiming his Colt Python at another charging warrior and squeezing the trigger. The bullet shattered the man's forearm and sent him to the ground, clutching ruined, bloody flesh in his good hand.

"Guys! Trouble behind us!" Mildred called out, making heads turn. Krysty's mouth fell open when she saw what was coming their way.

A shambling horde of at least two dozen stickies were running their way, attacking anyone they found. Those Bunker guards able to function after the blast from the APCs had just formed a ragged line when the muties tore through them. Although several got shots off from their strange-looking weapons that seemed to fire quiet bursts of bullets, the stickies' flesh absorbed the rounds without seeming to injure them too much, enabling them to wreak terrible havoc. One man was grabbed by two of the creatures and literally had his arms pulled off, screaming in agony until his limbs separated from his body and he passed out from shock. Others were set upon by the crazed beings, which peeled strips of skin off limbs and faces with their suckers, hooting and snuffling gleefully as they sprayed blood and flesh everywhere.

"Reload, reload, reload!" J.B. called, looking around for another weapon, any weapon that would do more permanent damage to the oncoming horde. Spotting a holstered blaster on a belt slung over the shoulder of the warrior Jak had shot, J.B. kicked him in the face, knocking him unconscious, and yanked the belt off. Grabbing the weapon, an ancient, dusty Beretta 92S, he pulled back the slide and threw the belt with its two additional magazines over his shoulder.

"They're coming!" Mildred yelled, bracing her left hand with her right and taking aim.

"More blueskins comin'!" Jak shouted, his chromed Python winking in the sunlight.

"J.B., we can't stay here! They'll tear us apart!" Krysty said.

"Know that already, thanks." The Armorer glanced around, his eyebrows lifting in surprise. "Why hasn't that APC moved yet?"

Krysty followed his gaze to see the last Bunker wag standing by itself on the far end. Her eyes met the other man's, and they both had the same idea.

"Everybody run for the APC! Lead the stickies into the Indians!" Krysty said, snapping off two shots at the nearest muties only a few yards away. With Jak in the lead, the group ran straight at the nearest cluster of blue warriors, who were just starting their own charge into the melee. The two groups clashed on a flat plain, the five friends against a half dozen frenzied, screaming warriors.

With the group's deadly skills all together, it was no contest.

Jak drew first blood the moment he saw the point warrior emerge from the pall of smoke. Taking three long steps, he launched himself into the air, leading with his booted foot, now turned into a deadly projectile. The running Native American smashed his face into the sole, crushing his nose and snapping his head back with such force his neck vertebrae snapped, killing him before the pain of his pulverized face could register in his brain. Jak sailed over the still-twitching corpse and kept going, Magnum blaster in one hand, Doc's cane sheath in the other.

Krysty and Mildred kept it simple, their blasters out and aiming at anyone who came too close. Well-placed shots took out two more warriors, although one got close enough to almost touch her with his war club, made from a converted wooden longblaster stock. She sidestepped the weak blow and kicked his legs out from under him, then ended his struggles with a bullet to the head.

Doc also faced two adversaries, but the old scholar was also well prepared to receive his enemies. Thumbing back the hammer on his LeMat, he let fly with the shotgun barrel of the blaster, the heavy lead balls smashing into one blue face, pulping his mouth and jaw and leaving a bloody hole filled with shattered teeth and a mangled tongue. The wounded man clapped both hands over his face and fell to his knees, making thick, unintelligible noises from his ruined face.

The second fighter, wielding a rusty cavalry saber in both hands, didn't pause, but lunged forward, the blade raised high above his head to split Doc's skull in two. The old man didn't flinch or hesitate, but threw up his blaster arm to block the warrior's attack while thrusting his own rapier into the man's stomach. The fierce expression on his adversary's face turned to a grimace of anguish as the steel ran him through, the point scraping off a rib to emerge from his back in a burst of blood. Doc pushed him away, withdrawing his blade and giving his mortally wounded enemy a quick salute with the blade in front of his face.

"Doc, quit fuckin' around and run!" J.B. called from the other side of the fight. He'd risked a precious second to check that the others were still with him, and also find out how close the stickies were, and had nearly lost his head as a result. Feeling a sudden wind on his left, he'd ducked just as a massive war club had swung through the space where his head had been a moment before.

J.B. turned back to see a mountain of a man, easily close to seven feet tall and at least 350 pounds, looming over him. He aimed the Beretta and pulled the trigger, only to have the blaster jam with a click. The huge warrior laughed at the sight, until J.B. hurled the weapon at his face. The projectile smashed into his mouth, crushing his lips, and making the man spit out blood and a rotten tooth before lumbering toward him. J.B. danced around him, trying to put him between himself and the approaching muties. The giant seemed unconcerned about anyone else, but concentrated solely on the Armorer, raising his club to brain the smaller man. The moment he brought it down, J.B. moved.

Not away from the man-mountain, but toward him. Stepping inside his reach, J.B. got close enough to smell his rotten breath as he darted around the man, his knife seeking a vital spot he could reach with relative ease—the giant's right hamstring. He sliced through both tendons on his way out, and ducked as a ham-size fist tried to grab him, the massive warrior being faster than he appeared to be. The turn made his wounded leg buckle, however, and he crashed to the ground, shouting in pain and surprise. Grabbing his bleeding joint, the warrior looked up to see three stickies staring down at him, lipless mouths opening and closing in their hairless faces, their protuberant, staring eyes evincing no reaction at the man lying before them. Bending over, they all went to work on him.

For J.B., the screams would echo in his dreams for

days afterward. At the moment, however, he wasn't concentrating on anything but reaching the APC. Most of the group had already made it to the protection of the vehicle's roof, with Doc being hoisted up by Krysty and Mildred while Jak kept a lookout for approaching stickies or blue-painted warriors.

Loud hoots from nearby let J.B. know he had been spotted, and he put on a burst of speed. The sounds of carnage were all around him as the stickies found the remaining warriors and attacked them with the same glee as they did any other living creature.

Hearing footsteps slapping the ground behind him, he pushed himself to the limit to reach the APC, making a final desperate leap to grab Krysty's and Mildred's outstretched hands. As they began to pull him up, a heavy weight grabbed his legs, pulling him back down.

"J.B., get rid of him. He's gonna pull you down!"

"Want to tell me how I should do that!" he barked.

Doc's snow-capped head appeared over the side of the APC, his LeMat in hand. "Fear not, John Barrymore, I will remove this ruffian from your person."

"Doc, you better have the goddamn right barrel selected!"

"Of course, my good man." Doc checked the blaster and twisted the barrel slightly before sighting down at him. "Just hold still."

"A little lower—just a little lower!" J.B. shouted, seeing the muzzle come dangerously close to his chest. Doc adjusted his aim one more time before pulling the trigger. A puff of smoke and flash of flame later, the weight fell away from J.B.'s legs, and the two women pulled him up.

"Great, we made it. Now how to we get inside?"

Mildred asked, wiping her sweaty brow with the back of her hand.

"What, isn't there a top hatch up here?"

Krysty pointed to a yard-square piece of dark metal with a seam running all around it. "Yeah, we think so, but it's locked from the inside."

J.B. knelt to take a look at it. "I didn't get up here just to fry in the sun or become some stickie's skin toy." He quickly located a small, armored panel, which slid aside at his touch, revealing a numeric keypad. "Jak, knife."

"Don't break tip like you did before." The albino teen handed over one of his slim throwing blades, which J.B. used to pry up the pad, exposing green circuit boards. Identifying which one controlled the power, he sat back on his heels and tried to figure out how to run a bypass without wire when the panel slid open, nearly throwing Doc over the side.

"Hey, you did it!" Krysty said.

"Not me." J.B. bent over to look inside and was greeted by the barrel of a short machine pistol shoved into his face.

"You got three seconds to explain yourselves, or you're worm food," the armored, helmeted sec man wielding the gun ordered.

Chapter Thirty-One

Ryan burst into action as the wave of stickies swarmed toward him and Josiah Carrington. Even as he leaped forward in what would surely be a vain attempt to save the old man, even as he brought up his Sig Sauer and aimed at the nearest one, a part of him wondered what the hell was making him try to save Josiah. Had he really bought into the man's vision of a true free city in the Deathlands, or was it simply that no one deserved to die like that?

Later, he'd realize that he'd never gotten an answer to his question, for as he charged in front of the old man, tracking and shooting stickies with head shots as fast as he could pull the trigger, there wasn't any time to consider what had brought him there. The dead muties made a small hole in the shambling horde, with several breaking off to find easier prey, but a large group kept advancing on them, heedless of the others dying under the accurate aim of the one-eyed man.

Five stickies fell to the ground, bleeding from punctured eye sockets or holed skulls, but the rest kept coming. Ryan tried to shove Josiah behind him, keeping himself between the man and the greedy horde only a few feet away now. He shot until his pistol's slide locked open, then reached for another magazine while elbowing the elder Carrington back, hoping he would take the hint and retreat, but knowing this was probably his last stand.

"Cawdor, get down!"

Ryan pushed backward with all his might, landing on Josiah and sending him to the ground. He covered the other man with his body as a blast of flame jetted over him, splashing onto the lead stickie and instantly setting him on fire. The tongue of flame licked farther out, enveloping the rest of the group in a sticky, liquid inferno. Ryan was too busy trying to roll Josiah out from underneath the jet of flame, otherwise he would have taken a moment to enjoy the immolation erupting all around him.

The knot of muties flew apart, each one capering and dancing madly even as they cooked under the jellied napalm. Some, true to their nature of being enraptured by large fires, watched the others burn even as they were consumed themselves, staring until the flames crisped their eyeballs and seared their lungs. Others tried to put out the persistent inferno consuming them, slapping at the dancing heat with their suckered hands, but to no avail. Slowly, each one fell over, thrashing and twisting on the ground in their death throes, but eventually each blackened form stopped moving, leaving the remaining flames to lick at the charred bodies.

Ryan looked back to see Sergeant Caddeus running toward them, holding a strange device that looked like two small propane gas tanks mounted above a handle, tubes and a flaming nozzle. Holding the device against his hip, ready to shoot in case any of the stickies moved again, he reached a hand down.

"Just in time," Ryan said as he grabbed it and was pulled up by the other man.

"Well, I had to repay you for helping me in that

hellhole under the plains." Caddeus bent down and helped Josiah to his feet, as well. "Where's Rachel?"

A scream from one of the trucks made all three of their heads turn. Tellen was behind the wheel of the wag, which belched black smoke as it lurched into motion.

"You've got to be shitting me," Ryan groaned as he watched the wag begin to drive away.

Josiah was near panic as he watched the wag begin to disappear into the distance. "What are you talking about? My daughter is in there. We have to go after him!"

"I've got to see if my people are safe first." Ryan turned, scanning the killing field, his hands already busy reloading his blaster. Small clusters of stickies were busy savaging Indians and Bunker sec men alike, while here and there pockets of resistance attempted to fend off the brutal mutie onslaught. In the distance, Ryan saw a motionless APC, and atop the roof was a figure topped by a shock of long, bright red hair that he knew so well, next to a rail of a boy with stark white hair. As he watched, another figure with dark skin and beaded plaits clambered up beside her, then a skinny man in a frock coat.

"Come on, J.B., come on." Ryan waited another moment, ignoring Josiah's pleas for help, until he saw the last member of his group climb up after Doc had apparently shot something near him.

"Let's go." Turning back to them, he legged it over to the second wag, which was being started by the panicking driver. The six-wheeled vehicle's engine had just roared into life when Ryan, accelerating into a run, leaped onto the running board, grabbing the large side mirror and pointing his blaster at the driver's head, just behind the ear. "Park it and get out."

Holding up one hand, the man did so, then tried to push Ryan off the truck by shoving the door open with him still hanging on. However, he'd failed to account of Sergeant Caddeus, who was waiting on the ground next to the wag, and jumped up to grab the driver, who had gone for a blaster hidden near his seat. A lightning-fast palm strike to the face, and Caddeus hauled the unconscious, bloody-nosed driver out of the seat and dumped him unceremoniously to the dirt. Slipping behind the wheel, he pulled the door closed, letting Ryan get his footing back on the truck. "You in or out?"

Beyond the black man, Ryan saw Josiah climb into the passenger seat, wheezing as he did so. "Just go. I'll be in the back." He grabbed one of the metal struts that had held the canvas up and swung into the cargo bed of the wag as it shot off after Tellen.

The wag swayed and bounced over the washboard plains, and Ryan was hard-pressed to keep his balance as they pursued the other vehicle. Caddeus handled the wheel deftly, avoiding the worst of the wind and flash-flood-carved ruts, and soon they were catching up to Tellen. Ryan saw a head appear out of the passenger-side window, and snapped off a shot at him, even though he knew he had almost no hope of hitting the guy at this range.

"Closer!" he shouted. Caddeus answered by coaxing a burst of speed out of the old wag, making it shudder as it narrowed the gap even further.

"What the hell are you doing?" Caddeus shouted over the roaring engine.

"Pull alongside him!" Ryan moved to the other side of the wag, one foot on the metal side of the cargo bed as Caddeus slowly drew abreast of the other truck. Tellen suddenly swung his vehicle hard left, smashing into the fender of Ryan's wag, and making it slew over, almost pitching him out.

"Son of a bitch!" Aiming his Sig Sauer at the nearest tire, he shot at it until it exploded in a spray of rubber fragments. The wag slowed a bit, but kept plowing forward, demolishing scrub bushes and anything else in its way.

"Fireblast, Caddeus, get me near that flatbed!" Ryan shouted as he shot out a second tire on the other truck. He looked up just in time to see the head pop up from the passenger window, this time carrying a stubby machine gun.

"Fuck!" Bringing up his own blaster, Ryan shot three times as the masked man leveled his weapon and sprayed a short burst across the truck. Ryan ducked for cover as bullets sparked off the fender and cab, starring the rear windshield glass.

The vehicle under him surged forward again, coming almost even with the front of the other wag. Ryan gauged the distance and leaped across, landing on his hands and knees in the cargo bed and rolling to the far side, jolting to a stop with a breath-stealing slam against the metal side. He'd kept his blaster pointed more or less up, and now turned to find himself staring down the barrel of the sec man's weapon as he pointed it at his head. Ryan tensed for the bullets to tear into him, only to roll back across the cargo bed as the wag lurched violently from Caddeus ramming his truck into the other one.

The man's burst went wild, and Ryan recovered first, rolling to his knees and aiming at the sec man's head. He squeezed the trigger just as the man ducked back into the cab, the bullet clipping his scalp, but doing no serious damage.

Ryan peered through the rear window of the truck, seeing the shooter spot him at the exact same time. He hit the floor as the sec man let loose with another 3-round burst, shattering the window and raining hundreds of tiny glass pellets on the one-eyed man. Brushing them off his face, he looked up just in time to see the subgun poke out of the window, aimed in his general direction.

Ryan grabbed the blaster and pulled hard, trying to wrest it from the sec man's grasp. Instead, he found the man's body coming through the window, so unwilling was he to let go of it. Reflexively squeezing the trigger, the man emptied the submachine gun's magazine, the bullets flying into the air, some punching through the cargo bed of the other wag, which was still trying to disable Tellen's truck by ramming the hell of out the left side fender.

For a moment, the shooter was stuck half in and half out of the cab, then gravity took over, and he fell on top of Ryan as he was trying to bring his blaster to bear. The Sig Sauer and Ryan's hand ended up pinned between the two of them, putting him at a severe disadvantage as the man used both hands to twist his weapon out of Ryan's grip, and then tried to brain him with its butt. He got a solid blow in to the side of the Deathlands warrior's head, making him see nothing but red and black for a moment. Levering his free hand between himself and his opponent, Ryan shoved as hard as he could, rolling over, pushing the guy away.

His vision clearing, Ryan rolled to his knees and brought up his Sig Sauer, only to feel a numbing blow on his wrist, making his fingers pop open and the blaster clatter to the metal floor. Tellen chose that moment to narrowly miss a hillock, the truck's left side jouncing high in the air before crashing back down to earth. The unexpected collision sent both men crashing to the patterned steel again, sliding toward the driver's side of the cargo bed.

Ryan recovered faster this time and grabbed the man's wrist as he swung the subgun toward his head, digging his thumb into the nerve cluster an inch from his hand to try to make him drop the weapon. The masked man grabbed Ryan's wrist with his other hand, trying to dislodge it, but Ryan gritted his teeth and held on even tighter, digging his fingernails into the man's skin and making him growl in pain. His empty blaster hand still numb from the hit it had taken, Ryan put it to work by punching the guy in the face with short, sharp blows. The combination of assaults made the man throw up the hand that had been gripping his adversary's arm to block his fist, while attempting to escape the wrist hold by twisting out of it. Ryan stayed with him, however, pressing into the tendons of the man's forearm until his fingers opened and the blaster fell to the truck bed.

The wag swerved again as Tellen sent it crashing into Caddeus's ride. This time the front fenders locked together, making a horrific screech as metal grated against metal, each truck's frame shuddering as it tried to overpower the other one. With a scream of a tortured engine and the shriek of an overstressed fender, the two wags peeled apart again, each running more slowly now, white smoke puffing from both engines.

The collision had forced both men apart, and Ryan rolled to his feet, turning to face his adversary who had drawn a thick-bladed combat knife with a serrated blade, ready to slash or stab in an instant.

Ryan reached down to his hip for his heavy panga, only to realize too late that it wasn't there. It must have fallen in the fight. But that wouldn't necessarily be an issue, unless the man knew how to handle his knife. As he approached, he wove a blurred pattern in the air, the black steel weaving crazily around in distracting, erratic movements. Ryan brought himself up short—this might have just become a problem. Spreading his legs apart a bit, balanced on the balls of his feet against the rocking of the wag underneath him, he kept his arms close to his body and waited for the man to make his move.

The masked man, one eye now swelling shut from the beating to his face, shuffled his feet as he approached, then feinted high with the knife before coming in with a downward stab aimed at Ryan's chest. Gauging the moment, the one-eyed grabbed the man's wrist again, pulling him forward and off balance with all of his strength, whipping him around in a half circle before just as suddenly letting him go. Already committed to his attack and still moving from the redirected inertia of Ryan's throw, the man staggered to the edge of the cargo bed, his lower legs hitting the side, and flailed to regain his balance. Unfortunately, Tellen chose just that moment to jog his wag to the right, and the man fell over the side—just as Caddeus wheeled his own truck over to smash into the other vehicle again.

Caught between the two wags, the man had enough time for one agonizing scream that was choked off almost immediately. The two trucks ground his chest into crushed bones and flesh before separating, his corpse falling to the ground, the large wheels pulping his limbs and head and leaving a mangled, unrecognizable corpse on the dusty ground.

Casting around for his blaster, Ryan saw it in a far corner of the cargo bed and crawled over to retrieve it. Gripping it in his hand, he rolled to the back of the cab just as Caddeus rammed his wheezing wag into Tellen's again, the jarring impact almost tipping the 6x6 up onto its right wheels for a second. Ryan slid down toward the right front corner of the cargo box, landing in the corner with a grunt. The wag crashed back to earth, and he saw Caddeus's truck fall behind, the white smoke billowing from its engine turning a dark gray.

Grasping the edge of the window frame with his free hand, Ryan popped up and jammed his blaster into Tellen's neck. "Stop the wag now!"

Out of the corner of his eye he saw Rachel in the passenger seat, her hands tied behind her back, her lower lip split and bleeding, and one eye beginning to swell into a dark shiner. At the same instant, he noticed the rebel leader had an angry, inflamed set of scratch marks running down the side of his face. Apparently she'd given as good as she got.

Tellen hunched over and jammed the accelerator to the floor, goosing a burst of speed out of the ancient machine. "Or what? You shoot me, this thing'll most likely flip, and then it's goodbye Rachel, you and me!"

"Just shoot the fucker!" Rachel shouted.

"Shut up!" Ryan and Tellen both shouted at the same time.

The rebel leader glanced back at him, the corner of his mouth quirking up in a grim smile. "If I had my way, I'd let both of you off right now—just to get this insane, irritating bitch out of my hair—and keep on drivin', but I don't think Daddy Carrington is gonna let this slide. So what do we do, Cawdor?"

"I don't give a flying fuck what Carrington wants. Now way would I let a rabid dog like you go free after what you did back there!" Ryan pressed the muzzle of his blaster into Tellen's neck even harder. "Stop the wag right now, or you'll be chilled no matter what!"

"No can do! Keeping this fucker moving is the only thing keeping me alive! I stop now, you put a bullet between my eyes. No thanks!"

"Fireblast, you just don't know when to quit!" Ryan moved his blaster three inches to the left, aiming at the instrument panel to try to disable the wag. The moment the blaster was withdrawn from Tellen's neck, he grabbed Ryan's wrist and yanked down hard, trying to dislocate the other man's elbow by smashing it into the windowsill. Ryan was forced to slide farther into the cab to keep his grip on the Sig Sauer. His finger tightened on the trigger, and a 9 mm round starred the windshield, sending spiderweb cracks all through it as the safety glass shattered, but didn't break apart.

"Fuck! Now I can't see where we're going!" Tellen made no move to stop the wag or try to break out the glass, but kept driving, pushing the truck for all it was worth.

Rachel leaned down over Ryan as he struggled to regain control of his blaster. "Would you just kill him already!"

"Make yourself useful and break the bastard windshield!" Ryan grunted. When wrenching his blaster arm free failed, he grabbed Tellen by the throat with his free hand and pulled his head backward. The wag swerved back and forth wildly as Tellen tried to maintain speed while fending Ryan off. Although the one-eyed man was taller and should have been stronger, the smaller man fought like a man possessed, his wiry body seeming to hold limitless reserves of stamina.

"Watch where you point that!" Rachel howled as the blaster's muzzle drifted close to her head before Ryan turned it back in Tellen's direction. She had managed to get her feet above the dashboard, and was pounding on the safety glass with her boots, which wasn't doing much to dislodge the windshield.

"Now tell me—you didn't do that—on purpose," Tellen said as he tried to keep Ryan from pointing the blaster back at his head again.

"Fuck you!" Ryan snarled, just as he had the strangest feeling of weightlessness for a moment before crashing back to the seat as the wag slammed into the ground, bottoming out the suspension and making everyone hit the ceiling as they bounced around the cab. Ryan ended up upside down between Rachel and Tellen, his head wedged between the curved lump of the floor above the drive train and his shoulder on the seat. Somehow, Tellen still held on to his blaster arm, and was trying to strip the Sig Sauer from his fingers.

Ryan saw red. Swinging back his booted foot, he clobbered Tellen in the side of the face, then did it a second and third time, the last blow actually making the other man's head ricochet off the frame of the cab. Stunned, Tellen slumped over the wheel just as Rachel gave the starred windshield one last good kick, popping out the entire piece and sending it tumbling off to the side. "Oh, shit! Ryan, get up here!"

Ryan managed to hook his fingers around the top of the seat back and pulled himself up to look out the window, the wind streaming in making his eye water. "What the hell are you— Son of a bitch!"

The truck was headed straight for the edge of a deep canyon, now only about a hundred yards away. "Time to go!" Shoving his blaster into his waistband, Ryan picked Rachel up by the waist and shoved her out the back window into the cargo bed.

"Hey, wait a minute... My hands! Ow!" Rachel shouted as she fell out of the cab.

Ryan was right behind her. "Go! Go! Go!" He tried to follow, but was held up by something snagging the collar of his jumpsuit. He looked back to see Tellen's bloodied face staring at him, his hand grasping Ryan's collar.

"You weren't thinking of leaving just yet, were you?"

Ryan grabbed his hand and bent the fingers back, breaking two of them along with his grip. "Watch me!" Releasing Tellen, he ran for the back of the cargo bed, grabbing Rachel's arm and pulling her with him. "Jump!"

They both stepped up onto the tailgate and leaped off, landing hard in the dirt. Ryan released her upon impact and rolled, coming up just in time to see the wag disappear over the canyon edge, clattering down the side in an avalanche of crumpling, crushed metal and a roaring engine, and ending with a thunderous crash at the bottom.

Exhausted, filthy and aching all over, Ryan walked slowly to the canyon edge and peered over. At least a hundred feet down, he saw the wreckage of the wag, mangled almost beyond recognition. The cab had been crushed to less than half its former size, and he saw no sign of Tellen, although a trickle of blood dripped steadily from a twisted corner of the passenger compartment.

"He dead?" Rachel had come up beside him, just as dusty and tired, looking over as well.

"Don't know many people who can walk away from that kind of wreck. I'm pretty sure Tellen isn't one of them."

She spit into the canyon. "Good fuckin' riddance. Now how about you cut me loose?"

Ryan turned and eyed her, a smile curving the corner of his mouth. "Don't know about that. You might be easier to handle like this."

"Oh, fuck you, Cawdor..." With an effort, Rachel reined herself in. "Look, thank you for saving my life—again—but please, untie me, cut me loose, whatever. I think my fingers are going numb."

"All right, hold still." Ryan examined her bonds, which consisted of a sturdy strip of plastic encircling both wrists, with one end going through a one-way fastener. "Have to find a rock or something. Don't have a blade on me."

Rachel stared at him in disbelief, her eyes wide. "You're kidding, right? Tell me you're kidding."

"Nope. We better start walking. We should catch up to Caddeus and your father in a mile or two." With that, Ryan took the first step of the long walk back to his friends, doing his best to shut out the constant stream of profanity spouting from Rachel's mouth, aimed at him, the situation and the world at large—but mostly at him.

Chapter Thirty-Two

"Are you sure there isn't anything else we can do for you?" Josiah Carrington asked as Ryan swung into the driver's seat of the mil wag. "Anything at all?"

Ryan thought about replying, but Doc beat him to it. "By the three Kennedys, good sir, you and your people have already done more for all of us than we have seen since I don't know when." The old man swept his arm out in a low bow. "Unfortunately, we must be on our way. However, we look forward to revisiting your fair city the next time we come through this area."

"Place'll look a damn sight better then, as well, I can tell you that." Over the past few days, Ryan and his group has rested and recovered at the Free City of Denver, with just about anything they desired at their beck and call. Josiah had also regained much of his strength and color during this time, and now extended a hand to Ryan, who gripped it back, both men shaking strongly. "We owe you damn near anything we can think of. With the Bunker on our side, I don't think there'll be any limit to what we can accomplish in the years to come."

Despite the inauspiciousness of their first meeting, Josiah and the rest of the Bunker's leaders had quickly come together in fast friendship. It had helped that J.B., Krysty and the others had smoothed the way by assisting in clearing what was left of the stickie and Indian assault once and for all with the massive APC's weapons. They had spent another day removing the remnants of Tellen's army in Boulder, which had already begun disintegrating once news of their leader's death had reached them. Even now the Armorer would occasionally look wistfully off to the east, mumbling under his breath about TOW missiles, or pressurized napalm flamethrowers or something even more esoteric and deadly. Watching him, Mildred would just roll her eyes and smile.

Ryan nodded. "A man I once knew—good friend of mine—said something about new ventures back when I ran with him—take it slow and steady, and you'll come out just fine on the other side."

"Sounds like a wise man," Carrington replied.

"Yeah." Ryan fired up the engine, Krysty sitting beside him, with Doc climbing into the backseat, still shaking hands with several of the townsfolk. The rear storage compartment was filled with supplies—food, tools, ammo. The second mil wag held J.B. at the wheel, Mildred beside him, and Jak manning the turret-mounted .30-caliber machine gun, with more supplies packed in and around them. The small caravan was ready to roll.

Rachel had also come out to see them off, with Caddeus right next to her—almost too close, Ryan thought. He stared at the pair, his eye widening in surprise as he saw their hands disengage from each other as they approached. He opened his mouth to say something, then closed it as he saw Caddeus shake his head almost imperceptibly. Ryan shook his head in amazement, grinning as he arched an eyebrow mouthed "good luck," and receiving a dazzling smile from the black man in return.

Even Rachel seemed to have calmed down since their adventure on the Colorado plains. She walked more sedately, and also extended a hand to Ryan. "Thank you, Ryan—for everything."

He nodded at her. "You're welcome. Like Doc said, next time we're in the area, we'll be sure to stop by."

"Our doors will always be open to you." Josiah stepped back from the vehicles and signaled the men manning the main gates to open them. Ryan put the Hummer in gear and drove out under the warm summer sun, enjoying the wind in his hair.

"By Gaia, I'll miss those clean sheets the most." Krysty had turned in her seat to watch the ville fade into the distance as they traveled north. "So, where to, lover? Back to the redoubt?"

"Not just yet." With a grin, Ryan pressed the accelerator down, letting the wag power down the cracked asphalt road, checking to make sure J.B. was following at an appropriate distance. "It'd be a shame to waste such a good day. Let's just head down this road a few miles, and see what comes."

With that, he revved the engine, and they took off down the highway.

Epilogue

Tellen limped into the shattered remains of his headquarters in Boulder, surveying the damage to what had once been an orderly command center for his army. Papers were scattered everywhere, furniture destroyed, the windows broken. Shoulders slumping, he sighed, the movement sending a flare of pain through the cracked ribs in his chest. His right arm was wrapped in a crude sling, and his brow was dappled in sweat, heralding the onset of a fever from an infection of some kind.

After waking up in the destroyed wag, curled up in a ball in the reduced passenger compartment, it had taken him half a day to extricate himself and another four days to get back to his base, living on whatever he could find and eat—mice, groundhogs, insects—and sucking the early-morning dew off the prairie grass. He'd wanted to lie down and die more during his journey back, but a small part of him still held out hope that his men would be here when he returned. Another part of his mind urged him onward, as well, insisting that he had to make his last report, otherwise his leader might reserve a fate worse than death if he didn't.

Leaning down, every inch of the movement causing pain to grate through his chest, Tellen picked up a chair and set it upright on the floor, then collapsed into it with a weary wheeze.

"Comfortable, are you?" The voice behind him,

soft and deep, made him start, and he glanced around wildly, heedless of the ache it caused. His head was suddenly gripped by cold, steel fingers, holding it perfectly still and straight, tightening just enough to cause his skull to flex painfully.

"I came to report on what happened out there—" Tellen coughed, and a spray of blood misted out of his mouth into the air.

"It seems you have done yourself damage in returning. You had better make your report, then, before something more permanent happens to you."

Squaring his shoulders, Tellen made his report as quickly and succinctly as he could, leaving nothing out, not even his failure to achieve even one of the goals he'd been assigned. When he'd finished, he took a breath as deep as his broken chest would allow and held it, waiting for his leader's reaction.

Strange whirs and clicks could be heard behind him as the man processed the data he had been given. "So, if I were to ascribe one overall factor in your failure to secure the Bunker or the Free City of Denver, it would be the interference of Ryan Cawdor and his group, yes?"

"Y-yes sir, that would be correct." Tellen tried to remain still, but couldn't help hunching his shoulders slightly, waiting for the bullet or knife blade or laser to pierce through him and end his life. When nothing happened after several seconds, he dared to let out the breath he had been holding.

As quickly as they had appeared, the hands on the sides of his head were removed. "Very well, Tellen. We had better see to those injuries of yours."

"You're…you're not angry?"

The man chuckled, a strange, sibilant sound that

resembled the hiss of air escaping a stoppered pipe at regular intervals that anything remotely resembling humor. "At you? No, you could not have foreseen how one man and his little group of friends could set in motion a chain of events that can destroy such well-laid plans as what you were tasked to carry out. And yet that is what Ryan Cawdor continues to do."

"You know him, sir?"

"Know him—yes and no. He is a thorn in my side that resists my most determined attempts to excise him from what remains of my flesh. To be sure, it has been a good while since I have made a determined effort to do so. Perhaps that time has come once more. Do you know what became of the one-eyed man and his amazingly resilient companions? Perhaps it is time that I sought them out."

"Heard they went north, don't know how long ago." A lightning bolt of pain shot through his chest, making Tellen double over in agony, spraying blood all over the floor. "I'm hurt bad, mebbe dying."

The man behind him tsk-tsked, the sound lacking any demonstrable human warmth or compassion. "Yes, this too, too solid flesh is certainly melting, is it not?"

Tellen felt himself being lifted as easily as if he were a child, those metal fingers digging into the flesh under his arms, cruelly cutting into the nerve clusters there. He whimpered as his cracked ribs shifted and grated in his chest as he hung in the air, forced to look into a face that he couldn't have imagined in a hundred years. A face made equally of flesh and metal, skin and steel, all assembled in a horrible mockery of life gone insane, melded to machines to become some crazed cybernetic clockwork monster.

Otherwise known as the Magus.

Tellen's leader carried him out of the ruined headquarters and over to a large, dark gray APC. "Perhaps I have been unkind in not bestowing the secrets I have learned upon others. Perhaps it is time to share what I know with the world. And you, Tellen, will be the first to receive the gifts that I can give." His stiff, plastic lips peeled back in a hideous mockery of a smile. "Does that not please you?"

Tellen couldn't speak, couldn't shake his head, couldn't do anything but piss his filthy trousers as the cyborg carried him up the stairs of the APC and into the chamber of horrors inside, the door closing behind them, and the large vehicle moving off toward the horizon, swallowing the former rebel leader, as if he had never existed.

* * * * *

Don Pendleton's

Mack Bolan®

Grave Mercy

An evil regime returns to unleash terror across the Caribbean

The horror of the Ton Ton Macoute has returned. This Haitian madman commands an army of machete-wielding hordes, stripped of their humanity by powerful toxins, and he's plotting a brutal invasion. Now the zealot is about to experience the Executioner's trademark version of hellfire—righteous, hardcore and everlasting.

Available September wherever books are sold.

Or order your copy now by sending your name, address, zip or postal code, along with a check or money order (please do not send cash) for $6.99 for each book ordered ($7.99 in Canada), plus 75¢ postage and handling ($1.00 in Canada), payable to Gold Eagle Books, to:

In the U.S.
Gold Eagle Books
3010 Walden Avenue
P.O. Box 9077
Buffalo, NY 14269-9077

In Canada
Gold Eagle Books
P.O. Box 636
Fort Erie, Ontario
L2A 5X3

Please specify book title with your order.
Canadian residents add applicable federal and provincial taxes.

GOLD EAGLE®

www.readgoldeagle.blogspot.com

GSB144